"Stella, I need to tell you something."

The serious tone in Jake's voice scared me. I took a deep breath and waited, assuming he was going to blame himself for Bitsy's death.

"After you and I broke up, Bitsy and I had a...short relationship." He looked at me. "A few years later, a couple of feds paid me a visit, doing a background check on Bitsy. They didn't tell me why, of course, but I figured it out. Bitsy was joining the spy club. She may have been on a job when she called you. She probably knew we were working together and didn't want to risk calling me directly."

Oh, great. So, Bitsy hadn't wanted to hire me, she wanted Jake. Didn't they all?

"You all right with this?" Jake asked.

I gave him my best smile. "Glad you told me. We'd better get to it."

I turned away and stared out my window as Jake drove. The real reason I was upset was not because Jake had information I didn't have. I was upset because Jake had lots of secrets, and they just seemed to keep popping up. How could I trust a man who had so many secrets?

Dear Reader,

Have you ever wished you could roll back the hands of time, even for a brief moment, and revise your own history? You know, "If I'd only known then what I know now!"

Well, Stella is my opportunity to revisit history. She's come home to the small town where I grew up (although I've made a few changes to protect the innocent as well as the guilty!), and she gets to do a lot of the things I could never quite accomplish. For one thing, she gets the guy! Jake is so much yummier than the boy I pined after in high school and Stella's got him right where she wants him. In real life, those guys grow up, they lose their hair, gain a spare tire and get sooo boring, but not Stella's Jake! He's grown up and he's gotten better with age and experience.

Stella takes on a case that involves an elderly woman in a nursing home. For the past two years, in my "real life," I've been consulting two days a week in some local nursing homes, doing psychotherapy with the residents. It has been an eye-opening, heartbreaking time for me. Very often I find myself trying to provide the hugs and love that my abandoned parents and grandparents crave. They are so alone, so forgotten, so...well, downright neglected. Stella finds herself caring as much for Baby as I do for my residents. I just couldn't resist the opportunity to once again point out that our elderly or our "mentally ill" are not disposable items—they are wise, giving and loving human beings, and we are lucky to have them among us.

But more than anything, this book is about love and its place in life's journey.

Have fun, dear reader!

Nancy

what
stella
wants

nancy
bartholomew

Silhouette®
BOMBSHELL™

Published by Silhouette Books

America's Publisher of Contemporary Romance

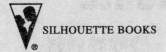 **SILHOUETTE BOOKS**

ISBN-13: 978-0-373-51413-7
ISBN-10:   0-373-51413-1

WHAT STELLA WANTS

Copyright © 2006 by Nancy Bartholomew

This edition published by arrangement with Harlequin Books S.A.

® and TM are trademarks of Harlequin Books S.A., used under license. Trademarks indicated with ® are registered in the United States Patent and Trademark Office, the Canadian Trade Marks Office and in other countries.

www.SilhouetteBombshell.com

Printed in U.S.A.

Books by Nancy Bartholomew

Silhouette Bombshell

Stella, Get Your Gun #13
Stella, Get Your Man #25
Sophie's Last Stand #41
Lethally Blonde #66
What Stella Wants #99

*stories featuring P.I. Stella Valocchi

NANCY BARTHOLOMEW

didn't seem like the Bombshell type at first. She grew up in Philadelphia as a gentle minister's daughter. Sometimes, though, true wildness simmers just below the surface. Nancy started singing country music in biker bars before she graduated from high school. And yes, Dad was there, sitting in the front row, watching over his little girl!

Nancy graduated from college with a degree in psychology and promptly moved into the inner city, where she found work dragging addicted, inner-city teenagers into drug and alcohol rehabilitation. She then moved south to Atlanta and worked as the director of a substance abuse treatment program for court-ordered offenders. Her patients were bikers and strippers and they taught her well...lock picking, exotic dancing, gun play for beginners and hot-wiring cars.

When the criminal life became less of a challenge, Nancy turned to the final frontier: parenthood. This drove her to writing. While her boys were toddlers, Nancy spent their naptimes creating alternate realities. She lives in North Carolina where she rides with the police on a regular basis, raises two hooligan teenage boys and tries to keep up with her writing, her psychotherapy practice and her garden. She thanks you from the bottom of her heart for reading this book!

For my dad—my mentor and role model in
life's journey. I could only wish to one day
be so loving and wise! I love you, Dad!

Chapter 1

It was about time my luck changed.

In the past month I'd been beaten up, shot at, lied to and seduced. In my opinion, other than the seduction, I'd been on the short end of the karma scale. At least this stake-out and surveillance, while in the middle of winter, was indoors. Okay, so there wasn't any heat in the garage, but I wasn't standing outside in a blizzard, either. And our "target" was slow-moving and not very dangerous. She was an old lady. The bad news was she was my Aunt Lucy.

My partner, Jake Carpenter, also known as the man voted most likely to get under my skin and into my bed, was crouched down next to me, peering out the grimy garage window and into Aunt Lucy's kitchen.

"She let him in," he said. "Why hasn't she brought him back to the kitchen? She brings everybody to the kitchen."

I looked at Jake. Tall, dark, handsome and sometimes completely clueless. Still, a lot had changed about the man since high school, since he'd left me waiting at the altar in a failed elopement that was now just a distant memory. He'd grown up, but then so had I.

"Oh, I don't know, Jake. What do you think? Do you think they just went straight down the hall to her bedroom, or what?"

I guess the sarcastic tone gave me away. Jake actually managed to look hurt. "Damn, Stella, I was just asking."

I arched an eyebrow and tried not to notice the way his eyes were traveling the length of my body, stopping at all the good parts—the parts that had so readily responded to his touch just hours before.

"Jake, it's my aunt, for God's sake! She's been widowed what, six months, and some mysterious guy from her past surfaces and she doesn't say word one about who it is or what he wants, and you think I shouldn't be so sensitive? He could be a con man. He could be a killer. He could be…"

I stopped, trying to come up with more possibilities, which gave Jake the window he was looking for. "He could be looking to get laid. Aunt Lucy's old, but she's not dead!"

I punched him, and his responding grunt was loud enough to let me know I hadn't lost my touch. Police training and conditioning is no joke, and I wasn't about to let it go by the wayside just because I was no longer a cop. Private investigators need muscles and endurance, too, maybe even more. They don't have an entire police force ready to back them up—they just have a partner or two if they're lucky. Jake was solid muscle and ex-Special Forces, but he was only one guy. I was the other half of the team. I needed to retain my edge…even if I was only tailing my elderly aunt at the moment.

As we watched, the back door suddenly flew open and my aunt Lucy came rushing down the steps, a white plastic trash bag in hand and a grim look on her face. She headed straight for the garage.

"Hide!" I yelped and dove behind a bunch of boxes.

Jake wasted no time joining me and together we crouched, waiting for my aunt to pull open the old wooden door and head for the trash cans that lined the far wall.

"Nothing good comes of spying on relatives," I muttered.

"It was your idea," Jake reminded me.

I wanted to smack him but didn't dare with Aunt Lucy mere seconds from entering the ancient garage.

"It's for a good cause," I reminded him. "I'm only saying that, even if our intent is good, God might not look too kindly on the effort, that's all."

"And God doesn't take intent into account?"

I pinched his earlobe, the only readily available, exposed flesh I could reach.

"Ouch!"

"Shhh!"

The garage door creaked open and Aunt Lucy could be heard walking briskly across the concrete floor to the battered metal trash cans. She pulled a lid off, dumped her bag inside, replaced the lid and started to stomp off. Without warning she stopped, parallel to our hiding place and as we listened, she sniffed, loudly, cautiously, and I was certain she'd discovered us.

"Humph!" She snorted. "Nothing worse than the smell of dead fish!"

Then, without further comment, she left, slamming the garage door securely behind her and continuing on her way across the rectangular back yard. A moment later we heard the back porch door slam and knew we were in the clear.

"I thought she was going to nail us," Jake said. "The woman's psychic, I swear she is."

My cell phone began to vibrate, humming softly in the still garage.

I fished it out of my parka pocket, flipped it open and said, "Valocchi Investigations."

Jake gave me his usual and customary hard look as I said the name. For some reason the man thought that because we were partners, his name should be on the door. I wasn't sure I was ready for the partnership to become permanent, so why change things before I had a feel for the potential duration? Look what happened the last time we tried to form a partnership...I'd wound up hurt and alone, trying to explain running away to marry Jake to my disappointed aunt Lucy and uncle Benny. No, I needed to wait this relationship out before I made another foolish commitment.

"Stella, is that you?" The voice, female and anxious, sounded distinctly familiar.

"Yes?"

"Stella, it's Bitsy Blankenship—well it's Margolies now, but it was Blankenship. Marygrace Llewellen said you'd moved back home and opened a private investigation office. I need to see you. Right now!"

I closed my eyes. Elizabeth "Bitsy" Blankenship. Blond, cheerleader, airhead and high maintenance in high school. Sounded like nothing had changed, at least not in the maintenance department. I remembered hearing she'd married a junior diplomat and was now leading the high life of embassy parties and overseas assignments. Figured she'd land on her designer heels. But the demanding, "everything's urgent and about me" tone to her voice brought out the rebellious adolescent in me.

"Uh, sorry," I said. "My first available appointment

won't be for another…" I opened my eyes and stared up at the old garage rafters, aware of Jake's confused expression because he knew we were next to unemployed in terms of busy. "I guess I could squeeze you in tomorrow, late morning."

"No! I mean, please, Stella, this is an emergency. I need to see you now!"

I sighed, pushed the sleeve up on my parka and looked at my watch. It was almost noon. "Okay, I suppose I could see you at two, but I might be a few minutes late. We're in the middle of an important surveillance."

"Two?" Bitsy's anguished wail was almost satisfying, especially when I remembered that Jake had briefly dated Bitsy, shortly after he'd failed to show for our elopement to Maryland. "Really, Stella, you can't see me any sooner?"

Damn, what did the woman want, blood? "I'm sorry. Two is my absolute earliest time and I'll be pushing it at that."

I could hear the sound of a car's engine in the background as Bitsy considered whether to take the appointment or not. She was driving, and I wondered if she were in town yet or on her way in from D.C.

"Oh, all right! I'll do two. I suppose I can waste a couple of hours visiting my grandmother in the nursing home or something."

Visiting her grandmother was a waste of her time? Oh, I was so glad I was putting Mrs. High-and-Mighty on the back burner!

"Okay, you know where the office is? It's across from the old newsstand, off Main."

"I'll find it. And, Stella, listen, it's really important that you don't tell anybody about this, okay? I don't want anyone to know I'm in town or that we're meeting. It could be a matter of life and death."

I rolled my eyes at Jake. What had he ever seen in this dingbat? Jake frowned and mouthed the words, "What? Who is it?" But I just smiled and shook my head.

"Don't worry, I won't tell a soul. See you at two!"

I snapped the phone shut and smiled even bigger at Jake. "Guess what, buddy? Your old girlfriend, Bitsy, is coming to town and she wants to hire me."

"Us," Jake corrected, still stuck on the pride of ownership. "She wants to hire us."

"She didn't mention you," I taunted. "If she'd wanted you, I suppose she would've called you."

"What's wrong with Bitsy?" Jake was all concerned now.

I shrugged and returned my attention to my aunt's kitchen window. "Don't know, don't care. I just hope she has deep pockets. Why don't you slip back around front and see if you can get the guy's license plate number when his driver comes back? I'm going to see if I can get a little closer to the house."

Jake started to protest, caught himself, and shrugged. "It's your party," he said. I could tell he thought sneaking around in broad daylight was a bad idea, but what else could I do? Aunt Lucy hadn't entertained the guy at night. So far, all she'd done was disappear during the daytime, only to return a few hours later with this stupid smile on her face and vague answers when we asked where she'd been and with whom.

Even Lloyd the Dog was left out of the loop. Considering the fact that, until very recently, Aunt Lucy had considered my Australian shepherd to be her deceased husband, Benny, reincarnated, I found her reluctance to confide in him troubling. True, Lloyd the Dog had found love himself in the form of an overwhelmingly large part-wolf named Fang, but that was no reason for Aunt Lucy's sudden secrecy.

I watched as Jake eased out the back door of the garage and into the alley before I considered my stealth opportunities. Aunt Lucy had been anxious to get us out of the house for the day. She'd found a very necessary and quite convoluted errand for my scattered cousin, Nina, and her girlfriend, Spike, to run in downtown Philadelphia. She'd asked me and Jake to run out to Lancaster to take a set of architectural plans to her Amish carpenter friend, Max. She'd been so insistent we leave that I'd known for certain this was the big day; the day Aunt Lucy had invited the mysterious man to her home.

So we called Max and blew him off. We made a big show of driving away from Aunt Lucy's ancient, brick row house and returned in a borrowed conversion van with tinted windows to park and hide. A mere twenty minutes later our efforts were rewarded by the arrival of a long, black, chauffer-driven sedan.

I was expecting someone as huge as the limousine, someone large, ostentatious, maybe a Donald Trump type. What we got was a short, elderly, white-haired man in a charcoal-gray overcoat carrying a small bouquet of purple violets.

"What the hell?" Jake murmured. As we watched, the little man ascended the steps to the brownstone and rang the doorbell.

Aunt Lucy answered the door moments later, looked down the street in both directions and hastily pulled her visitor inside. This forced us out of the van and around the back of the house to the garage where we hoped to watch my aunt entertaining her visitor in the kitchen. Aunt Lucy always brought company back to her kitchen. Except for this visitor. What was up? I had to get closer to the house. I had to know what was happening inside.

I slipped out the back door of the garage, edged around

the far side of the wooden building and began creeping past the thick lilac bushes that lined the edge of my aunt's yard. I glanced up nervously at the kitchen window and saw no movement inside.

I began working my way up the side of the house, passing the back porch and stopping beneath my aunt's bedroom window. I am not proud of what I did next, but you need to understand, I thought Aunt Lucy was in danger...maybe. I slipped the miniature sound amplifier out of my pocket, fitted the tiny earpiece into my right ear and reached up stealthily to attach the little bug to the glass windowpane.

My aunt's voice reverberated inside my head. "Oh, right there!" she cried. "You've almost got it! Come on, you can get it! Please!" There was a pause and then a soft, excited cry. "Oh, yes! That's it! Oh, you got it!"

Oh. My. God! I ripped the earpiece out, snatched the listening device off the window and ran, full tilt, the length of the house and out onto the front sidewalk. Where was Jake? Oh. My. God! They were...they were....having... sex! My aunt, my uncle Benny's widow, was having S.E.X.! I didn't know people that *old* even had sex!

I sprinted for the street, darted through parked cars and banged on the passenger-side door of the van.

Jake greeted me with a knowing smile. "Well, well... just when I was wondering how to pass the time."

"Shut up!"

"Hey, a little edgy, aren't we?"

I glared at him. "They are in her bedroom. They are... she's...he was..."

Comprehension dawned slowly in Jake's eyes. "No, they weren't!"

I nodded.

"You sure about that?"

I just looked at him.

"No way. Damn! Well, who knew? I guess getting old won't be so bad after all."

"Jake, shut up!"

I peered out into the street, looking for the limousine. With the exception of Aunt Lucy's neighbor Mrs. Talluchi's ancient black Plymouth, there were no black sedans in sight.

"He must have told the driver to leave," Jake said, anticipating my next question. "We wait him out."

The way he said it, the way he moved up behind me left no doubt as to how Jake Carpenter thought we'd pass the time. His breath, hot on my neck, tingled, sending shivers of anticipation surging to every raw, hungry nerve ending in my body. When his hands slid around my waist and pulled me back against his body, I fought the urge to give in and turned on him.

"Jake, not now! Honestly! Is that all you think about?"

Jake's grin was infectious, and any other time I might have given in, but I'd just heard Aunt Lucy in the throes of passion and it didn't exactly do a whole lot for my libido.

"Come on, Stel, lighten up!"

Lighten up. Wasn't that just like a man. I pushed the sleeve up on my parka and stared at my watch. It was only 11:30. I tugged the plaid curtains apart on the back side window and looked out through the darkly tinted glass at my aunt's tiny row house. It looked so normal, so peaceful, so…Jake's thumb stroked the spot he knew all too well behind my ear, breaking my concentration and sending shivers down the side of my neck. A tiny flame caught and held deep inside my body. I was in trouble.

When his tongue followed his thumb, knowingly tracing the fire line along my neck, I couldn't help myself. A sigh escaped my lips and I turned, letting my body mold into his as we kissed. When would I ever learn? I am putty in Jake's hands, willing, soft, mushy putty. Oh, well, if you can't beat 'em, you might as well join 'em.

"I love conversion vans, don't you, Jake?" I breathed the words in a whisper as he slowly moved me to the thickly padded day bed that hugged the back of the cavernous vehicle.

"Mmm-hmm," he said, and unzipped my parka.

A moment later, before I could feel the cold, I discovered the pile of quilts and blankets conveniently placed at one end of the well-stocked van.

"Hey, who'd you borrow this from, anyway?"

Jake opened up a thick, multi-colored quilt and smiled. "Buddy of mine."

"You knew this would happen, didn't you?" Suspicion dawned in my gullible brain. He was not nearly as interested in tracking down Aunt Lucy's mysterious visitor as I was.

"Now, Stella, you know that wasn't it. I just like to be prepared, that's all."

I felt my spine stiffen. "Prepared, my ass!" Wasn't that just like a man? I'd left Florida and a promising career in law enforcement to get away from a no-good, cheating scoundrel only to wind up back in my old home town with the very first con artist to break my heart. What was it with me, anyway? When was I going to learn?

Jake leaned down and kissed me so thoroughly I began to appreciate the beauty of thoughtful preparation. So what if he was prepared? So what if he didn't care about Aunt Lucy's boyfriend as much as— *Oh, please keep touching me there!*

I reached for Jake, grabbing the waistband of his jeans and pulling him closer. My fingers found the top button and I knew there was about to be no turning back.

"What if the limo comes?" I murmured, my lips never leaving his.

"We'll hear it," he assured me. "I'll listen out for it. I have unbelievable ears."

Jake's fingers slipped under my bra and began softly stroking and tugging at my nipples.

"You have unbelievable fingers," I whispered, and sighed as my body gave itself over to his slow seduction.

"You're no slouch yourself," he answered.

I smiled and pushed his jeans down over his hips. Another moment and we were naked beneath a pile of warm afghans and quilts. Outside, the street was silent. With the exception of the old people, like Aunt Lucy and her best friend, crazy Sylvia Talluchi, all the other inhabitants on the block were at work.

Jake's knowing hand moved slowly down across my stomach, teasing me with its leisurely approach. I heard someone moan and knew it was me. Here we were, naked in a van, about to make wild crazy love while also trying not to make enough noise to rouse the curiosity of any inadvertent passersby. It was illicit, steamy and a complete turn-on. Jake, I realized, was a brilliant man. He knew what this unexpected opportunity would do to me, and he was totally prepared to take full advantage of it. You just had to love a man like that.

Or did you?

In the past few months our relationship had kindled into far more than the adolescent fumbling that had been our high school romance. We'd gotten past, kind of, Jake jilting me at the altar in a failed, underage elopement. We'd survived my uncle Benny's murder investigation in which Jake had been one of the prime suspects. We'd even gone into business as private investigators and resumed our personal relationship with the wisdom that

only age and experience can bring. But in the past few
months, the chemistry between us had exploded into an
all-consuming fire that frankly scared the hell out of me.

I'd tried to play it cool. I'd forced myself to spend time
away from him. He'd let me down before, and while we're
on the subject, so had every other man I'd every had a
personal relationship with, even my father. He and Mom
had had the nerve to take a second honeymoon to Ireland,
without me, and had managed to die in a fiery plane crash.
I just had to be sure about Jake before I got so hopelessly
entangled in the relationship that I couldn't survive the
loss of it.

"Oh, Jake!" His tongue was following his fingers. I felt
my body explode into a bonfire of need and without
thinking I reached for him, pulling and positioning my
body beneath him. What was wrong with me? How could
I not trust someone who made me feel like this? This was
so incredibly good! This was better than anything I'd ever
felt in my entire…

Outside, the van walls began violently shaking as
someone beat the door with their fists. Maybe more than
one someone was beating on the van. The loud noise
seemed to come from everywhere, surrounding us.

"What the—" Jake jumped to his feet, completely naked
except for his unbuttoned, plaid flannel shirt. I had a full
frontal flash of what I was about to miss before I, too,
jumped up and joined him in the frantic dash to reclothe ourselves.

"Who in the—" I gasped, struggling into my jeans.

"They're in there. I saw them!"

"No, no, no!" I moaned softly. Sylvia Talluchi, the
world's most active busybody and self-appointed watch-
dog for the entire neighborhood, had seen us and pulled
the alarm.

"Stella, are you in there?"

Oh, we were dead. Aunt Lucy was banging on the other side of the van. There was going to be total hell to pay.

Jake looked at me, wide-eyed, as the same realization hit him.

"Let me handle this." I pushed my way past him, pulling on and zipping my parka as I went. I didn't even wait for Jake to answer me. It was my aunt and my execution.

I flung open the door and was momentarily blinded by the brilliant winter sunlight.

"Stella! *Marone!* What are you doing in there?"

"Lucia, you don't know?" Mrs. Talluchi's querulous tone grated like fingernails on a chalkboard. "They were doing the nasty if you ask me!"

My eyes adjusted in time to see my aunt shoot her best friend a dark look before she leveled the same gaze at me.

"Well?"

I forced a broad smile and stepped down the two metal stairs onto the sidewalk where Sylvia Talluchi and Aunt Lucy stood waiting. Jake stood framed in the doorway behind me and I prayed he had the sense to smile as well.

"No, of course we weren't 'doing the nasty' as you so succinctly put it, Mrs. Talluchi. Jake and I were about to stop back by the house before we went out on surveillance. You see, we were on our way to Lancaster to see Max when we got this call and…"

I stopped in midsentence. At the far end of the street, a limousine slowly crept past on Johnston Avenue.

"Who is that?" I demanded, pointing so there'd be no doubt about the vehicle in question.

Aunt Lucy and Sylvia Talluchi spun on their heels just as the long black sedan's tail lights vanished from view.

"Who was what?" my aunt asked, turning back to face

me. "Never mind that! What were you doing out here? Have you no sense of common decency? In the van, for all the world to witness? Have you no shame?"

Jake stepped down out of the van to join me on the sidewalk. "Mrs. Valocchi, we noticed you had company and I said we shouldn't disturb you, so we were just waiting."

I wanted to slap him. How could he think my aunt, a former CIA chemist, could possibly be so stupid? But it was too late. Jake had wandered into the minefield.

"You noticed I had company? How did you notice that, Jake?"

"Well, we saw the limousine pull up and..."

"Saw the limousine, did you?" she echoed dangerously.

Jake nodded. A slight smile tugged at the corners of Sylvia Talluchi's lips as my aunt let Jake swallow the bait.

"So you've been waiting outside my house for almost an hour, have you?"

Jake, former Special Forces operative, suddenly realized now how badly he'd underestimated my aunt.

"Yes, ma'am." It was a weak tone for such a big man.

"Right out here in the van, were you?"

He nodded.

"Both of you?" she murmured, her eyes boring into my soul.

"Aunt Lucy, you've been disappearing for hours at a time without any explanation ever since we got back from the beach. We were worried. There were those flowers that kept arriving mysteriously and then the notes. You gotta admit, you were worried, too. We were only trying to protect you!"

Damn. Too late for Stella Valocchi the Brilliant Former Cop, too.

"So, I suppose it didn't occur to you that if I was no longer worried and if I chose not to say where I'd been that I might no longer feel concerned about my secret admirer? Furthermore," she said, her voice rising just enough to let me know the depth of emotion that lay behind the words, "did it ever occur to you that perhaps my private life is none of your business?"

"And what if this man was conning you? What if he…"

My aunt cut me off with a look. "So, now I'm not capable of discerning danger for myself? Now I'm suddenly feeble-minded and incompetent? What next, we have a hearing and I get placed in one of those homes?"

"Sweet mother in heaven!" Sylvia Talluchi cried. "Betrayed, by your own family!" She crossed herself and looked up at the sky above our heads. "Father, forgive them," she whispered.

"No, nothing like that!"

"Humph! I think it's exactly like that."

Okay, not withstanding the fact that Aunt Lucy thought Lloyd was Uncle Benny reincarnated, she was one of the sanest women I knew. And I had hurt her beyond all comprehension. I saw it in her eyes.

"Aunt Lucy, I was just worried. I'm sorry. I should've know better."

Aunt Lucy slowly shook her head, looking at me with a mournful gaze that completely broke my heart.

"Yes, *cara mia*, you should have known better, but you didn't."

She let her gaze shift to Jake, the man I knew she loved almost more than she loved me, the man more like a son to her than a family friend. Slowly her eyes traveled the length of his body, down to his feet and back up again.

"And you," she said. "*Stunade!* You have broken my heart."

"Aunt Lucy, I…"

"You lied to me! Both of you lied to me!" Her eyes glittered with anger and pain.

"We only wanted what was best for you. We didn't want to see you get hurt!" I cried.

Aunt Lucy sniffed imperiously.

"I don't need that kind of help," she said softly. "I need love and I need family, but I don't need to be treated like a child. If I want privacy, you should respect my wishes."

Now my back was up. I had acted out of love. I wanted to protect my aunt.

"Well, I was only trying to look out for you," I said, stung. "I didn't realize you needed so much privacy. I thought we were closer than that. Maybe you need more privacy than I thought." Jake dug his elbow into my ribs in a warning but I was too far gone to stop. "Maybe I've overstayed my welcome."

"Maybe you have," Aunt Lucy said quietly. Without another word, she turned and walked back across the empty street, up the steps to her row house and inside, closing the door firmly. In the echoing silence that followed I heard the solid click of the dead bolt as it shot home.

Mrs. Talluchi, not to be outdone, glared at me. *"Puttan!"* she spat. Turning to Jake, she narrowed her eyes and stared hard at his chest. "Ha! I was right!"

She stomped off down the street and up the spotless marble steps to her row house. I turned to Jake, puzzled until I caught sight of his chest. He'd buttoned his shirt wrong, making his shirttails uneven and leaving no doubt as to what we'd been doing in the van. To further seal the verdict, his fly was undone and he was only wearing one sock.

"Great!" I said. "Look at you."

Jake looked down and shrugged. "Well, it's not like you gave me an option," he grumbled. "You threw open the door and I did the best I could."

I looked across the street at my aunt's front door. "What are we going to do now?"

It was a rhetorical question. I moved past Jake and climbed back into the van, this time settling myself in the passenger seat where I waited for him to slide behind the wheel.

"Where to, boss?" he asked as we pulled away from the curb.

I shrugged. I was already going to hell, what did it matter where we went in the interim? And then I remembered Bitsy Blankenship.

"The office. If I'm going to need to rent an apartment, I'd better start making enough money to pay for it. Let's do a little background work before Bitsy comes at two."

Jake nodded. Neither one of us was as enthusiastic as we would've usually been about the prospect of new business, not with Aunt Lucy feeling as she did. How had our good intentions suddenly turned to shit?

I reached into my jacket pocket, retrieved my cell phone and punched in my younger cousin, Nina's, number. I needed to share the misery.

She answered on the first ring. "Peace, baby!" she cried. She sounded so happy I almost hated to burst her bubble with my worries, but the hesitation was overridden by the need to find a soft shoulder to cry on.

"Oh, no, you didn't." Nina sounded horrified.

So much for sympathy.

This was followed by more questions, muffled relays of information to her girlfriend, Spike, the former assistant D.A. turned performance artist, and more cries of disbelief. Apparently, Nina "resonated"

with my aunt's "cosmic energy" and was as appalled as
Aunt Lucy had been.

"I don't know, Stel," she said finally. "I've gotta look
up your chart again. I think your sun is in some serious
retrograde."

"Let me talk to Spike," I said, disgusted.

"Where are you?" Spike said without preamble.

"Heading into the office. We've got a new client in
about an hour and a half."

"We'll meet you there," she said and severed the connection.

That was Spike for you. Sensible. Level-headed. The
polar opposite of my cousin, Nina. How the two ever fell
in love was a complete mystery to me, but love it was.
They'd been seeing each other for almost two years and
they never seemed to hit a bump in the road. Their love
just grew with every passing day. Why couldn't I be
certain that a man could love me like Spike loved Nina?

"They're going to meet us at the office," I told Jake.

He nodded, lost in his own thoughts. He looked as
miserable as I felt.

Neither of us spoke on the short drive across town.
Glenn Ford, Pennsylvania, is idyllic in many ways. It sits
an hour outside of Philadelphia, close to Amish country,
and is lush with verdant farmland and historic fieldstone
houses. It was a wonderful small-town environment to
grow up in and a great place to return to when my life fell
apart in Florida, but today it was just a bit too small for
my liking. There was nowhere to hide from the remind-
ers of the importance of Aunt Lucy in my life.

She was everywhere; in the park behind the elemen-
tary school where she'd spent hours with me after my
parents' deaths, consoling, talking and, more often than
not, just sitting silently, a witness to the tears of loss and

longing. I remembered countless shopping expeditions to Guinta's Grocery Store or Reeder's Newsstand, or any number of small shops that lined Lancaster Avenue. By the time we'd reached the offices of Valocchi Investigations, it was all I could do to hold back the tears.

Jake avoided looking at me as he unlocked the front door to the entryway that led to our office and climbed the flight of steps to the second floor. I knew he felt my misery and was giving me time to pull myself together.

Once inside, I went immediately to the computer, determined to throw myself into busywork until Bitsy Blankenship arrived for her two-o'clock appointment.

I Googled Bitsy's name, her maiden as well as her married name, Margolies, and began searching for anything that would tell me about her life since high school. It was just better to know a bit about potential clients before they came strolling in to give you a story that usually had gaps or outright fabrications included. Knowing Bitsy from high school precluded the matter of aliases, so catching up, I figured, would be easy.

Not so. Bitsy, deceptively brilliant for a blond, cheerleader, girly-girl type, had attended Virginia Tech after high school, majoring in electrical engineering of all things. The next fifty or so articles detailed Bitsy's engagement and subsequent marriage to David Margolies, whom she apparently met sometime during her college career. Margolies was a junior diplomat, an attaché with the U.S. mission in Slovenia. He was also apparently a shining star because he and Bitsy had been moved around frequently as David gained more authority and climbed the diplomatic ladder.

I was reading a detailed account of a party Bitsy and David had attended at the British Embassy when Nina and Spike arrived. Nina's face was flushed and she was out of breath from her run up the flight of steps to the office. Her blond hair, streaked this week with metallic purple, stood out at wild angles all over her head. Spike followed her at a more leisurely pace. Cool, calm and collected as usual, she strolled into the room with not one long brunette hair out of place.

Nina, as usual, did the talking for the two of them, her words accented by wild arm movements.

"Oh. My. God!" she cried. "I'm sorry we're late, but ohmigod! We were at the mall, you know, and like, there was just total chaos!"

I looked past Nina to Spike for verification. She nodded, as if Nina was absolutely right and the mall was a complete mob scene.

"Really? Big sale, huh?"

Nina's eyes widened. "No! Do you two not listen to the radio or what?"

Jake came into my office, drawn by Nina's increasingly excited tone.

"What's all the excitement?"

I rolled my eyes. "Nina was at the mall and it was a zoo."

Nina stomped her foot impatiently. "No, really! We thought we'd never get out, I think every fire truck and police car in town was there. They cordoned off the entire west side of the mall parking and they were hustling people out of the area and telling them the mall was closing!"

"Bomb scare?" Jake prompted.

Nina shook her head. "No, a bomb. A real bomb!"

"You're kidding, right?"

"Turn on the news if you don't believe me. Some lady's car blew up with her inside it! It was like, just so totally gruesome!"

She had our complete attention now.

Spike walked over to the tiny television set that sat on my bookcase, picked up the remote and hit the power button. Sure enough, a reporter stood in front of the mall, the yellow crime-scene tape running the length of the screen behind her, fire trucks and police cruisers everywhere. She looked grim as she leaned forward to speak to her audience.

"The sedan, a late model Lexus, had diplomatic plates, but the victim, a woman in her late twenties, has not been formally identified pending a positive identification and notification of her family."

I looked up at the clock on the wall and realized it was 2:10. Somehow time had slipped away from me. I looked back at the burnt-out shell of a car in the mall parking lot with growing apprehension. Bitsy Blankenship was ten minutes late.

Chapter 2

Back in the day when we attended Glenn Ford High School, Marygrace Llewellen was the "go-to" girl for any and all information pertaining to the comings and goings of our other classmates. She was also an expert at forging parental signatures. This added to her repository of information, as she knew who was skipping and with whom. It also gave her the capacity to blackmail any and all of us at any time, should she desire additional tidbits of gossip that had somehow eluded her.

While Marygrace never exactly extorted information from anyone, the threat was always there when she came to you for information. She was sweet about it. She never used her powers for evil, preferring mostly to matchmake her fellow classmates or gently sway them into various activities that she felt strongly about, like Save the Planet Day or Senior Skip Day. I admired Marygrace's easy way with others. Everyone liked her while simultaneously fearing her. It was a pretty cool talent she had there and she knew it.

So when she appeared in the doorway of Valocchi Investigations the day after my Aunt Lucy fiasco and Bitsy's probable death, I was glad to see her and also a bit apprehensive.

"Hi, guys!" She greeted me as if it hadn't been twelve years since we'd last seen each other and as if it were the most normal and casual thing in the world for her to be stopping by. My internal alarm bell didn't even ring.

"Marygrace!" Jake rushed over to pick her up in an affectionate bear hug. She squealed, a short butterball of exuberance and enthusiasm, her little feet dangling in the air as Jake whirled her around. "I haven't seen you since…" He broke off, trying to remember.

"Since you married that bimbo you call your ex-wife. I gave you guys a toaster. You know, I knew you were headed down the wrong road with that one. She never even wrote me a thank-you note. I think she was threatened by me. Poor breeding will do that to you every time, won't it?"

Jake was momentarily thrown by Marygrace's summation, but I saw Nina grinning in agreement.

"So," she said, turning her radar my way, "I hear you two are finally an item. Good, right?" Her hazel eyes bore into mine like lie detectors, and I felt my face flame.

"It's all good, Marygrace," I said. "How've you been?"

Marygrace still wore her strawberry-blond hair the way she had in high school. It fell just below her chin in a pageboy bob that somehow suited her. When she shook her head as if putting off my question, her hair swung back and forth like a shampoo commercial. I found myself staring at it, unconcerned that she had no intention of answering me and was now asking a new question.

"How come you two are partners but it only says Valocchi Investigations on the door?"

That got my attention. Unfortunately, it got everyone else's attention, too, including Nina's. For some reason, she decided to save me.

"Hey, Marygrace, who was in the car at the mall?"

Marygrace almost seemed to quiver, the way a dog does when it catches scent of something really, really good.

"The police haven't released her name to the media yet, but I already know on account of them telling her mother and calling me. It was Bitsy Blankenship," she said, turning to me. "That's why I'm here. See, her grandmother is a patient of mine." Marygrace caught my puzzled expression and rushed on. "I'm a social worker now, Stella, out at Brookhaven Manor Nursing Home. I know, I know." She held up her hand. "Why is a good social worker working in a nursing home? You think only loser social workers work in rest homes but that's just a myth. There are some really good social workers taking care of the elderly, but that's not why I'm here."

Marygrace barely seemed to stop for breath between thoughts. I had to work hard to follow her.

"Bitsy's grandmother is one of my patients." Marygrace looked at us with an anxious furrow between her brows. "This is confidential, what I say in here, isn't it?"

"Well, technically, Marygrace, only if you're a client, and then only within certain parameters," Spike said, being cautious. "Is that why you're here? Do you want to hire us?"

Marygrace cocked her head to one side and seemed to consider the matter for a second before answering.

"Well, yeah, I guess. I mean, Bitsy's grandmother is a lost ball in high weeds. Some days she thinks we're working at the paper mill and some days she seems just fine, but obviously *she* can't hire you!"

"Huh?" Even Nina was getting lost now.

Marygrace looked around the room at the four of us. "Do I need to sign papers first or give you a check or what?" Before anyone could answer, she sped on. "Well, I'll just tell you. It's not like Baby Blankenship's gonna sue me or anything. Like I said, she can't even remember who I am half the time, so she sure won't sue me for telling you about her! Besides, everybody knows social workers aren't in it for the money, and Baby wouldn't be in a nursing home if she had the money for private care, so there you are!"

"Is this about Bitsy's death?" I asked, wishing Marygrace had a shortcut button.

Marygrace's eyes widened. "Well, that's why I'm here. Somebody breaks into the woman's room and takes her stuff, then Bitsy turns up dead. Call me paranoid, but I gotta wonder."

"Wouldn't that be a police matter?" Jake asked.

Marygrace looked at him, hands on hips, with a frustrated frown. "Oh, yeah, right, like they'll give a rat's ass. Baby's just an old lady to them. There wasn't anything of any real value in her room. I told you, she's poor. Don't you know anything about nursing homes? Stuff gets stolen out of people's rooms all the time. If it isn't nailed down— and sometimes even if it is—it gets stolen."

"Okay, so, you want us to find out if there's a connection between Bitsy and whoever's stealing worthless stuff from Baby Blankenship's room even though she doesn't probably even remember what it is and probably doesn't care?" I tried not to look as if I thought Marygrace was nuts, but I was beginning to wonder.

"Who said she doesn't know what's going on or what's missing? I told you, some days she doesn't remember who she is, but the rest of the time, Baby's a sharp old cookie. She told me someone came into her room and believe me, when I went in after the head nurse called, Baby's room was trashed. She said someone came in and was looking everywhere and they took something."

"So, what did they steal?" I asked.

Marygrace shrugged and for the first time seemed a little bit disconcerted. "She doesn't know. She can't remember. That's what you guys are supposed to find out. You're detectives aren't you?"

"Whoa!" Nina said softly. "Now that's totally a case to sink your teeth into!"

"You think?" I said reflexively.

"Aw, come on, man!" Marygrace said impatiently. "She's an old woman. Her granddaughter's just been killed, maybe by terrorists, and someone came into her room and took something. I'm asking you guys to do something, as a public service. It'll be good publicity. Don't you need to get the word out about your agency?"

I shook my head, hoping to clear the confusion of facts and questions in Marygrace's rapid-fire statement.

"Hold up here, girlfriend," I said, hoping to apply the brakes to Marygrace's mouth before I became eternally lost in her next rush of words. "Let me just get a few things straight."

"What makes you think it was a terrorist?" Jake interrupted me and set Marygrace off again.

"Hey, I watch TV. I can read between the lines. Her husband's a diplomat. Bitsy's car was just sitting there. It's not like she threw a match in the gas tank or anything. It had to be terrorists. Who else? I hear Bitsy's mama is just all to pieces." Marygrace turned bright red and clapped a hand over her wayward mouth. "Oh, Lord, I mean she's upset, not all to…pieces!"

Jake looked at me over the top of Marygrace's head. She would have no way of knowing about Bitsy's urgent phone call. It had been almost the only thing Jake and I had thought about since hearing of the mysterious explosion at the mall. Now here was Marygrace saying Bitsy had definitely been the one in the car and her grandmother was the victim of petty larceny. Maybe that's why Bitsy had called for an appointment. Maybe she'd wanted us to look into her grandmother's problem. If there was a connection, we'd need to make sure the authorities took it seriously.

A wave of relief washed over me. The load of guilt that had been sitting on my shoulders since I'd heard about the explosion lifted a tiny bit. Maybe Bitsy hadn't been calling me about a matter of life and death. She probably wanted her grandmother to feel as if something was being done. Bitsy wasn't dead because I spitefully put her appointment off when I could've met her earlier.

Except—Bitsy had called me before going to the nursing home. How could she have known about the theft?

"Sure, Marygrace," I said. At that point, with my roller coaster of emotions, I would've promised Marygrace anything. "I would be more than happy to investigate Baby Blankenship's missing belongings, whatever they are." I sobered up, thinking of Bitsy and how much her death would affect her family. "She must be devastated by Bitsy's death. How's she doing with that?"

Marygrace sighed and shrugged her shoulders. "Well, I hate to say it, but I doubt Baby even remembers Bitsy. She hadn't seen her in years before yesterday. If Baby remembered Bitsy at all, it was as a little girl."

Well, at least Baby got to see Bitsy grown-up one time. Poor Bitsy. Wonder what made her decide to stop by and see her grandmother after so many years? I glanced over at my cousin, the believer in all things New Age. She'd probably tell me Bitsy had unconsciously sensed her impending demise and wanted to tie up loose ends.

"So, why did Bitsy stop by to see her grandmother yesterday, I mean, after so many years?" I voiced my question.

Marygrace just shook her head. "Who knows? She came racing in, barely said 'Hi' to me, asked what room her granny was in and took off down the hallway. You'd have thought it was a race to the finish line. And then, she only stayed for like, five minutes before she took off! I just never could figure that Bitsy out. For someone so smart, she sure was stupid."

Spike had been listening to Marygrace's tale with growing interest. "How was she stupid?" she asked.

"Well, she had book sense but the girl didn't have a bit of common sense. Look at that geek she married." Marygrace's eyes twinkled as she looked around the room, drawing us in to her story. "She eloped, you know."

"But I read about her…"

Marygrace nodded. "Oh, they had a wedding, all right. Brenda, her mama, threatened to disown her if they didn't come back and put on a show. Otherwise, people would've thought the worst."

"What?" Nina asked. "What's worse than getting married?"

Jake sputtered, choking on the coffee he'd been trying to drink, and turned red. I figured it was only his karma paying him back. After all, the man had abandoned me at the altar when we were in high school and scheduled to elope ourselves.

"Yeah, Marygrace," I echoed. "What's worse than getting married?"

"Aw, come on, man. You know. Her mama said people would think she was knocked up!"

"Damn!" Nina breathed. "I just like, totally don't get some people."

"When did Bitsy stop by the nursing home?" Jake asked, pulling us back to the matter at hand.

"It had to be after she called me," I muttered to Jake.

Marygrace cocked her head to one side and appeared to be giving Jake's question serious consideration. "Let's see. It was after ten o'clock bingo and a little before lunch. Yeah, that's right. I remember because old Mrs. Maxwell expired around four and I was trying to take care of the arrangements when all hell broke loose in Baby's room."

Marygrace twitched, clutched her side and reached inside her brightly colored jacket. A moment later she pulled a tiny cell phone out and flipped it open.

"I'm sorry," she said. "I'm on call. I have to take this."

As we watched, Marygrace listened, the frown on her face deepening with each passing moment.

"Don't give me that!" she cried. "How can it happen again without anybody seeing anything? Where were you people?"

Marygrace looked up from her conversation and mouthed the word, "Baby" before returning to the conversation.

"Where's Darren? Well, tell him I'm coming back right now, and this time we're calling the police. If one of those CNAs laid a hand on Baby, I'll have their job and their ass. Call Stephanie and get her in to see Baby right now. If she can't come, call a fucking ambulance and have her transported to the E.R."

There was a brief hesitation as the person on the other end apparently questioned Marygrace's orders. I watched her eyes darken and her scowl deepen, thinking only a fool would ignore a dynamo like Marygrace when she was riled up.

"I don't give a flying rat's ass what Medicaid'll pay for. Get her there and get her there now!"

Marygrace slammed the lid shut on her tiny phone.

"Let's go!" Marygrace was already halfway out the door. When nobody moved to follow her, she spun back around. "Well? Come on! Baby's room got hit again and this time she got hurt. Are you guys gonna sit around with your thumbs up your butts or are you coming?"

"We'll be right behind you, Marygrace," I answered. "I've got to get a couple of things started before we head out, that's all. We're coming."

Marygrace's eyes glittered with unshed tears and her face and neck flushed. She clenched and unclenched her fists. In that one moment I understood her feelings completely and saw the woman she'd become. Marygrace had simply taken all the skills she'd used for fun and diversion in high school and channeled them into her career as a social worker.

She was no longer the champion of her fellow fun-loving teenagers. She had evolved into a champion of lost causes and underdogs. Marygrace fought for her patients with the same fervor and intensity I'd had on the police force. I hated to think what would happen if she were the one to encounter Baby Blankenship's abuser.

"Just hurry up, okay?" she said finally. "This scares me."

She was gone before I could answer her. I swallowed hard, ignoring the tight feeling in my throat and the naked emotion in Nina's eyes. "All right, you two, Jake and I will take the nursing home. While we're there, I want you to get me some background information."

Spike nodded, her chin resting on Nina's head. "What do you need?"

"I know you still have contacts in the police department," I said. "I want to know what they know about Bitsy's death. I want to know everything you can find out."

Spike looked momentarily puzzled. "Okay. As soon as they ID'd the car, the feds wouldn've taken over."

I shrugged. "I don't know. I'm covering all the bases. Bitsy was coming to see us and she'd said it was urgent. She never made it, and I want to know why. I'll take any bit of information I can get."

"What do you want me to do?" Nina asked, her voice muffled by Spike's shoulder.

"As soon as I can get a list of employees on duty today and at the time of the first incident, I'll call you. I want you and Spike to do the background checks."

Jake was strapping on his shoulder holster while I talked. So, he was expecting trouble, too. I didn't know why our subconscious alarm systems had suddenly kicked in, but they had, and it was always best to trust your instincts in this business. There was no doubt in my mind that Bitsy Blankenship's death and the attack on her grandmother were somehow related. Now it was up to us to figure out how and to prevent anything else from happening.

"You ready?" Jake was already halfway out the back exit.

"Be right there!"

I crossed the room to my gun safe, punched in the combination and, when the door swung open, considered the cache inside carefully. Not the Glock; no safety. I discarded the Sig; too bulky. I reached past the Beretta and pulled out my Lady Smith 9 mm. Perfect. Small, easily concealed. "Tasteful, elegant but not ostentatious," I murmured as I pulled out a pancake holster and stuck the gun inside it. "Just the right little accessory for a visit to a nursing home."

I reached for my blazer, grabbed my purse and ran

down the back steps and out into the cold winter air. The
sky was clouding up ominously, and a gust of wind blew
in from the northeast. Not a good sign. I sniffed. The air
smelled like snow.

Jake punched the accelerator of his newly purchased
'98 black Viper. It was his way of saying, "Hurry the hell
up!" When I hopped into the passenger seat he spun out
of the parking lot, barely waiting for me to close the door.

"Calm down!" I yelled. "There's no sense in getting us
killed, too."

He didn't answer me and he didn't slow down.

"Jake, I mean it! What's wrong with you?"

He took the road toward the outskirts of town well
over the speed limit. We headed into a sharp turn, careen-
ing around a massive granite boulder outcropping, and
swerved right into the path of an oncoming concrete truck.

There wasn't even time to scream. I grabbed the edges
of my seat and stopped breathing. Jake fishtailed through
the narrow gap between the truck's bumper and the guard-
rail, accelerated and cleared the truck with a two-inch
margin. A second later he pulled over onto the side of the
road and cut the engine.

We sat for a long moment without speaking. Finally
Jake broke the silence.

"Stella, I need to tell you something about Bitsy," he
said. He was staring at a spot on the dashboard instead of
looking at me. "I need to tell you something about *me* and
Bitsy. Now. Before this goes any further."

The serious tone in his voice scared me. What could
Jake possibly have to tell me that was this desperate? And
what did he mean, "Before this goes any further?" Was
he talking about the investigation or did he mean our relationship? I took a deep breath, forced my body to relax
back into the leather bucket seat and waited.

"After you and I broke up, well, Bitsy and I had a… short relationship." He looked at me, scanning my face for a reaction, and when I didn't show one, went on. "It didn't mean much. I mean, it didn't last long. It was just one of those summer things and I guess I pretty much forgot about it. Then a few years later, when I was in Special Forces, a couple of suits paid me a visit."

"Suits?"

"Feds, spooks, you know, CIA types. They were doing a routine background investigation on Bitsy. They didn't tell me why, of course, but I got curious and eventually I figured it out. Bitsy was joining the club."

"Shut *up!* Bitsy? She's not spy material. She's a dingbat."

Jake smiled. "She's a genius playing a dingbat, Stella. The girl was brilliant. She was the third brightest in our graduating class, and I know she could've walked off with the best G.P.A., only it wouldn't have fit with her party-girl image."

"So she dummied down?"

Jake nodded. "Just enough to still get into a good school but not be called a geek."

"And this is what you wanted to tell me?"

Jake looked uncomfortable. "Not exactly. A few years later, right before she got married, we ran into each other again. It was a strange set of circumstances. Both of us were far away from home, doing things other people would hopefully never know, and well, it was fairly high risk, so…"

Great. Jake and Bitsy.

"Weren't you still married then?" Okay, so I was sticking the knife in and twisting it a little bit.

"Yeah." Jake looked so miserable I started to feel bad.

"So, then what happened?"

Jake looked out his window for a long moment.

"Nothing. We finished doing what we had to do and that was that. I never saw her again. She got married about a month later and I kept on…"

"Wait a minute. Bitsy got married a *month* later? After she had an affair with you?"

Jake nodded. "She didn't love him, Stella. In fact, she never even mentioned him. I doubt Bitsy even knew the man at the time."

This wasn't making sense to me. It didn't sound like the Bitsy I remembered, but then, she'd eloped and that wasn't her, either.

"I'm confused, Jake."

This made him smile. "Me, too, baby. What I'm trying to say is that Bitsy may have been on the job when she called. She probably knew we were working together but didn't want to risk calling me directly."

Oh. I was starting to feel stupid. "So you think Bitsy wanted you, not me. You think she was in some kind of trouble and remembered you?"

Jake nodded. "She knew I had a certain…skill set. She probably knew I was out of the service and so I wouldn't be on anybody's radar if she needed something and had to stay under the wire. Marygrace probably told her how to reach me."

Oh, great. So Bitsy hadn't wanted my help at all! She wanted Jake. Well, didn't they all?

"I'm just saying, if you were for any reason blaming yourself for Bitsy not making it in, don't. This has nothing to do with you. It's my fault. I should've put it together and had you call her back. I guess I just thought she'd be out of it by now. People like Bitsy get promoted into administration. They don't stay out in the field."

So that explained the squirrelly driving. Jake was blaming himself for Bitsy's death.

"I'm telling you this after the fact because I think we should be extra cautious on this one. There probably is a connection between what's going on at the nursing home and Bitsy."

I nodded. There was no way I could've seen this coming. I knew there was no reason to beat myself up for somehow not being able to divine this bit of information, but I felt suddenly out of the loop.

Jake reached over to start the engine then turned to study my expression, once again trying to read me.

"You all right about this?" he asked.

I gave him my best smile and nodded. "Glad you told me. I'll be on the lookout." I motioned toward the road. "We'd better get to it. I don't want Marygrace Llewellen on my back."

I turned away and stared out my window as Jake drove. As we made our way toward Brookhaven Manor, a realization suddenly hit me. The real reason I was upset was not because Jake had information I didn't have. I was upset because Jake had a secret. In fact, Jake had lots of secrets and they just seemed to keep popping up. What else was he holding back? And how could I trust and love a man who had so many secrets?

Chapter 3

Brookhaven Manor sat on a small knoll overlooking the bypass just outside Glenn Ford. It could've been any generic nursing home in any town in America with its low-slung, redbrick exterior and the long front porch lined with white rocking chairs. I stared up at the building wondering if rocking chairs were a requirement of aging. Every assisted-living and retirement home I'd ever visited had them.

Jake parked in the small visitors' lot and studied the grounds. "Nice for old people, bad for security," he muttered.

I surveyed the tree-filled grounds, noting the many paths and benches tucked away into what would normally be cozy nooks for chatting or reading but were now a haven for hiding out or trespassing unseen.

"A regular nightmare," I agreed.

We hadn't even reached the massive glass front doors

before Marygrace Llewellen was outside, hurrying toward us with a grim expression on her face.

"Don't go in yet," she said. "I want to tell you something." She looked over her shoulder, as if checking for pursuers, then turned back. "I've talked to some of the staff and apparently there was an as-needed PRN attendant on duty last night. She was sent by the staffing service we regularly use but it was her first time with us."

"Was she assigned to Baby?" I asked.

"No, but one of the nurses saw her in that hall and directed her back to her assigned post. At the time she figured the girl was just lost, but in light of what happened later…"

Marygrace looked back over her shoulder again, obviously nervous. "She's back again today, that's what I wanted to tell you. I haven't spoken with her and the police haven't made it out here yet to take their report, either, so I thought I'd leave her to you guys."

I smiled. "Good thinking, Marygrace. Where is she?"

"Follow me. They have her working on the North Hall today. I asked the charge nurse to have her wait for me in the conference room." Marygrace turned and set off rapidly through the entrance doors, across the wide linoleum foyer and down a hallway that ran to the left of the entry.

When we reached the North Hall nurses' station, Marygrace stopped and motioned to a large, heavy-set black woman in white scrubs.

"Is she in the conference room?"

The woman nodded. "Should be. That's where I told her to go, but her English isn't too good." The nurse shook her head. "I wish they'd send us some help that we can actually communicate with. Half the time they babble off something and I don't know what they're saying."

Marygrace pointed to a room at the end of the hallway as Jake's pager went off, startling both of us and causing a little man in a wheelchair to stop and stare at Jake.

"It's a call-out, ain't it?" he said. He looked irritated. "Damned things! Tell 'em I'm off and ain't no way I'm coming in!" With this, he rolled off down the hallway.

Marygrace smiled. "He's a retired firefighter. He thinks he's still on duty."

Jake's expression changed imperceptibly but I saw his eyes darken and knew something was up.

"Go on ahead and get started with her," he said, reaching into his pocket. "I'd better check in with Spike." He withdrew his cell phone from his pocket and turned to walk away from us. Whatever it was, it was serious and it was not something he wanted Marygrace to overhear.

I covered for him by starting off toward the conference room with Marygrace. "Now, I don't want to scare her, so why don't you introduce me as a friend of Baby's instead of a P.I.?"

Marygrace bobbed her head up and down in agreement as she reached for the door handle and led me into the large room. Windows overlooking a pond and the woods beyond them lined the far wall and gave the room a feeling of unending space. A massive conference table flanked by leather chairs took up most of the room. I looked around, noting the sparse countertops that lined the other walls and the impersonal art that had been hung in an attempt to add warmth to the stiff furniture. It was the standard conference room. It was also empty.

Marygrace took one look and stuck her head out the door. "Sandra, she's not in here. Page her, would you?"

Someone else walked by the room and I heard Marygrace asking her if she'd seen the CNA.

"I saw her go into the ladies' room about five minutes ago," the female voice answered.

I intervened. "Where's the ladies' room?" I asked Marygrace. "I think I'll go check. Give me her name and a brief description." My internal alarm system was beginning to sound the red alert. I scanned the hallway for Jake and didn't see him anywhere. This wasn't going so well and we'd only just arrived.

"The ladies' room is back off the lobby next to the dining room. The girl's name is Aida. She's tall, with long, dirty-blond hair that's got a perm, you know, so it sort of falls in ringlets. She's thin and she'll be wearing scrubs, probably green. The agency we use gives their temps complementary uniforms and most of them wear those."

I started off down the hallway with Marygrace on my heels.

"You'd better stay back there, in case Aida comes back. We wouldn't want to miss her."

Surprisingly, Marygrace didn't question me and returned to the room.

I kept looking for Jake as I walked up the hallway but he was nowhere to be found. As I passed the lobby, I looked down the opposite hallway, but he wasn't there, either. Now where had he disappeared to?

The ladies' room was clearly labeled in big white letters. I paused in front of the door, pulled my Lady Smith out of its holster and dropped it into my jacket pocket just in case, then slowly entered the restroom.

It was a small, three-stall room with two sinks and a window above the heating unit at the far end of the room. As I watched, a green ass and a pair of legs vanished through the open window.

"Hey!" I cried and went into autopilot. I ran, scaled the

metal heater and scrambled up the side of the wall and through the open window.

There was a six-foot drop to the ground below. I looked up and saw a figure in green scrubs running across the back parking lot, headed for the woods and thought, why me? Where's Jake? Damn!

I jumped, dropping hard to my knees before straightening and pursuing my quarry into the woods. She had a good head start on me but I was in shape, and with effort, I began to slowly close the gap between us. And then she disappeared. She simply vanished into the thick stand of pine trees in front of me.

I stopped, stuck my hand into my jacket pocket and brought out the gun.

"Aida," I called. "I just want to talk to you."

I stood still, listening. The air was thick with the humidity that signaled an oncoming snowstorm and all the small ordinary sounds. Where was she? I tried to remember the area around the nursing home, searching for a mental map in my mind that would let me guess how she might try to escape so I could anticipate her next move.

Where the hell was Jake when I needed backup?

I crept slowly forward, still listening, barely breathing as I scanned the fir trees ahead of me. I slipped the safety off the Lady Smith and slid my forefinger along the smooth barrel of the gun.

I never saw her coming.

She landed the first blow to the side of my head, a swift, strong punch that I'm certain left knuckle indentations in my skull and sent my gun flying out of my hand. She had a good jump on me, but I landed the next punch. I whirled around, caught sight of cold, green eyes and faked right before upper-cutting her with a solid left.

Neither of us said a word. We fought in silence, each too intent on landing the finishing blow. I felt the air sail out of her lungs as I landed a kick to her solar plexus. Her answering move threw me off my feet and onto the hard ground. I saw my gun lying a short distance away and rolled to grab it. My fingers had just closed around the firm metal grip when lights exploded somewhere behind my left ear and the world around me swirled into an inky darkness.

When I came to, Aida had vanished. I thought I heard footsteps running away in the distance, but it could easily have been the anguished pounding of my head. I struggled to my feet, leaned against a nearby pine tree and waited for the world to stop spinning around me. What had that girl hit me with?

"Stella!"

Great. Now he shows up. I could hear Jake getting closer but when I tried to answer the only sound that escaped was a thin, high-pitched squeak. When he finally caught sight of me, he stopped and stared.

"What did you do, hit a tree?"

I just looked at him. Well, actually, I looked at two of him for a moment before my vision cleared. Jake was attempting to play, but his concern was evident in his eyes. I'd scared him.

"I opened a can of whoop ass on this tree here and then I used what I had left over on that little nurse's aide Marygrace wanted us to interview."

Jake looked around the clearing. "What'd you do then, bury her?"

I let go of the tree and took a few uncertain steps toward him. "No, idiot, I let her crawl off into the woods to die. It was the only honorable thing to do."

He nodded. "She cold-cocked you and got away, huh?"

I looked past him and started walking back toward the nursing home. "Yeah, something like that."

Jake stopped me, studying my face before gently tracing the area around my left eye with his thumb.

"Ouch! Stop that!"

He smiled softly. "You're gonna have a hell of a shiner."

"Yeah, well you should see her!"

Jake sighed as I shrugged off his attempt to support me while I walked.

"Where were you, anyway? Here I am, attempting to whoop some scrawny girl's ass and you're chatting with Spike on the phone. Where's your sense of duty? You're supposed to back up your partner."

Jake's expression darkened. "I hope you're kidding. If somebody hadn't seen you running and told Marygrace, I'd still be looking for you. I had no idea you'd get into something so fast."

"Yes, I was kidding. What did Spike want?"

"Among other things, she called to tell me the coroner was about to send Bitsy's body to the state forensic lab for identification when the feds stepped in and claimed it."

"How'd they explain that?"

"They told the coroner she was married to a member of the diplomatic corps and that he'd requested it."

"Which was bullshit, right?"

Jake nodded. "Yep. Guess there's no doubt about it. She was still on the payroll."

We'd reached the front entrance to the building, and Marygrace was waiting for us. When she caught sight of me, her expression ran the gamut from surprised to horrified to professionally neutral. I figured I had to look pretty scary to make her pull out her job face.

"Looks like you need a little doctoring," she said. "Our physician's assistant, Stephanie, can take a look at you."

"I'm fine. I just got a little scraped up, that's all."

Marygrace raised an eyebrow. "Well, I just thought you might not want to scare the residents. Come on. Let her patch you up. Besides, I figured you'd want to talk to her anyway. She's the one who usually looks after the residents in place of the doctor."

I nodded, wishing my head didn't hurt so much. "You don't have a doctor on staff?"

Marygrace was scuttling down the hallway but the mention of expense and doctors made her pause momentarily. "With Medicaid paying? Hell, places like this don't get real doctors. We get their P.A. and if it's really bad, we might see them at the end of the day, when they're already too tired and could care less about whether one old person lives or dies." She apparently thought better of this because she quickly tacked on a disclaimer. "Not all of them are sharks. I'm just saying most of them are."

"The doc here, is he a shark?"

"No comment," she answered grimly. "But I like Stephanie."

"Was she the one who initially treated Baby today?"

Marygrace shook her head. "Nope. She was seeing patients in Dr. Alonzo's office when Baby got hurt. The charge nurse sent her on to the hospital and she's still there. But Stephanie saw her after she reported someone had been in her room two days ago."

Jake was walking along with us, the frown on his face deepening with every step. When Marygrace stopped to speak to a resident, I took him aside. "What's wrong?"

"I'm just trying to put this all together. I mean, why go out a bathroom window and not a door?"

"Oh, that's easy," Marygrace said, rejoining us and shamelessly eavesdropping. "All the doors are locked.

You can only get out by punching in the code on the keypad that's located next to each door."

"And don't all the employees have the code?"

"Sure," Marygrace said, grinning. "Unless you change it and don't tell them. That's what I did as soon as I got back here. I wanted to control who was coming and going until the police got here. The front door was the only door with open access and I had the front desk clerk writing down the names of everyone who arrived or departed."

"So, why didn't she just walk out the front door?"

"Look at him!" Marygrace said, gesturing to Jake. "He's got cop written all over him! He's big. He's got a bulge under his suit coat and he was outside talking on the cell phone right in front of the building. I'd take the window too, if I'd been in her shoes."

I nodded, making a mental note to get the name of the staffing agency the nursing home used to hire Aida. They'd be reluctant to talk, if not downright uncooperative, fearing a lawsuit from the nursing home and citing confidentiality, but we could still try.

A tall woman with close-cropped wiry black hair stood in front of the North Hall nurses' station, writing in a thick chart. She wore a spotless white lab coat, open to reveal a downright sexy pink knit top that crisscrossed her ample chest and highlighted the rich mocha color of her skin. As we approached, she looked up, took one look at my face and turned away from her paperwork.

"You don't have enough to do, Marygrace, you gotta go gathering people up from the parking lot for me to see?"

Marygrace went off into one of her long, rapid-fire explanations punctuated with requests for medical attention and information. Within moments I was sitting in a chair in the conference room wincing as Stephanie dabbed Betadine on the scrape above my eye and Jake peppered her with questions about Baby Blankenship.

"Without Baby or her P.O.A. signing a release, I can't talk to you about her condition or any treatment I may or may not have provided. As I understand it, you two have been retained by Marygrace to investigate the theft of items from Ms. Blankenship's room. Frankly, I don't see how I can help you."

Great. What now? I looked to Marygrace and saw her deep in thought. She cocked her head to the side and smiled at the physician's assistant.

"Of course you can't talk about Baby, specifically, but you could speak generally about people like Baby, people who…I don't know, let's say, elderly people with maybe midstage Alzheimer's."

Marygrace was fairly levitating with the possibilities of obtaining information from Stephanie without breaking the laws pertaining to confidentiality.

"How about this," Marygrace continued. "Suppose someone with a fair amount of memory loss encountered a trauma and lost something important to them. Suppose they then forgot what they'd lost. Would there be a chance that they could wake up tomorrow and perhaps remember more details, like the specific item that was missing or the description of the person who'd taken it?"

Stephanie smiled. "Perhaps. It happens. Of course, they could wake up tomorrow and have forgotten the entire incident, too."

Jake was worse at hiding his frustration than I was. He fidgeted impatiently and finally turned to Marygrace. "Can we see her room?"

Marygrace sighed. "Sure. I told the staff to leave the room untouched, but I was too late. They were already trying to put things in order by the time I got back to the facility. They didn't know. I guess they don't watch those police shows like I do." She smiled ruefully. "Come on. I'll show you her room while Stephanie finishes doctoring Stella."

"Wait a minute! We're done, aren't we?" I jumped up off the stool despite Stephanie's attempts to continue dabbing me with swabs and ointments and took off after Jake and Marygrace. No way was I getting the short end of this investigation.

"Thanks, Stephanie," I called over my shoulder, drowning out her protests.

I reached the door to Baby Blankenship's room just as the other two were walking into it. It looked like any room in any hospital or nursing home in America, with the exception of a wall covered in family photographs and some other brightly colored knickknacks scattered around.

I had just begun carefully inspecting a photograph of a much younger Bitsy, surrounded by the rest of her family at what appeared to be a birthday party for Baby, when my cell phone rang.

"Stella?" Nina's voice sounded strange, as if she had a cold or was trying not to cry.

"What's wrong?"

"I was trying to help," she said and sniffed loudly.

"Nina, tell me what's going on."

Jake and Marygrace were both studying me with concerned expressions.

"Well, after you guys left I remembered I had a hair appointment later and like, well, I have this paint chip I wanted Verna to see, you know, so she'd know what color I wanted for the highlights this time?"

"Uh-huh."

It would do no good to rush Nina. It would only make

her back up and start the tale all over again. The best thing I could do was pray she wound it up in short order.

"Well, you know how you were talking about that limo and all and Aunt Lucy being so pissed?"

"Uh-huh."

"It was there! He was dropping her off! So I like, got the license plate number and— Oh, God, Stella! It's awful!"

Nina began to sob. When she gulped air, I broke in.

"Nina, what's awful?"

"Oh!" she wailed. "I didn't know I was so good!"

"Nina, what are you talking about?"

My cousin sniffed loudly, sounding offended. "Stella! For pity's sake, try and follow what I'm saying! I am just like, totally good at this detective crap! I found out who he is and…and…"

"And?" I wanted to jump through the phone and throttle the girl.

"And, well, I found out too much, that's what!"

This was followed by a renewed burst of crying, punctuated by loud sniffs and snorts.

"Nina," I said, trying to be heard over the sheer volume of her sobbing. "Where is Spike? Let me talk to her."

"She…she…can't come. She went to see the…D.A." More crying followed and I silently counted to ten and prayed for patience.

"Okay, Nina, now try and get hold of yourself. I need to know what you found out."

Nina snuffled, blew her nose loudly and said, "All right." She drew in a deep breath and said absolutely nothing.

"Nina, who is he? What did you learn about the man? Is he a criminal? What is it?"

"I can't tell you over the phone!"

"Nina! Why not?"

Silence from her end of the line and then the infernal tear machine cranked up and she was off and running.

"You…you…you have to come here…to Aunt Lucy's. Right now! Oh, this is awful!"

"Has something happened to Aunt Lucy?" Fear rose in my chest, tightening my throat as visions of Aunt Lucy at the hands of an evil stranger snapped in a rapid-fire slide-show of possibilities.

"No! She's out again somewhere…probably with… him."

Jake was mouthing "What? Why is she crying?"

All I could do was shake my head and frown. It was impossible to explain while also trying to calm Nina down.

"All right, honey," I said finally. "We'll be there as soon as we can. It shouldn't be more than a half hour at the most."

"A half hour?" she wailed.

"Twenty minutes."

"Oh…oh…oh!" She was hiccupping now. "What… what…ever!"

I snapped the cell shut and rolled my eyes at Jake. "I don't know what's going on, but it doesn't sound good, and Spike's out working on the D.A. I don't think there's a lot we can accomplish here right now. Maybe we should return when Baby gets back from the hospital and has had some time to rest."

Marygrace's eyes widened. "You guys can't stay away too long. What if Baby comes back and something else happens? I want you to protect her!"

Jake looked puzzled. "I thought you wanted us to find whatever got stolen. You didn't say anything about protection."

Marygrace stamped her tiny foot and glared at him.

"Aw, come on man! Do I have to spell out everything? Baby got hurt and that aide beat up Stella. I'd say the woman needs protection!"

A little muscle in Jake's jaw began to twitch and I knew he was getting frustrated with Marygrace's impatience.

"Okay, Marygrace, if you want to hire private protection…"

Marygrace held up her hand, stopping me. "Whoa, now exactly how much is that going to cost? I mean, I am a social worker. Money doesn't just grow on trees, you know. Anyway, I guess the facility might pay, but I need to check it out. In the meantime, we have to take care of Baby. Where's your—"

I broke her off before she could question my civic-mindedness.

"All right! All right! Jake, how about you drop me at Aunt Lucy's and go on to the hospital so you can keep an eye on Baby. I'll go see what's got Nina so upset, then relieve you at six, either there or here, depending on when they release her."

Jake nodded but before he could add anything else, his cell phone rang.

After he said hello all I could hear was the sound of Nina sobbing. I snatched the phone out of his hand and pressed the receiver to my ear.

"All right! We're coming! You don't have to call Jake to ride herd on me, okay?"

"It's a matter…of…life and death," she said shakily. "I thought I might've forgotten to…tell you…that."

The cell phone went dead as Nina severed the connection. Oh, this was just too unbelievable. We finally get a case that has nothing to do with insurance fraud or cheating spouses and what happens? We develop a rash of personal problems! Somebody give me a break!

   Still, a little flame of apprehension ignited inside my
chest, growing stronger the closer I got to my office. Nina
was a dingbat, no doubt about it, but she rarely got upset
without cause. In fact, Nina never overreacted, at least not
in the presence of real danger. So something was wrong,
all right, and if Nina was on target, it *would* be a matter
of life and death.

Chapter 4

Nina had stopped crying by the time we reached the brick row house she, Spike and I shared with Aunt Lucy. My Australian sheepdog, Lloyd, sat in my uncle Benny's old place at the kitchen table, the seat of honor he'd been given ever since Lloyd and I had returned from Florida and Aunt Lucy had decided he was my uncle reincarnated. Nina sat next to him, her eyes swollen and red, nursing a cup of herbal tea. Aunt Lucy's newest adoptee, Fang, the part-wolf dog, lay at Nina's feet.

"Stella, what happened to you?"

I frowned, momentarily having forgotten that my eye was swollen and by now turning black.

"It's a long story. There's more to the nursing home situation than we thought, but tell me about Aunt Lucy first."

Nina sighed and shook her head sadly. "I guess the

whole world's got problems. Now Fang and Lloyd aren't getting along."

As if on cue, Fang lifted one lip to expose a nasty-looking canine tooth and snarled softly at Lloyd. On her worst day, Fang could eat Lloyd for a snack and not feel satisfied, but this had never been an issue. Lloyd and Fang had met on the beach in New Jersey and from that first moment, they'd been inseparable. When Fang's owner decided to move to the Caribbean, it seemed only natural that my generous aunt would bring the monstrous beast into the family.

"What about Aunt Lucy's boyfriend?" I asked, ignoring the dog issues. "You said it was a matter of life and death."

Nina's momentary calm dissolved. Her chin quivered and tears filled her eyes. "It's sooo sad," she wailed.

"Nina! Just tell me what's going on!"

"Well, I told you I got the license plate number and well, you know I have that friend, Micky, at the D.M.V.?"

I nodded, encouraging her.

"Well, she got his name." This produced a fresh spill-over of tears. "It's Arnold Koslovski. He graduated from Glenn Ford High School in 1951, went into the army, then to Villa Nova on a VA loan and then, for some unknown reason, moved to Michigan. I guess that's where he met his wife, Elizabeth. Anyway, he stayed there and eventually opened his own company. He was some big entrepreneur, owned one of the first chains of electronics stores and then he discovered computers. Everything he touched turned to money. He's like a gazillionaire or something. There were all these articles about him and his wife doing good deeds and giving away millions."

Nina blew her nose as the tears continued to fall. Jake squatted down to pet Fang but drew his hand back when Fang snarled.

"Man, she is testy today! Think she could be sick?"

Leave it to a man to change the subject whenever feelings get involved!

"She doesn't look sick to me. She looks fat and lazy. Maybe living the good life is starting to get on her nerves."

Lloyd whined and gave his beloved Fang a concerned look. Nina blew her nose again and continued on with her convoluted report.

"Arnold and Aunt Lucy were in the same class," Nina said. "I found Aunt Lucy's old yearbook lying out on the coffee table. She must've been looking through it." Nina reached down into her lap and drew an ancient volume up from beneath the table. A napkin marked the page where Arnold Koslovski's teenage face smiled out at us.

"Nina, this is all well and good, but if there's a life-threatening situation here, could you just cut to the chase and tell me about it?"

Mistake. Big mistake. Never rush Nina, it only makes the situation and the story last that much longer. My cousin sniffed and scowled at me.

"I am like, totally telling you about this!" she snapped. "You have to know the history and background to understand the gravity of Aunt Lucy's situation."

"All right, all right! Do it your way!"

"I will. As I was saying…Aunt Lucy's been receiving anonymous flowers and cards ever since Uncle Benny died. Then when we were at the beach, you know, on our last case, the flowers started coming there, and there were groceries, too. Well, Arnold must've hired people to watch Aunt Lucy. How else could he have found out where we'd gone? And, like, I thought it was totally creepy until I found this!"

Nina shoved a piece of paper at me. It was a copy of an old newspaper article dated 1971. "Kidnapped Koslovski Heiress Found Dead," was the headline. I read the piece with Jake leaning over my shoulder.

"So the guy's only kid was killed in a bungled kidnapping?" Jake clearly didn't get the connection to my aunt.

"Isn't that awful?" Nina looked at the two of us and seemed to be waiting for us to "get" it. "So, like, the guy doesn't want anything bad to ever happen to people he loves," she said with a tone of exaggerated patience. "So, he's been watching over Aunt Lucy for, like, ever. That's how he knew Uncle Benny died."

"Nina, that doesn't make sense. Why would some guy Aunt Lucy went to high school with have private investigators watch her when she's married to another guy? *That* is creepy."

"No, look!" Nina snatched up the yearbook and flipped to another page she'd marked with a napkin. "See!"

Jake and I stared down at the picture of my aunt as a young girl. "She looks like you," Jake murmured. "Look at those huge, dark eyes and that hair!" Jake looked at me with a speculative eye. "You had black hair just like hers in high school. What's with the blond?"

In truth, the blond was a stakeout cover on my first and only big case with the Garden Beach, Florida, Police Department but I liked it and so, as part of starting over, I'd kept it. I ignored Jake and turned my attention back to the yearbook. Spidery blue script covered the margin next to my aunt's picture.

"Can you read that?" I asked Nina.

"It says, 'Lucille, wait for me. Our love is eternal. A.' You see? That proves it!"

"Proves what?"

"That he loved her, even though she didn't wait and married Uncle Benny. 'Our love is eternal.' Isn't that just too romantic?"

"Not when the guy stalks her for the rest of her life," I said, concern growing with every new fact Nina trotted out. She didn't seem at all concerned about this part of Aunt Lucy's relationship with Arnold Koslovski, so what was bothering her?

"Didn't you say the guy's married?" Jake was obviously trying to hone in on the "life or death" issue, too.

"His wife died two years ago," Nina said. "She had leukemia." The tears were back in Nina's eyes. We were getting closer to what was bothering her. "And now…now he's back in town, looking for his beloved Lucille before…before…"

"Before?"

"Before he dies! Arnold's dying!"

Okay. *Now* we had an issue. Aunt Lucy had gone half-crazy after Uncle Benny died. If this Arnold person was dying, how would she take a second loss of a love?

"How do you know the guy's dying? Are you sure?"

Nina nodded miserably. "Yeah. He was going to buy the old Proctor place, signed the contract and everything, but then he reneged."

"Nina, how do you know all this? We were only gone, what, half an hour and you found out all this?"

Nina looked even more miserable. "Yeah, told you I'm good."

"Honey, just because Arnold didn't buy the Proctor place, it doesn't mean he's dying."

Nina nodded. "I know. I found out about the Proctor deal from Cindy Evans, she works at Burgess Realty and I knew she'd know if somebody like Arnold Koslovski moved back to town. She's the one who gave me his new address and that's how come I know he's dying!"

Jake couldn't stand another second of this. "What in the hell does that have to do with the man's health?"

"Because," Nina said as she looked up at him, "it's the

hospice unit in Honeybrook. Arnold Koslovski couldn't live there if he wasn't dying!"

Nina started sobbing and my cell phone began vibrating. I ignored it. A minute later Jake's cell also went off. Marygrace Llewellen was an impatient woman.

"Guess she wants to know why we haven't made it to the hospital yet."

Jake gave me a look that said "And we took this case on as a public service because...why?"

I ignored him and reached for my cell phone. "Go ahead. I'll take care of her and *this* situation too." Nina was still snuffling into a wad of tissues, too lost in her own conclusions about Arnold Koslovski and his relationship with my aunt to pay any attention to us.

"Good luck!" Jake was gone in an instant, probably relieved to have a valid excuse to take off. For once I couldn't blame him. I looked down at my sodden cousin, took a deep breath and once again tried to convince her that she was jumping to conclusions but it did no good. Nina remained adamant in her beliefs about Arnold Koslovski. When Spike arrived home from her information-gathering trip to the D.A.'s office, I gladly relinquished my responsibilities for my cousin's happiness and refocused my thoughts on Bitsy and Baby Blankenship.

I started by responding to Marygrace's third page in thirty minutes, launching into an offensive before she could tackle me with another one of her verbal onslaughts.

"Jake's on his way to the hospital now," I said as soon as she came on the line. "We were checking with some of our informants, you know, for recently fenced stolen property that might've belonged to an elderly woman. It was a shot in the dark, what with most of your pawns consisting of tools and elec—"

"Never mind that!" Marygrace whispered into the phone. "We've got bigger fish to fry over here! The State's in, and I don't mean your regular auditor types. I think they're feds!"

"What?" I looked up at the ceiling, hoping I was communicating directly with the Person or Persons in Charge. *Why me?* I asked silently. *Is this paybacks for spying on Aunt Lucy? I'm telling you, I was only trying to protect her! And if this is about putting off Bitsy... Well, don't you think I'm already feeling bad enough, now you gotta add feds to the mix? I could lose my license if they get pissy about things.*

"Stella," Marygrace snapped, forgetting to whisper. "Pay attention! The State comes in to audit nursing homes once a year. They come in any other time they feel like it, but most often it's because someone's made a complaint about something we're doing or not doing to the old people. Well, they're here, only I know all the State people and I've never seen these two, no matter what their credentials say."

"Are they doing the regular things the State does when they come?"

"Hell, no! They asked for Baby's chart and then they went into her room! She's not there. There isn't any reason for them to go in there, and the charge nurse says they've been looking all over her room. I think you'd better get Jake to lay low until they leave. I don't want any more questions."

"So, you want us to back off and let Baby come on back to the nursing home without any coverage."

Marygrace sighed. "No. I want Jake to lay low, you know, don't let the feds know who he is and what he's doing."

Right. Now that would be easy. What was he supposed to do, dress up like a nurse?

I hung up and dialed Jake's cell phone number.

"Dr. Carpenter." No hello. Just Jake sounding very professional and lying his ass off.

"This is Nurse Barbie calling. Wanna check my temperature?"

"I'm with a patient. Can it wait?"

"Jake, Marygrace just called. She thinks she's got feds at the old folks home and she wants you to stick to Baby like glue, but disguise yourself."

"No can do," he said cryptically. "They are probably familiar with my work."

"Nurse Barbie's familiar with your work, too," I said, and felt a familiar rush of warmth as I remembered his last house call.

"I think you should probably do the consult yourself. I'm in the middle of completing a consultation on a patient who's about to be discharged."

"You've got an audience and it's more than Baby Blankenship, huh?"

"I'm sure your qualifications will more than meet the need."

"Yours too, Doctor," I cooed. "I guess I'll see what I can round up before Baby gets back to the home. So, they're about to ship her out?"

"Yes, absolutely. Within the hour. Feel free to consult with me after you've assessed the patient."

"Oh, Doc, I do love it when you talk dirty!" I said and hung up.

Great. I had to go undercover at the nursing home where too many people had already seen me, and my black eye from the earlier tangle would be a certain giveaway. How was I going to pull this one off?

Thirty minutes later, after a visit to the attic and a search through a multitude of chests and boxes, I emerged from my room a changed woman. If Aunt Lucy arrived before I walked out the door, I was dead meat. I could justify it as having been done for a worthy cause, but knowing my aunt, this would cut no sway with her. Sacrilege is sacrilege.

When I walked into the kitchen, Spike looked up and did a double-take. Nina reflexively crossed herself.

"Oh no you didn't!" she gasped. "That's Aunt Cathy's!"

"Was," I corrected, crossing myself and murmuring. "May she rest in peace."

Spike's nose wrinkled. "You smell like cedar."

"You look like..." Nina started, but I was already sweeping past her, headed for the door. "You'd better go to confession!" she yelled after me.

When I arrived at the nursing home, no one recognized me. Even Marygrace lowered her head and made the sign of the cross.

"Sister," she said softly. "May I help you."

I couldn't help it. I giggled. "Yeah, Marygrace, you can introduce me as the new chaplaincy intern, here for the next few weeks."

"Shit!" she cried, eyes widening. "Stella, is that you?" She got up from her desk and walked around to inspect me more closely. "Damn, you smell like mothballs or something!"

"It's my great-aunt Cathy's habit from back when she was in the convent."

"What'd you do to your face to hide those bruises? You look pale."

I smiled. "Well, the wimple hid most of the damage, but I had to use under-eye concealer to get the rest."

Marygrace frowned at the heavy white cloth that framed my face. "Stella, do nuns even still wear habits? I thought they dressed in street clothes nowadays."

I gave her a look. "I don't know what they wear and it doesn't really matter. All you have to do is make everyone believe I come from a small, conservative outfit that still does things the old-fashioned way. Besides, I doubt anybody'll have the nerve to ask me about my wardrobe."

A grim-faced trio entered the room led by a large, red-headed man in a gray suit. They stopped short as soon as they recognized my outfit.

"Oh, Marygrace, excuse us," the redheaded man said. "I didn't know you were busy."

Marygrace smiled nervously, her fingers twisting the lanyard that held her nametag. "Oh, Darren, this is the new...chaplaincy intern, Sister..."

I stepped forward, held out my hand and tried to look severe and imposing. "Sister Angelina Jo-Joseph." I looked straight into the administrator's eyes, knowing he had to know Marygrace was lying because he'd have been informed of a new intern on staff, but daring him to give us away.

Darren looked startled, his pale skin reddening just slightly beneath the freckled surface.

"Glad to have you with us...Sister." He glanced past me to Marygrace. "I hate to interrupt, but these gentlemen have a few questions for you concerning the record audits they've been doing."

I took the social cue and smiled gracefully. "Well, if you don't need me, Marygrace, I'll just go down to the west wing and say a few prayers."

Marygrace's mouth opened, but she was at a loss for words. I made my way past the two broad-shouldered men in dark suits, committing their faces and general descriptions to memory as I went. The chances were slim that Jake would recognize them from my generic depiction; still I tried to pick out distinguishing characteristics. Crew cuts aside, they were both well over six feet tall, but one had a half-moon-shaped scar circling his left eyebrow and the other had the tip missing from his left ring finger.

The two men certainly looked like government agents, but there was something I couldn't quite put my finger on that made me wonder if they were *our* government agents. They just didn't have that fresh-scrubbed Bureau air, and yet I couldn't say for sure that they didn't fit the profile. I left the room but lingered outside the door long enough to hear one of them speak. No trace of a foreign accent. Nope, I was probably letting my imagination run away with me and seeing terrorists everywhere.

I reached the corridor leading to Baby Blankenship's room just as two uniformed ambulance drivers wheeled a gurney through the back door. A thin, white-haired woman with vivid blue eyes was propped up in a sitting position and seemed to be taking great interest in everything going on around her.

"Hey, I know you!" The little elderly firefighter from our earlier visit sat in his wheelchair at the opening to his room. He was looking right at me and scowling. "I've seen you around here, Sister, and believe me, it takes more than a bunch of black and white cloth to hide that package!" He cackled but I was frozen, wondering who'd heard him.

"Mr. Heinz, that's no way to talk!" A young woman dressed in aqua scrubs emerged from the room across the hall and stood, hands on hips, shaking her head at the little man.

"Don't pay him no mind, Sister," she said, smiling at me. "He don't mean a thing by it."

"I do, too!" Mr. Heinz sputtered. "I'm old, girly, not

crazy! She may smell like a mothball but she's all woman underneath that get-up! I seen her!"

I hated to do it but it was his sanity or mine. "In the name of the Father, the Son and the Holy Spirit, let us pray," I murmured softly.

The little man dropped his head as the aide walked away. "Forgive me, Sister, for I have sinned," he said slowly.

I couldn't do it. God might not strike me dead for lying but Aunt Lucy certainly would.

"I'm just praying, son," I whispered. "It's not confession time yet."

The white-haired man peeked up at me. "The hell it ain't, Sister. You're hotter than a two-dollar pistol, and I've got lust in my heart!"

Before I could move away, my admirer shot out his hand, grabbed a sizable portion of my posterior and squeezed.

"Mr. Heinz!" The aide materialized from another room just in time to catch her patient in action.

The retired firefighter drew his hand back and smiled up innocently at the girl. "Ah, Kenya, there you are! I was looking for you!"

"Not like that you weren't!" she groused. "Come on. You're not fooling me or the sister." She looked up at me and shook her head. "He's got selective dementia," she said. "He picks and chooses when to forget his manners. I'm sorry."

I raised one hand and smiled my best pure-of-heart smile. "Go in peace, child," I said, and was amazed when lightning didn't strike me dead. I turned to walk away and found Baby Blankenship watching me.

"One time," she said, her voice quavering with the

effort to speak. "One time that old coot did the same thing to me. I wasn't as Christian to him as you just were."

I smiled as I approached the gurney. "What did you do?"

Baby Blankenship smiled. "I told him to go fuck himself!"

The entire nursing station fell silent for a long moment before one of the nurses gave the tall, skinny ambulance attendant a sharp glance.

"I take it the doctor didn't order Mrs. Blankenship some Ativan before you left?"

"Apparently not." The guy started to grin, remembered who I was, and stopped.

"Don't worry about it," I said pleasantly. "She's not fully cognizant of what she's saying. I've worked in nursing homes before. I know how it is."

The ambulance attendants, accompanied by the nurse, rolled Baby into her room and as I watched, gently deposited the frail woman back into her bed. When they'd gone, I quickly entered the room and closed the door behind me.

"Mrs. Blankenship?" I said, approaching her bedside. The woman's eyes were closed, but at the mention of her name, they popped open and for a moment she appeared frightened.

"Am I dying?" Baby asked in her shaky voice.

I smiled and patted her arm. "No, dear, not that I know of. I wanted to talk to you about what happened earlier today."

Baby gave me an understanding wink. "I see. You heard about that, did you?"

A wave of relief spread through me. Baby was having one of her lucid periods.

"Yes, I heard. It's just terrible! Can you tell me what happened?"

Outside Baby's room I heard footsteps stop and Mary-grace's voice as she spoke to whoever was with her.

"The door's closed. The aide is probably with her, getting her changed and back into bed. We'd better not go in just yet. I really don't think it's in Mrs. Blankenship's best interest to talk to you now. Surely this can wait until morning?"

Marygrace had pitched her voice just high enough to carry into the room, signaling me. The deep rumble of an insistent male voice told me that time was of the essence. I turned back to Baby and smiled.

"Baby, did someone come in here and take something that belonged to you? Is that how you got hurt?"

Baby frowned. As I watched her lower lip began to tremble as her watery blue eyes filled with unshed tears.

"Oh, did they? How awful!" she murmured. "I thought that girl wanted something. She was mean to me!"

"Who was mean, Baby? Was it your aide?"

Baby shook her head emphatically. "No, not Lunta. Lunta's good to me." She picked nervously at her cotton coverlet. "Barbara came to see me the other day. She's almost grown-up now." Baby closed her eyes and appeared to have fallen asleep.

"Baby?"

Her eyelids fluttered as she focused on my face, smiling. "Oh, hello. Am I dead?"

I sighed silently. This was not going to be something I could rush. "No, dear. I'm a chaplain. I came to see if you're all right and to keep you safe." I decided to take a risk. "Your granddaughter, Bitsy, sent me. She said someone took something that belongs to you and I'm here to help get it back."

The door creaked open and instead of turning around

I began to pray, hoping it would deter Baby's visitors from entering the room. "Our Father who art in Heaven…"

Baby obediently closed her eyes and I kept on praying until I heard the door click shut again.

"Baby?"

This time she was truly sleeping. I slipped my hand into the deep pocket of my robe, pulled out my cell phone and dialed Jake.

"Hey, what's going on?" he answered.

"Marygrace is trying to keep two guys out of Baby's room and I'm in here with her. She's sleeping. I asked her about what happened earlier and if someone had taken anything from her room but she's not all there. I got nothing."

Jake chuckled softly. "She apparently thought I was one of her old boyfriends but she did tell me Bitsy came to see her."

"Well, you got further than I did."

I looked around the spare little room, feeling sad for the small woman lying asleep in her bed. What an awful way to spend the last days of your life.

"Maybe we ought to look at this from the other end," Jake said. "Maybe we should find out why Bitsy was in such a hurry to talk to us."

I looked back at Baby's door and saw shadows moving past the bottom of the door frame. I had no doubt the feds, or whoever they really were, wouldn't give up and leave without coming into the old woman's room and questioning her for themselves.

"Those guys are still here," I said.

"I know. I'm in the woods behind the parking lot. Open Baby's blinds and I'll be able to see which room she's in."

I crossed to the window, pulled open the blinds and saw nothing but darkness. The sun had slipped below the horizon, and night had fallen in the short time I'd been inside Brookhaven Manor.

"Nice get-up," Jake murmured. "I was looking forward to Nurse Barbie but now this is something…"

"Jake!" I warned. "This really isn't the time for games. Can you call Nina and see if she can come relieve me later? That should free us up to pursue the Bitsy angle."

Jake chuckled softly before switching gears and returning to the business at hand. "I'll call her. You want her to come as an aide?"

Before I could answer, the door began to open behind me. I slipped the tiny cell phone back into my pocket and turned just as the two alleged state "investigators" entered the room, accompanied by Marygrace and her boss.

"I'm sorry, Sister," Marygrace said, not looking the least bit sorry. "These gentlemen are with the state adult services division and need to talk with Mrs. Blankenship about an episode that occurred earlier today. Would it be too much trouble…"

I interrupted her before she could finish. "Gentlemen, this lady is exhausted, not to mention, heavily sedated. I doubt you'll be able to rouse her before tomorrow. I was here when the ambulance attendants gave their report. Her doctor gave her the medication right before she left the hospital." I looked at Baby and smiled. "The poor dear fought the sedative as long as she could and only agreed to close her eyes if I stayed with her." I looked back up at the two men, letting the smile fade as I gave them my best-remembered impression of the meanest nun in my parochial school. "I'll be sitting right here by her side when she awakens in the morning. I suggest you come back in the afternoon if you want to talk to her. It would be cruel to awaken the dear."

I lingered over the word *cruel* until I was certain I had their attention before going in for the close.

"If need be, I'll be glad to speak to your supervisor about the need for Mrs. Blankenship to have her rest…"

I let the threat linger while the two men reluctantly considered their options. It would look very odd if they insisted on waking a sleeping patient. I had no doubt they wouldn't have hesitated to override the nursing home staff because of the state's clout with nursing home operations, but now they were going up against one of God's employees. Even phony state investigators had to pretend to honor their higher power.

"Certainly, Sister," the man with the half-moon scar said. "We'll just come back in the morning."

I stiffened and frowned at him, enjoying my role immensely. "Not before lunch, young man."

"S'ter," he said, accepting defeat.

"I'll be right here by her bedside all night," I cautioned. "So don't you worry. I'll watch over her."

Marygrace ushered everyone out of the room but held her hand behind her back long enough to give me a thumbs-up sign. The door closed behind them and I pulled the room's lone armchair over beside the bed, settling back into its cold vinyl cushions. It was going to be a long night.

When Nina shook my shoulder a few hours later, I sat up startled and had to take a few moments to remember where I was. Nina stood beside me, her spiky blond hair tamed down with hair gel, wearing dull-green scrubs and no makeup. It was obvious, from her swollen, red-rimmed eyes, that she'd been crying again.

"Did you talk to Aunt Lucy?"

Nina shook her head. "No. Jake said I'm supposed to tell everyone I'm Mrs. Blankenship's private sitter. And he said to tell you those two men are in a blue sedan in the back parking lot."

I nodded. "Are you sure you're all right to stay?" Nina looked awful, pale and as if she might fall to pieces at any moment.

Nina looked at the sleeping woman in the bed and smiled. "I like old folks. It'll take my mind off things at home." But the smile crumpled as Nina's lower lip quivered.

"Nina, what's going on?"

"Spike wants to move. She says we should have our own place, and I was all for it in the beginning, but now Aunt Lucy's hanging out with a walking-dead guy and she's all mad at you and Jake and I just can't go!"

A fat tear escaped to run down my cousin's cheek.

"Oh, honey," I said, pulling her down to sit on the arm of my chair. "Aunt Lucy's fine. We'll get everything worked out. Besides, we don't know for sure that her boyfriend's dying. Maybe he just gave the real estate company that address so they'd leave him alone."

Nina brightened at this. "You think? Maybe you're right. I thought you had to be…you know…like almost dead to be in a hospice."

I shrugged. "That's what I think too. So, you see, maybe it's not as dark as it seems."

Nina still seemed a little uncertain. "Well, yeah, but what about you and…"

"Nina, Aunt Lucy and I can work things out without you living in the house. I can always call you guys if we need you. I mean, you're not thinking of moving far away are you?"

Nina shook her head but frowned harder. "Spike wants a new house in Exton and I don't like new houses! I want something with character. We've been out looking some, but we just haven't seen anything we love."

I sighed. "That's not a big deal," I said, reassuring her. "You two will work it out."

Nina looked down at me. "I don't know. I don't want to get married." She held up her hand before I could remind her that same-sex marriages weren't legal in Pennsylvania so it wasn't really an issue anyway. "She wants to have a commitment ceremony, but I'm not so sure I want to be that...well, you know...conventional."

I stood up and stretched. This was certainly nothing that couldn't be talked out and dealt with later.

"Honey, relationships take time and energy and compromise. Don't try and sort out the entire deal tonight. When and if the time comes and you two decide to get your own place, don't worry, I'll help you with Aunt Lucy." I looked over at Baby, who lay so still in her bed I had to watch to make sure she was still breathing.

"Call me if she tells you anything about the break-in or what's been taken."

I was about to open the door when I heard Baby Blankenship's distinctive voice.

"Bitsy," she called. "Bitsy, wait a minute!"

I turned around and saw Baby staring at me, her eyes wide with what appeared to be apprehension.

"Yes, Grandma?" I answered.

"You will be careful, won't you? I never did like him, you know. I want you safe..."

Before I could answer her, she'd fallen back to sleep, leaving me to wonder who she'd been talking about and how she'd sensed her granddaughter was in danger.

Chapter 5

Jake's apartment was in the center of town over the top of what had once been his auto repair business. I turned onto his street and slowly approached the building, checking to see if he'd waited up for me. A light was on in his back bedroom and so I turned into the narrow driveway that led to the small parking lot behind the building and parked.

The streetlight that usually illuminated the alleyway was out, making my progress toward Jake's fire escape entrance difficult, particularly in a nun's habit. I tripped over a rock, stumbled and swore under my breath. Why hadn't I just settled for calling him and filling him in on the details? Surely we couldn't do any more on the investigation tonight.

Oh, who was I kidding. I stopped by because I couldn't stay away.

I reached the bottom of the fire escape, stretched out

my hand to grasp the railing and felt a strong arm reach out to clap a hand over my mouth. With his other hand, my attacker grabbed me around the waist and pulled me back against his rock-solid body.

I fought as best I could but was hampered by the element of surprise and the bulky nun's habit. The man whirled me around and propelled me up against the brick wall of Jake's building. His breath was hot in my ear as he spoke in a muffled whisper.

"Don't move, Sister," he said.

I spun around, trying to make him out in the darkness. "Jake, you scared the shit out of me!"

He leaned down, scooped me up in his arms and slung me over his shoulder, walking with an unwavering stride through the back door to the empty lower floor of the room that had once been his office. When he put me down, I squirmed away.

"I said, freeze."

I stopped moving, my heart pounding as the familiar fire caught low in my body and began to ignite every nerve ending in its path. My eyes began to adjust to the darkened room. He was against the wall, watching me.

"Your gown, Sister…take it off."

"No," I breathed, but my fingers flew to do his bidding. The headpiece dropped to the floor. I fumbled with the buttons to the robe and practically tore it off in my hurry to feel his fingers on my skin.

When the robe fell to the floor beside the wimple, I reached for my silk camisole.

"Stop!" he commanded. "Now. Take it off, slowly. I want you to undress for me."

Suddenly I was self-conscious. I tried to move slowly but felt awkward, as if this were the first time, ever, with anyone…

The camisole slid slowly over my head and dropped to the ground. I hooked a thumb into the thin straps of my black lace thong and slowly began to work them over my hips.

"Nice," Jake whispered in the darkness, "very nice."

I heard him moving toward me, closing the distance between the two of us. "Now," he murmured. "I want to see you touch yourself."

"No! I can't! Don't…"

I saw the outline of his body in front of me, felt the warmth of fingers trail down my skin.

"You're mine," he whispered and closed the gap between us. His breath tickled my ear. His tongue flicked behind my earlobe, down my neck to circle the tightening bud of my left nipple. I sighed, felt my body weakening and relaxed into his arms as he gently scooped me up to carry me across the room. He bent and deposited me on a mattress. Before I could move to touch him, he was on me again. His fingers and tongue were everywhere, taunting and teasing each responsive nerve ending in my body. He owned me and he knew it.

"Jake," I murmured.

"Tell me what you want," he murmured, but his fingers already knew the way.

"Jake, I want…I want you to…"

The shrill screech of his pager going off was amplified by the emptiness of the room.

"Ignore it, baby," he growled. "Tell me what you want."

I reached for his T-shirt, grabbing at any scrap of fabric I could reach and tearing it up and off of his body.

"I want…"

The pager went off a second time.

"Damn! Just once I want your damned pager to get left behind where it won't bother us!"

"Ignore it," he said, but the words were clipped and strained. Who was he kidding? We couldn't ignore a page when we were on a job. For that matter, we couldn't *ever* ignore a page, because if we weren't working, we were looking for work!

"Get it," I said. "See who it is. Neither one of us will relax until we know."

"Shit!" Jake was up and off me, sitting on the side of the narrow mattress as he fumbled to pull his pager from its holster and read the message.

"Damn. I have to take this. It's my contact at the CIA."

That got my full attention. I knew his contact at the CIA. One of the hazards of dating a handsome man is that he leaves a string of former lovers behind him. Shelia Martin had found a way to stay involved in Jake's life, through carefully doled-out information and "friendly" lunches every now and then to keep Jake "current" on the agency's latest changes. But make no mistake about Shelia: there was nothing innocent about that woman. I knew it, and she knew that I knew it. She wanted Jake back.

Shelia Martin would play the game skillfully. She wouldn't push; she'd just wait, hoping that Jake would tire of me. That's when she'd make her move.

Jake was up and moving, gathering the scattered pieces of my nun's habit and handing them to me as if it were just understood that he had to go.

"So, where are we meeting her?" I had to ask, even though I knew the answer.

"Stella, you know she won't…"

I rose from the mattress and began dressing. Game over. "I know. Shelia won't tell you anything if I'm around. It's enough of a risk for her to tell you. Okay. So at least tell me where you two are meeting."

"A hotel on the Main Line, near Narberth," he answered cryptically. "But she'll probably give me a new location once I get there, she's cautious like that."

Cautious, my ass. Shelia just didn't want me showing up unexpectedly.

"Right. Well, I'll page you if anything happens tonight. Will you call me as soon as you leave? I'd like to hear what she's found out."

Jake pulled me to him in what was meant to be a reassuring hug. "Of course, Stel. You know Shelia and I are…"

I finished the phrase for him. "Just old friends with a history. There's nothing to it."

"Well, it's true," Jake said. "If I wanted to be with Shelia, I would've acted on it long ago. I'm where I want to be."

So why didn't I quite believe that? Why was I feeling so insecure about him? Was it because we had a history or was it more than that?

I yawned and stretched away from him. "Nothing like leaving a woman sexually frustrated to make her sleepy," I said. "I'm going home."

I waited for him to tell me to stay, to wait for him in his bed. When he didn't I felt stung, hurt by the knowledge that he was in a hurry to get to her.

His car's taillights disappeared out of the parking lot and into the distance before I could pull out onto the main street leading back over to my side of town.

I slipped into Aunt Lucy's house through the back door and tiptoed quietly down the hallway that led to my aunt's bedroom, up the stairs, past the room where Spike was probably sleeping, without Nina, and into the room I'd had since my parents' deaths. I threw my rumpled nun's habit over the back of a chair and climbed into bed. I was exhausted but too wound up to sleep. My mind raced as I mentally reviewed the events of the day and tried not to wonder how long Jake would stay with Shelia.

Sometime after two, I called his apartment. When there was no answer, I tried his cell. After one ring it went straight to voice mail. Damn that man!

At some point, I drifted off into an uneasy sleep, awakening hours later to a sunlit morning and a cell phone that showed no missed calls. It was almost seven. Where was he? For that matter, where was Nina? Had Spike relieved her?

The smell of coffee and the sound of voices drifted up from downstairs. I started to call Jake, thought better of it, stuffed the cell phone in my bathrobe pocket and hurried downstairs. I reached the kitchen just as Aunt Lucy set a plate of fried eggs and bacon down on the table in front of Lloyd. Nina was almost finished with her breakfast. She sat holding on to a coffee mug like a punch-drunk fighter. Her eyes were bloodshot and dark with fatigue but she smiled when I walked into the kitchen and sat down across from her.

Aunt Lucy placed a steaming mug full of black coffee in front of me but said nothing. We were going on day three of the silent treatment.

"Thanks," I said to her retreating back.

"Nina," Aunt Lucy said without acknowledging me. "Ask *her* what she wants for breakfast."

Nina rolled her eyes but did as she'd been instructed.

"I'm not hungry." This was akin to saying I intended to convert to another religion in my aunt's book and I knew it. You did not refuse a meal in my aunt's house. It simply wasn't done. "But thank you anyway," I finished.

"Fine, then," she said, still not directing her remarks to me. "I'll fix her usual."

Nina shrugged and looked at me. "Spike relieved me around six."

I cradled my coffee cup, feeling the warmth radiate through my hands. "Did Baby wake up during the night?"

Nina shook her head. "No, and no one tried to bother her, either. They checked her vital signs a couple of times but that was it."

"Were those men still in the parking lot when you left?"

Nina nodded. "Yep. I think they were sleeping but I couldn't really tell. The car was parked kind of in the back of the lot, and I didn't want to act like I was staring at them."

I nodded. Aunt Lucy busied herself at the stove, muttering in Italian and slinging frying pans and pots around in a display of ill humor. When was she going to let it go?

"I wish she'd understand that I was only worried about her," I said in a loud voice. "I never meant to spy exactly. Nina, I just wanted to know she was all right."

"You tell Miss Busybody over there that I've done a fine job of taking care of myself all of my life. If she was so concerned, why not just ask me?"

"Nina," I said, getting up to pour myself another cup of coffee. "It didn't become necessary for me to check up on my beloved aunt until she refused to tell us anything about her new suitor…and this after the man stalked her and scared her half to death."

Nina was looking increasingly more uncomfortable, but I figured it was the fatigue setting in. Unfortunately, I was wrong.

"We know who he is now, Aunt Lucy, and I think it's sweet Mr. Koslovski watched over you all these…"

"What?" Aunt Lucy whirled around so fast it scared Lloyd into barking which brought Fang running into the room. "How do you know his name?"

"Oh, shit," I muttered. "Here we go!"

Nina's eyes widened and filled with tears. "My friend, Cindy, told me he almost bought the Procter place but then he didn't. She says he lives in…in…" I could see her summoning up her courage. "He lives in the hospice in Honeybrook! Aunt Lucy, is he dying?"

The world came to a grinding halt as Aunt Lucy stared at Nina as if she had suddenly sprouted two heads.

"What…did…you…say?" she asked slowly.

Nina shrank back against her chair and seemed to become a frightened child again.

"I just wondered if Mr. Koslovski was sick or something because he…he…lives where people go to die. Did you know that?" she finished weakly. "I mean, maybe he's a doctor or something…" But of course, Nina knew Arnold Koslovski was nothing of the sort.

Lloyd whined and hopped down from the table, leaving his breakfast unfinished as he trotted over to stand beside my aunt. The gesture of loyalty went unnoticed as Aunt Lucy continued to stare at Nina. It was as if Aunt Lucy was incapable of understanding Nina's question. She just stood there, looking at Nina, while the girl grew increasingly flustered.

"I didn't spy, if that's what you're thinking because, um, people have a right to do— Well, I mean, I just saw the limousine and then Cindy said— So, okay, maybe I called this girl I know and…"

When the cell phone in my pocket chirped, interrupting Nina with its loud ring, I don't know which of the two of us was more grateful, me or Nina. She turned with an exaggerated show of interest and focused all of her attention on me.

It was Jake's number on the caller ID and had it not been for our professional relationship and need not to die at Aunt Lucy's hands, I would've let the thing go straight to voice mail.

"Yes?" I answered coolly.

"Where's Nina?"

I frowned at the phone. "Sitting next to me."

"Who's watching Mrs. Blankenship?"

"Spike is. Why? Has something happened? Is Baby all right?"

At the mention of Baby's name, Nina's interest moved from pretend to panicked.

"Is Spike okay?" she interrupted.

Jake's response was momentarily drowned out by the sound of sirens, loud and close by.

"Jake, what's going on?"

"All hell's breaking loose at Brookhaven Manor," he said, raising his voice above the background noise. "They just found our two friends shot to death in their car. I gotta go."

Jake hung up on me. I sat there for a stunned moment, still holding the phone to my ear while Nina became increasingly agitated.

"Where the hell is Spike? Ask him if she's all right!"

I stood up, shoving the phone into my bathrobe pocket as I moved. "The two guys in the car weren't sleeping," I said. "They're dead."

I looked over at Aunt Lucy. "Listen," I said. "I know you're mad at me and Nina, but I think we just took something on that's getting bigger than any case we've had before. I think we're going to need your expertise. Will you please call a truce long enough to get this resolved and make sure everyone comes out alive?"

Aunt Lucy turned her back on me and switched off the heat on the front two burners of her ancient gas stove. When she turned around again, her cheeks were flushed and she was looking directly into my eyes.

"Why are you two still standing there? Get dressed! Go find Spike!" As we ran from the room, I overheard her talking to Lloyd and Fang. "Benito," she said, calling Lloyd by my uncle's name. "You can't go with them. Fang and I need you need to stick with us."

Five minutes later, Nina and I were circling the block that housed Brookhaven Manor, trying to figure a way through the phalanx of police cars, fire trucks and barricades that stood between us and Spike Montgomery, former Assistant District Attorney for Chester County, turned performance artist, turned part-time private attorney and employee of Valocchi Investigations.

"Pull over right there!" Nina cried, indicating an empty field. "I see somebody I know!"

Without hesitating, I drove my ancient white VW up over the curb and into what had once been pastureland for a farm. Nina had the window down and was waving frantically at a young police officer. "Beatlejuice!" she cried. "Hey!"

"Beatlejuice?" I echoed.

Nina didn't look back at me when she answered. "Yeah, I dated him back in high school, before I quit the team."

"Before you quit the team? What team?" Nina was the most unathletic girl I could think of.

"The blue team, silly!"

Then she was gone, sprinting across the field to the barricade that blocked the entrance to Brookhaven Manor. I followed her, watching as she grabbed the officer's arm and began talking with great animation and gesturing toward the brick building behind him. He shook his head and seemed to be firmly insisting that he couldn't help her, but Nina was not taking no for an answer.

"You married Louise, didn't you?" Nina was saying.

The way she asked the question made me wonder if Nina was about to commit a felony. When I heard the next statement, I knew we were about to go to jail. "Bobby, does Louise know about..." Nina stood on tiptoe and stretched to whisper something in the cop's ear that made his face turn scarlet and his eyes widen.

"Nina!" Bobby the cop's voice cracked like a kid in the throes of puberty. "You wouldn't..."

Nina was all business. "I assure you I would. Now let us through!"

"I could lose my job!"

I almost felt sorry for the kid.

"Bobby, we're with the medical examiner's office!" Nina lied. "That's all you have to say! See ya!"

She didn't even wait to see if I was following her. Nina was going to get to her beloved Spike no matter what. The fact that there were more cops standing at the front door to the nursing home didn't seem to factor into Nina's awareness, and had Spike not been standing just a few feet in front of that doorway, talking to a plainclothes detective, I truly believe she would've plowed right on through the officers guarding the doorway.

"Hey!" Nina cried and began running toward Spike. "Hey!"

Spike turned, and for one split second her usually calm demeanor left her as the absolute need for Nina showed in her smile and the way her eyes lit up. As I watched, the two women ran toward each other and at the very last moment, stopped, suddenly aware of their surroundings, before greeting each other with a chaste hug. I stood back watching the brief interchange and felt a little piece of my heart break for them. It must be awful to be so much in love and yet unable to express it, even in a time when you most need comfort and support.

I would've fallen into Jake's arms, relieved to know he'd found me, cradled by his strong, secure— Oh, hell! What was I thinking? Jake hadn't even bothered to call me last night and I knew it wasn't because he'd forgotten. I'd sensed there was a good reason to hold off on letting myself go with Jake, professionally or personally, and last night was just the sickening proof I needed.

I waited for Nina to release Spike before approaching and giving her a hug myself.

"What happened?" I asked.

Spike smiled ruefully. "I wish I knew. I relieved Nina around 6:30. Mrs. Blankenship was still sleeping and everything was quiet. Then, around 7:10, all hell broke loose." She looked over her shoulder at the detective she'd been talking with when we arrived. "J.T.'s the lead assigned to the case. He said a call came in from the nursing home around 7:05 saying there were two men in a car, apparently shot to death. They got here, cordoned off the area and, as a precaution, called the fire and ambulance guys. I think the whole department's a little jumpy. I mean, Glenn Ford doesn't usually see more than six homicides a year and within the past forty-eight hours they've had three."

"So, Bitsy's death was definitely intentional?"

Spike's expression was grim. "J.T. thinks so. But they'd no sooner gotten the body ready to ship off to the state crime lab for autopsy and positive identification when the feds showed up and claimed it."

"What?"

Spike nodded. "They're claiming jurisdiction because of the diplomatic tie-in. It doesn't matter that Bitsy is the wife of a junior diplomat or was up here visiting family— because the plates were on the car, the government is claiming jurisdiction." Spike gave me one of her raised-eyebrow, skeptical glances. "And, yeah, I think that's weird, too."

I scanned the area surrounding the nursing home. There was no sign of Jake, leaving me to wonder—if this was the most important event in our case, what else was so significant that he wasn't here?

"Is Jake with Baby?"

Spike shook her head. "No. He called my cell and told me about the men in the parking lot but didn't say how he knew. He said he had somewhere to go but that he was going to call you and you'd decide what our next move is."

Great. Once again, Jake had decided to act on his own and had bailed on me.

Marygrace Llewellen emerged from inside the nursing home looking haggard and pale. As she made her way toward us I found myself wondering how far she'd go to keep her favorite patient safe. Surely she wouldn't shoot people just to prevent them from interviewing Baby. What a crazy thought! Still, Marygrace had always been a zealot for her causes. Stress and fatigue could make people impulsive and irrational. But not Marygrace.

When she reached us, she immediately grabbed my arm and drew me aside. "I think I made a mistake," she said. "We've got to fix it."

How was it that Marygrace just assumed I would jump to be her personal crisis resolution manager?

"What do you mean, fix it?"

Marygrace looked down at her feet for a brief moment before spilling the beans. "I just called Brenda Blankenship, Baby's daughter. I just thought with all the hullabaloo, I should let her know about this latest turn of events. I mean, I'm legally obligated to inform her of anything that happens to Baby, or of any change in her condition, so really, I had to do it."

I nodded, waiting for her to rush on in her customary fashion.

"Well, I certainly didn't think she'd freak out like she did. I mean, it's not as if she's been over here more than once or twice this entire year, and she only lives five minutes away, but she just got hysterical."

Nina and Spike were acting as if they weren't listening, but it was obvious that they were. They stopped speaking and were almost leaning sideways to hear.

"I should've known better," Marygrace said regretfully. "I mean, she's just lost her daughter and now I have to tell her that her mother's been robbed and I've hired private investigators. It was just too much for her." Marygrace shrugged. "What else could I do? She was going to hear about those two dead men on T.V. anyway. If I hadn't told her there could be a possible connection to her mother and then she found out on her own…" Marygrace shuddered. "Isn't it amazing how people just drop their elderly family off like dry cleaning and then claim to be all upset when something happens?"

I patted Marygrace's ample shoulder and tried to reassure her. "Baby's fine. I'm sure her daughter was grateful to you for…"

"No, that's just it! Brenda didn't see it like that at all. She started talking about suing us and taking Baby out of Brookhaven Manor. She can't do that! This is the only home Baby really knows…of course," she mused, sidetracking, "she'd forget all about it in a day or so, but that's beside the point. We love her here. Nowhere else would treat her as well as we do, I just know they wouldn't!"

Jake's unmistakable black Viper rounded the corner and slowly crept past the police barricade. I felt my stomach lurch as my pulse kicked up and sent an all-points bulletin to the rest of my body. No matter what I told myself, Jake Carpenter had gotten under my skin and there seemed to be no controlling my feelings for him.

"Now, Marygrace, I want you to remember that Brenda's upset right now. She probably won't remember half of what she's said to you. I wouldn't expect her to act on it, not with a funeral to plan. She's overwhelmed and probably lashing out at anyone who crosses her path."

Marygrace shook her head. "I wish I could believe that. I've just got a bad feeling about it. You should've heard her! I told her you and Jake were here watching out for her mother as a personal favor to me but that wasn't good enough. She said she had connections and her mother didn't need—". Marygrace broke off and looked at me apologetically. "You're right, she was just upset."

"What did she say, Marygrace? Tell me. I won't get upset."

"She said she didn't want amateurs looking after her mother, and then she hung up on me!"

"Amateurs?" Nina cried, forgetting she was eavesdropping. "We're not amateurs!"

Spike laid a hand on Nina's arm in an attempt to calm her down before she drew too much attention to us, but Nina was just as adamant about her causes as Marygrace was about her own.

"I'll have you know Stella caught one of the most notorious rapists in Florida, and Jake is a decorated former Special Forces operative. Our agency has more experience in its little finger than all the bodyguards and police officers in Chester County combined!"

"Nina!"

I gave her a dark look and turned my attention back to Marygrace, but she was already walking away, responding to a summons from a woman who stood framed in the open doorway of the nursing home.

"What do we do now?" Nina asked.

"We do just what we've been doing," I answered. "We watch Baby. You go home and sleep. Spike, you stay here. If any of your police contacts find out anything, call me. In the meantime, I'm going back to the office. I think everything that's happened to Baby can be tied directly to Bitsy's visit. I need to find out what Bitsy's been up to and what she might've brought with her that could've put her and her grandmother in danger."

I looked at Nina and saw the anxiety in her eyes as she said goodbye to her girlfriend. "I'm worried about you, honey," she was saying. "What if there's more trouble?"

Spike smiled reassuringly. "Hey, you forget I can handle myself. I used to be a district attorney. We thrive on trouble. Besides," she added, patting her black leather backpack, "I brought one of my girlfriends with me."

Nina gave the backpack a suspicious once-over. "Which one?"

Spike whispered, "The Sig Saur, but don't say anything. I sort of forgot to get a permit to carry concealed."

This law-breaking streak in Spike seemed to meet with Nina's approval because she smiled and nodded. "Good. Then I guess I'll see you at home later, huh?"

The look they gave each other was sickeningly full of promise. Lovebirds! You wouldn't see me getting that sappy over anybody. Not ever!

"Come on, Nina. You need your sleep and I've got business to take care of."

I kept looking out for Jake as we walked back to the car, certain he'd be lurking around the corner, waiting for me. When there was no sign of him, I felt strangely let down. I told myself it wasn't because I wanted to see him. No, it was more that I was anticipating the showdown that would come when I confronted him about being gone all night and not answering his cell phone. Jake Carpenter wasn't going to be able to wiggle his way out of this one. Not this time!

Chapter 6

Jake wasn't waiting for me at the office, either, but someone else was. A long, gray sedan with dark-tinted windows was parked across the street from the office. The diplomatic plates on the back of the car were a dead giveaway.

I drove past the car, pulled around to the back of the building and took the back stairs up to my office. Where in the hell was Jake? Without turning the lights on, I walked to the front window in the reception area and peeked through the slats in the blinds, down to the street below. What in the world was going on? Was the car waiting for me or for Jake?

I took a deep breath, exhaled slowly and decided I'd never know anything if I sat in a darkened office, thinking. I walked down the stairs to the front door, unlocked it, went back upstairs and began switching on every light in the suite. I checked the answering machine, saw we had no messages and was sitting at my desk pretending to work when I heard the downstairs door open softly.

One of the smartest investments Valocchi Investigations had made in the past few months was the purchase of a small hidden security video system. Without the newcomer knowing, I was able to switch on a monitor beside my desk and watch his slow ascent up to my second-floor office.

Bitsy Blankenship's husband, David Margolies, was almost unrecognizable from the young, blond-headed wonder boy in the photographs I'd seen while researching Bitsy's life since high school. He trudged up the stairs slowly, his face gray with fatigue and I supposed grief. When he rounded the corner of the reception area, I was ready for him.

I looked up from my desk with an expression of polite inquiry on my face and smiled pleasantly.

"May I help you?"

Bitsy's husband sighed. The bags under his large brown eyes made him look like a human basset hound. His cheeks sagged, seeming to drag his nose and ears along with them, making me wonder if David Margolies drank and ate too much too frequently.

"I'm looking for Jake Carpenter or Stella Valocchi. Are they around?"

I stood and walked around the desk to extend my hand. "I'm Stella."

David Margolies wasn't too tired or grief stricken to notice me. No. His eyes traveled the length of my body slowly before coming to rest on my face.

"I've lost my wife," he said slowly. "And I was wondering if you could help me."

His lanky frame seemed to shrink, and for a moment I thought his knees might give way.

"I'm so sorry," I murmured. "Won't you come into my office and sit down?"

I didn't want him to know I knew who he was, so I couldn't offer condolences without giving myself away. Most people who've "lost" someone in my business are looking to find them again when they come to see me.

I ushered him into the chair across from my desk, offered him water, which he declined and finally sat down in my safe, leather seat behind my battered antique lawyer's table and waited.

After a few, seemingly interminable moments, my visitor began to speak again.

"My name is David Margolies. My wife, Bitsy, was on her way to New York from our home in D.C. two days ago." He looked at me somberly.

I gasped convincingly, I hoped, and said, "Oh, I'm sorry! I had no idea Bitsy was your…"

"*Is* my wife," he corrected. "You see, there's been a terrible mistake. Bitsy's not dead. I need to find her before something dreadful happens to her."

Oh, boy. Nutcase on my hands, delusional husband can't accept wife's tragic death, probably blames himself…. All these thoughts raced through my head as I looked at him and tried to figure out my next move. Where was Jake, anyway?

"I'm sorry," I said. "I thought there had been a positive identification…"

"No, it couldn't be!" he snapped. "This is a small town. The coroner is inexperienced. That's why I had them bring the remains back to Washington. I wanted forensic experts to conduct the autopsy, but what do they know? Little shreds of bone and cloth. That doesn't mean it was my Bits! But she could be hurt. Don't you see?" he said, leaning forward, pleading. "I've got to find her."

Double nutcase, and I felt very sorry for him. He must've loved Bitsy terribly.

"Mr. Margolies, I'm sorry, but I don't see what I can—"

"I know she called you the afternoon she was passing through town. I also know she went to visit her grandmother. I've spoken with the people at the nursing home, and they tell me that Bitsy's grandmother was missing something or had something stolen on or about the time Bitsy came to visit her and that she was upset. I thought perhaps that's why she called you. I just have to know. We have to find her."

David looked desperate and not a little bit crazed so I decided not to waste time stalling.

"She said she needed to see me professionally," I said. "But that was before she went to visit her grandmother. Jake and I were involved on another case and so I was unable to see her until later in the afternoon. By that time it was too late. The accident had happened and she…never made it in."

David frowned, as if trying to comprehend the words. "Then why have you been working for Baby?"

This part was easy. "Because when Marygrace Llewellen called and said Baby was upset and something was missing, I felt I owed it to Bitsy. I guess I felt badly that I couldn't be here when she needed me, so I decided to do what I could for her grandmother."

David's scowl deepened. "Then who's paying you?"

"Nobody."

"What was missing from her grandmother's room?"

"I don't know."

"Let me see if I understand," Margolies began. "You're looking for God knows what and you're doing it for free because you couldn't help Bits? That doesn't make sense,

Ms. Valocchi. I want to know what's really going on and what you're looking for and I want to know right now!"

David Margolies stood up and leaned over the desk, his knuckles white against the golden-oak surface.

"I don't think you understand how very serious I am," he said. His voice had become menacing and harsh. His eyes were bloodshot and he smelled of body odor and alcohol.

"Sit down, Mr. Margolies," I said, dropping the chill factor in my voice by a good twenty degrees and bringing out just enough of the cop to ensure there was no misunderstanding I meant business. "I understand you're upset but I don't talk to people who threaten me."

Margolies seemed to deflate. He sank down into the chair and dropped his head into his huge hands. "I'm sorry," he said, his voice muffled by his fingers. "I'm just so damned upset. No one is listening to me! I know she's not dead. Why won't anyone help me find her?"

"David, have your people in D.C. confirmed that it was Bitsy in that car?"

"Yes." The word uttered in one long, despairing syllable.

"You said yourself they're the experts. Why don't you believe them?"

His head came up and the wild-eyed look was back. "Do you always believe what the government says?"

"Why would they lie to you?" I asked softly.

"I don't know! That's what I want to find out. I thought maybe if she was in trouble, or running away and perhaps left something with her grandmother, something that would explain all of this, it would help me find her."

Okay, so maybe he wasn't a complete nutcase. I nodded and looked at him sympathetically. "I see. I wish I could tell you something that would help, but I'm afraid

Bitsy didn't know anything was missing when she went to see her grandmother. When I talked to Baby, all she'd say was that she lost something but she can't remember what."

I thought about the aide who'd escaped after searching Baby's room and about the two men who had purported to be state Medicaid auditors but were now dead, and wondered.

"Suppose Bitsy did give her grandmother something to keep for her. What would she have that could make others so desperate to get it that Bitsy would be in danger? And why aren't the federal authorities looking into this, if that's the case? Why isn't anyone helping you?"

I watched David's face as he answered me, saw the closed, dead-end shroud that replaced the pleading, puppy dog expression and knew that whatever came next would be a lie.

"They say I can't accept the truth about Bits. That's what they all say." He stood up, looked across the desk at me and shook his head. "I suppose they're probably right. I don't know what Bitsy could've gotten into that would've gotten her killed. They tell me it must've been a case of mistaken identity. I guess we'll never know. That secret died with my wife." He looked up at me. "I'm sorry. I guess I hoped you'd tell me something that I could hold on to. I hoped Bitsy had told you something, but apparently she didn't."

He stretched his hand into his suitcoat pocket, drew out a billfold and started pulling bills from it.

"Put that away," I said. "I told you, I was helping a friend."

David Margolies pulled out six one-hundred-dollar bills and attempted to give them to me. "It would make me feel better if you'd take this," he said. "As a thank-you from the family. Bitsy's mother will be taking Baby out of that Godforsaken rathole. We'll keep her at home or place her in a better facility where she won't have to worry about thieving staff stealing her trinkets."

"Mr. Margolies, really, I wish you wouldn't blame the facility. They really seem to love Baby."

Margolies shrugged. "I think we realize the importance of keeping our family close to us now," he said, the mournful tone back in his voice. "Perhaps that's one lesson Bitsy's death has taught us."

When I wouldn't take the money from his outstretched hand, he dropped it onto the desk. "Thank you for trying to help Bitsy and her grandmother. I'm sorry for any personal inconvenience it may've caused."

He left and I sank back down into my chair and closed my eyes. Crazy people are exhausting. I tried to review what had happened and make sense out of it, but Margolies had been such a whirlwind of contradictions. First, Bitsy was missing and in danger. Then, suddenly, and without much seeming justification, Bitsy was dead and he was going to accept it. It didn't make sense, unless David Margolies was lying or really crazy.

I picked up the phone and punched in Marygrace's cell phone number. It was time for me to turn to a head-case professional.

"He didn't act like that when I saw him," she said, sounding puzzled. "He came in here with Baby's daughter, Brenda, acting like he was the lord of the manor and we were all less-thans. Told us they were taking Baby out of the place and that she was to be ready right after the funeral! Now, how are they going to take care of Baby? She can't be left alone. She needs constant supervision."

"Did he mention Bitsy?"

Marygrace didn't hesitate. "Well, of course, it was the first thing we talked about when they arrived. We offered our condolences, and while Brenda got choked up, that son-in-law of hers just ignored us. I mean, sure, he could've been in denial—that *is* one of the normal stages of grieving. But it didn't feel like that to me. It felt like he couldn't be bothered. All he wanted to do was get down to Baby's room and help Brenda start taking some of Baby's things away. Of course, Baby thought she was being robbed again!"

"Wait, Marygrace, the man just lost his wife. What's he doing helping Brenda pack up Baby's room?"

"Good question. Not like I had time to think about it then. Cops have been absolutely crawling all over this place, and on top of that, the real feds showed up. There are more people investigating us than there are patients staying here!"

Before I could ask another question, she was gone, called off to another emergency while I sat in my office trying to piece together little bits of conflicting information. The hell of it was, it didn't matter what I figured out. Bitsy's death was in the hands of local and federal authorities. Baby was leaving her nursing home and returning home to the bosom of her family. At least David Margolies was right about one thing: Baby wouldn't be robbed by strangers in Brenda Blankenship's snooty household. But would Baby be safe there?

I got up and busied myself by making coffee. I tried to think things through logically, but in the midst of thinking about Baby and Bitsy, all sorts of other thoughts began to crowd into my head, distracting me. Where the hell was Jake? Why had he cruised by the nursing home but not so much as called me back after I paged him? Was David Margolies right, was Bitsy alive? Who was lying, then, the feds or Bitsy's ex-husband? Who were the dead guys in the nursing home parking lot? And had Jake spent the night with Shelia Martin or had something else happened to call him away?

I pulled a thick, brown mug down from the shelf above the coffeepot and stared at the clay sign attached to the front of it. Bite Me, it read. My sentiments exactly. What was wrong with me? Why did I keep picking guys who were apparently unsatisfied with just one woman? I'd left a career in law enforcement because of one failed romance. It was the reason I'd returned home to Pennsylvania. What was I going to do now, if Jake and I didn't work out? Run away again? Start over again?

"I think not," I muttered. "Not this time."

"Taken up talking to yourself, huh? Not a good sign, Valocchi."

Jake stood, framed in the doorway of the reception room behind me. I hadn't even heard him come up the stairs, let alone into the office suite. I glanced over my shoulder, long enough to see he wasn't wearing the same clothes he'd left in, long enough to know he'd shaved but his eyes were bloodshot.

"They say talking to yourself is only a bad thing when you answer yourself, too." I had to work hard to sound unaffected by his recent absence, as if I hadn't even really noticed and certainly didn't care.

"You want to catch me up on what's been happening around here?" he asked. His tone was wary, as if he knew there had to be a trap somewhere and he was just moving slowly to avoid springing it.

"Sure." I picked up my mug, crossed the room and sat down at my desk. "Where do you want me to start? You know about the double homicide because you told me. Did you find them?"

Jake nodded. "Yeah, I did a little recon right before daylight and realized they'd been hit."

I nodded, as if this were not at all unusual. "Were you also the one who called it in?"

"No. I was hoping to get Spike out before the cops sealed the place. I didn't get to her in time."

I wasn't giving him a thing to go on. I nodded without saying I'd seen him drive by the crime scene.

"What did Margolies want?"

So, Jake knew about his visit, too. Had he seen me enter the office? Had the car's plates tipped him off? Had he then sat outside and waited for the man to leave? What was this, cat and mouse? The anger I'd been working to swallow welled up inside me and exploded with a soft burst of energy that only began to tap the keg of dynamite I was sitting on.

"Before we go any further with that, why don't you tell me what Shelia Martin wanted that made you forget we work together." Let alone that we sleep together. No, I wasn't going to lose that piece of my pride. Forget that!

"Excuse me?" Jake's jaw tightened until I saw the familiar little muscle jump that meant he was working to control his temper.

"I called your cell and your apartment last night. You said you'd call when you left Shelia's. Either you never left or you just decided to turn your phone off and take a little vacation." I leaned back in my chair and studied him. "You don't look like the type to take a vacation in the middle of a case, so I suppose I can answer that question for myself."

"Brilliant. Well, I suppose you'd better start worrying about this habit you have of talking to yourself because now you're not only asking the questions, you're answering them, too. What do you need me for? You're having this conversation all by yourself."

"Good question. What *do* I need you for?"

"You know, I don't like being interrogated. Either we're partners and you trust me, or we're not and you don't. Partners give each other the benefit of the doubt, but I don't have that with you and I guess I never have. Hell, I guess I can answer that one for myself. You don't trust me. I don't suppose you ever will." Jake stood up, face flushed, jaw clenched and stared down at me. "Stella, what happened between us in high school was almost twelve years ago. It was two teenagers being impulsive, wanting to run away and get married and live happily ever after, but it was wrong. I didn't show up. I couldn't call you. Are you going to hold that one against me forever?" He shrugged. "I guess I know the answer to that one, too."

Without another word, Jake turned and walked out of the office. A few moments later the downstairs door slammed, followed by the sound of his Viper roaring to life and driving away in a harsh squeal of rubber streaking onto asphalt.

I sat there watching the steam rise and disappear into the air above my mug, feeling as if every ounce of strength and hope I had were vanishing along with the curling tendrils of mist. Somehow Jake had turned the tables on my righteous indignation, leaving me to wonder if I'd been the one in the wrong and not him at all. What if I'd been a more trusting person? What if I'd let go of our foolish youthful past enough to take a good look at the present? Outside of our high school romance, what had Jake ever done to make me distrust him?

Jake's words gnawed into my bottomless pit of insecurity and created an even larger hole in my chest. I'd run to Florida to forget Jake but left there ten years later, after another disastrous love affair with an untrustworthy man.

Now I was back in my old hometown, experiencing Déjà vu all over again. Sure, I was older, but was I any wiser? I was even letting the past make a total mess of my new career.

I'd allowed myself to become sidetracked, choosing to spy on my aunt's new boyfriend rather than take care of my own life. Then, when a real client had called for an appointment I'd blown her off. Why? Because Jake had dated her after we broke up…eleven years ago, in high school, for pity's sake! Then I'd felt so guilty when Bitsy died that I took on her grandmother's petty-theft case for whatever cash-poor Marygrace could scrounge up.

I took a sip of cold coffee and shook my head in disgust. Maybe Jake was right. Maybe I was stuck in a child's-eye view of the past. Maybe it was time to get back to the bread and butter of our young, struggling agency; the insurance scam cases and the skip traces. My heart sank. I'd have to do those cases alone now. I'd just chased off the partner whom I hadn't even allowed to be a true partner…yet.

Could the day get much worse? Apparently so. Still, I was surprised to arrive home later that afternoon and find total chaos erupting in Aunt Lucy's kitchen.

I walked into the house through the back door, my head swimming from all the phone calls and e-mails I'd sent out trying to drum up new business, and for a moment failed to take in the full extent of the pandemonium. But when I realized Aunt Lucy had tied aprons around Lloyd and Fang's necks and was talking to them as if they were capable of understanding her, I knew it was time to pay attention.

Nina, Spike, Lloyd, Fang, Aunt Lucy and a short, elderly man were all crowded around my aunt's long wooden table, completely consumed in Aunt Lucy's current project. It wasn't exactly unusual for Aunt Lucy to be concocting some new potion or cleaning product, after all, she was one of the government's top research chemists, but this was obviously not the case today.

Stockpots boiled away furiously on the stove, and cooling jars of my aunt's tomato gravy sat out on every surrounding countertop. It seemed Aunt Lucy had decided to make up a large batch of her special sauce, something she normally did in the late summer, when the tomatoes were fresh and plentiful. Then I noticed the other jars. Quart-size jars filled with clear liquid and lemon peels. This explained the chaos.

For the first time since my uncle Benny's death, *limoncello*—lemon liqueur—was being made in the Valocchi household. I blinked hard, as hot tears fought to spill over onto my cheeks. *Limoncello.* Only Uncle Benny made the *limoncello.* But here they all were, with a stranger, making my uncle's liqueur in his kitchen with him not even dead a full year!

"What's going on?" I said, and was surprised when no one seemed to hear me…except for Lloyd. Lloyd the Dog always remembered who brought him out of Florida and up north to the household where dogs were king. Lloyd hopped down from his chair and ran over to lick my hand. I knelt down, buried my face in the warm black fur covering his neck and fought to regain control of my emotions.

"Stella!" Nina called. "You're home!" Was it my imagination or was she talking just a little bit louder than usual? "Hey, everybody! Stella's home!"

Spike looked up, distracted, grimaced and dropped the knife she held. "Ouch! Damn. I cut my finger."

"Baby!" Nina cried.

The elderly man, who I knew had to be Arnold Koslovski, grabbed a paper towel up off of the table and wrapped it around Spike's finger. He squeezed her finger tight with one hand and handed her an ice-filled tumblerful of a yellow liquid with the other.

"I don't know what's in this stuff exactly," he with the faint trace of a flat, midwestern accent. "But it oughta cure what ails ya!"

Aunt Lucy smiled at him affectionately. "Is good, Arnie." She reached across the table, her hand extended as if she were going to smack him, like she did with all of us, but stopped short and ruffled his hair gently.

How could she be doing this? How could my aunt actually be making *limoncello* with a stranger in the home she had shared with my uncle for over fifty years? It was one thing to socialize, but to actually… I thought back to the conversation I'd overheard between them in Aunt Lucy's bedroom. The one where she said, *Oh, right there! You're so close! Please!* and shuddered. What was Aunt Lucy thinking?

I glanced around the room and saw they were all oblivious to this horrible realization. Everyone was fawning over Spike and laughing like partygoers. They were cooking and making liqueur as if there were nothing at all wrong…as if…as if they were… Why, they were! Not the dogs, of course, but the rest of them certainly were…every single one of them was drunk!

"It's four o'clock in the afternoon," I murmured. "How long has this been going on?"

Aunt Lucy couldn't have heard me, but as if she sensed my disapproval, she turned around and smiled. It was Aunt Lucy's warning smile.

"Ah, Stella, you're home," she said. Her cheeks were flushed and she fanned herself with her hand. "Come and meet my friend, Arnold Koslovski."

I gave Lloyd a final pat on the head and crossed the room to meet the interloper.

"Hello," I said cautiously.

Arnold Koslovski did not look like a self-made multimillionaire. He merely looked like someone's grandfather. His eyes twinkled when he smiled and while I was certain he knew all about my surveillance of his earlier visit to my aunt's house, he didn't seem to harbor any unpleasant feelings toward me. He was about Uncle Benny's height, perhaps an inch or two shorter, and equally round. While Uncle Benny had been quiet and less apt to become boisterous, Arnold Koslovski never met a stranger.

"Ah, Stella! Have some of this lemonade drink! It's a little cocktail I invented for your aunt. We were just trying to come up with a name for it. What do you think?"

Nina handed him a squat tumbler filled with ice and watched, giggling, as the man opened a bottle labeled Everclear, and poured a shot into the glass, followed by a clear liquid poured from a measuring cup, lemon juice squeezed over the glass and topped with a splash of premium vodka. Potent, to say the least, as the Everclear was 190 proof grain alcohol.

"*Na Zdrowie!*" Arnold said, raising his glass.

Aunt Lucy, Nina and even Spike, followed suit, repeating the strange phrase as they took hearty swallows of their drinks.

"Go ahead, Stella!" Nina urged, weaving gently and bumping up against her girlfriend. "It's really, really good!"

"*Na Zdrowie!*" Arnold repeated, holding his glass up and gesturing toward me.

"Huh?"

"It means, to your health, in Polish," Spike explained. "Arnie's family is Polish."

very carefully and he certainly didn't try to make tomato gravy or drink cocktails while preparing it!

"And the tomatoes," Aunt Lucy cried. "He had them flown in as well."

Arnold squirmed a bit, uncomfortable, it seemed, with all the attention. "Well, the plane was already there and the tomatoes were ripe, so why not?"

Aunt Lucy smiled at me, happier than I'd seen her in months. "So, we will have gravy and more gravy!"

Before I could say another word, the phone rang and Aunt Lucy practically danced across the room to answer it. While Arnold tended to Spike's finger by mixing her another drink, I pulled Nina aside.

"Did you find out about the hospice yet?" I whispered.

Nina shook her head, glancing at my aunt and her boyfriend before answering. "No, but look at him. He's not dying, at least not anytime soon. I think you were right. It's some kind of misunderstanding."

Aunt Lucy was chattering away on the phone. "You must come for dinner," she was saying. "I insist!" There was a pause as the person on the other end of the phone apparently declined the invitation. "Do I ask you for much?" Aunt Lucy said, pouring on the existential Catholic guilt that just seemed inbred into my family. "Jake, I have someone I want you to meet."

My stomach lurched as my heart kicked into overdrive and I waited to hear the results of my aunt's pestering. Behind me, Fang growled low in her throat as Lloyd attempted to approach her.

"I don't know what's wrong with her," Nina said. "I think she hates him now. Maybe we shouldn't have taken her away from the beach. Maybe she liked it there."

Aunt Lucy said something to Jake and hung up, but I didn't hear what it was because Arnold had rounded the table to stand next to Nina, giving his opinion and drowning out Aunt Lucy's voice.

"I think I might have an idea," he said.

Aunt Lucy was walking back toward us, watching Arnie and Nina tend to Fang. I couldn't tell what Jake had said to her by her expression and didn't get a chance to ask either. My pager went off just as Arnold stretched out his hand toward Fang, startling the dog who reacted by snapping at the little man.

"Arnold!" Aunt Lucy cried. "*Marone!* Your hand is bleeding!"

"Shh," Arnold whispered. "She was frightened. It's just a scratch." As we watched, Arnold reached out to Fang again as she watched him with a wary eye. "There, girl," he soothed. "It's all right."

When Fang allowed Arnold to pet her, there was an audible sigh of relief from everyone standing by and I turned away before my pager could go off again. I looked down at the display and felt a pang of disappointment. It was not Jake. I pulled my cell phone out of my pocket and punched in Marygrace Llewellen's number, for the last time, I hoped.

"She wants to see you," Marygrace said without preamble.

"Who?"

"Aw, come on, man! You know who. Baby. She wants to talk to you."

I looked back over my shoulder as Arnold bent and began tenderly stroking Fang's stomach. Fang had actually rolled over onto her back for the man. What was he, the Pied Piper?

"Marygrace, Baby doesn't know who I am. She couldn't have asked for me. Besides, her son-in-law paid me a kiss-off visit today. He made it clear our services weren't needed."

Marygrace exhaled a long gust of frustration. "Stella, this isn't about that fancy-pants or Baby's family or any of that. It's about an old lady who's upset and asking for the girl in the nun get-up—that's what she calls you. Are you telling me you're gonna turn your back on her? Come on, man! She's going home with those assholes, and then there won't be anybody on her team. Just come talk to her, at least do that! You know Baby, she'll forget by tomorrow, but at least today, while she's on my watch, I can try and do what she wants. Stella, she wants to talk to you."

Damn. "All right," I said, giving in. It wasn't as if I had pressing business elsewhere. "But Marygrace, that's it. I'm not taking on any more wacko, lost-cause cases. We do it by the book, with the family's approval, or I don't do anything having to do with your people. Got it?"

"I owe you, Stel," Marygrace said. "Now get your ass over here!"

Chapter 7

Baby had been crying. Her pale skin showcased the red-rimmed eyes and puffy, swollen nose. She was lying propped up against her pillows in bed, wearing a pink polyester gown that made her look like a fragile porcelain doll and fingering the necklace around her neck nervously. An empty box of tissues sat on the bedspread in front of her, its crumpled-up remains scattered everywhere.

"Hello," she said when I walked in to see her. "I remember you."

I smiled. "And I remember you." I crossed the room and sat on the edge of the narrow hospital bed. "What's wrong, Baby? You've been crying."

"Have I?" Baby seemed a little disconcerted by this, but rallied. "I suppose I have." She looked into my eyes, studying me for a long moment before speaking. "Do you know they want me to come live in their house?"

"Who?"

"This woman who said she's my daughter. She's not my daughter. Brenda is a little girl! I think that lady was my mother or maybe she was my sister." Baby's brow furrowed as she tried to grasp the situation. "I don't know why they want me to come live with them."

"Are you going?"

Baby gave a little sigh and shrugged. "I don't have much choice, do I? I mean, I don't have any money. I can't work. I don't even know what happened to my house on Freemont Street."

"I'm sorry," I murmured. I had no idea what choices Baby had left. She couldn't care for herself or make decisions, not in her state, but did that mean her wishes carried no merit? It didn't seem fair.

"Oh, don't you worry, honey," she said, patting my hand. "I can take care of my mother. She's moody but I know how to handle her." Baby's worried expression returned. "I don't think that's why I wanted to see you though," she said thoughtfully.

"So, you really did ask to see me?"

Baby smiled. "Of course, honey. I'm old but I still have a right to my own thoughts, don't I?"

This made me laugh, and in turn she laughed.

"They certainly can't take your thoughts, Baby," I said.

But the frown was back and a moment later she reached out and took my hand. "Bitsy's in terrible trouble," she said softly. "She came to see me the other day. I hadn't seen her in years, you know, but she looked just like her mother did at that age. She said, 'Grandma, it's me, Bitsy.' So, I said 'Child, I know who you are!'"

The ticking of the clock punctuated the silence between Baby's thoughts. With each tiny click I felt the sense of urgency grow in Baby's voice, as if she were racing to complete her thoughts while she still had a hold on them.

"She said she was just visiting. She even brought me a little present. But I knew something was wrong. I was listening. She said someone was after her."

Baby fell silent, staring down at her hands and the tissue box in her lap.

"After her?" I prompted.

Baby looked up at me, startled. "Yes. But she said she had a friend who would help her, in New Jersey maybe, but I don't know…"

Baby was losing focus. The energy it took to keep it all together was slowly ebbing away.

"Did she tell you who she needed to see?" I asked gently.

Baby shook her head, drew in a deep breath and looked up at me. The fear in her eyes took my breath. "They're going to kill her," she whispered. "Please! You've got to find her and bring her back. I can help her. I know I can. She told me so!"

"How, Baby?" I asked, feeling the urgency in her words and knowing I couldn't tell her it was already too late for Bitsy. "How will you help her?"

Baby stared up at me, the desperation suddenly gone from her eyes, replaced by the more familiar confused expression. "Oh, I don't know, honey," she said. "I suppose we'll just talk about the old times, and then later I'll take her downtown to buy ice cream and a new necklace. Little girls like pretty things, you know."

Baby leaned back against her pillows and closed her eyes. When I left she was snoring softly and I paused in the doorway of her room, watching the even rise and fall of her chest beneath the thin white coverlet. There was just something about Baby that made me feel protective. I wanted to keep her safe. I wanted to know that she was happy, not troubled by clouded worries that came and went, scaring her with their urgency and reminding her of how much she was losing with each passing day.

It was dinnertime at the nursing home. As I stepped out into the hallway from Baby's room, two huge carts rolled by, pushed by attendants in netted caps. Other aides pushed wheelchairs or guided those more able to get around down the hallway toward the facility dining room. I stood there for a moment, watching and wondering if this was what it all came down to in the end. Would all of us one day wind up living in cramped rooms, wearing diapers and being tended to by bored workers instead of loving family?

Something about one of the women dispensing trays caught my attention. I turned to look at her retreating back as she carried food into a patient's room. Slim, tall. I waited for her to come back out of the room so I could see her face, but I was already moving in her direction. It was the sucker-punching aide from the day before.

She came out of the room fast, expecting me, but this time I was ready for her.

"Stop!"

Aida started running with me close on her heels. I reached out to snatch her, fastened on to her scrub top and felt it rip out of my hand. She turned abruptly, stopped and shoved me back hard with a stiff-armed move that momentarily took my breath away. Then she was gone, off and running out the front door.

I cursed myself for not bringing a gun and gave chase. I caught up with her again as she was trying to get into a small black car. This time I got the first blow in. I spun her around, drew my fist back and drove it into her solar plexus. The rewarding gasp told me I had her attention, but she didn't stay down. She straightened, lashed out with a kick, and the battle was on.

We were evenly matched in terms of fighting skills, but she was a good twenty pounds lighter than me. I didn't see how she could take such a beating and still find the stamina to keep on going, but she seemed tireless. I swung out again, grazing her left temple, and she swore softly in a language I didn't recognize.

"Who are you?" I asked. "What do you want? She's an old lady."

The girl's gray eyes were completely devoid of any emotion. She stared at me, then, without seeming to move, struck out with her left leg. I went down momentarily, but it was enough for her to make it into her car. I scrambled, half on my feet as I heard the engine roar to life and lurch forward, right toward me.

There wasn't time to get out of the way. Instead I threw myself forward and used the car's momentum to help push me across and off the Mini Cooper's hood. The little car sped out of the parking lot and was gone in an instant, blending in with the winter's early nightfall.

I stood, bent over and gasping for breath for a few minutes before I was able to move to my own car. It took another few minutes before I felt able to think or drive. I felt as if I'd been run over. What in the hell was going on?

When I pulled up into the parking lot behind Jake's building, I realized I'd been driving on instinct, homing in on the one person I knew to go to. Jake.

It took another five minutes to crawl out of my car and struggle up the stairs to his apartment. Every nerve ending, joint, muscle and bone in my body ached. I only hoped she felt as bad as I did. When I reached Jake's door, I stopped and leaned my head against the thick wooden frame. I wasn't sure I even had the strength to knock on his door.

I brought one fist up and let it land with a weak thud against the solid surface. Fortunately, that was enough. I heard him approach the door cautiously, knew he was looking out through the peephole and heard the door swing open a moment later.

"Damn, babe, you look rough."

He reached out, gently pulled me into him and led me inside his kitchen. "Let's get a look at you." He pushed me down into a chair and stepped back to survey the damage. "Well, I guess if you were worried about your black eye disappearing, you can rule that out. You're probably going to have a fresh shiner on top of that one."

He touched my cheek and I winced. "Yeah, nice scrape. The other guy look this bad too?"

"I certainly hope so," I mumbled. "She got away."

"No!" Jake feigned mock amazement. "Tell me it wasn't that same girl that whipped your ass out in the woods."

"I think she was working in the kitchen. When I found her, she was handing out trays."

"What were you doing at the nursing home?"

I sighed. "Marygrace. She said Baby wanted to talk to me."

Jake nodded, as if this made perfect sense to him. He walked out of the room and returned a short while later with his jumbo-size first-aid kit. He opened it on the kitchen table and appeared to be studying the contents.

"I'm thinking something in a basic white gauze and adhesive," he said finally. "Something that says, 'I've just had my ass kicked, but hey, I'm all right!' What do you think?"

He was acting as if nothing at all were wrong between us. He was just being Jake—cocky, unconcerned and upbeat. And I loved him. The realization just appeared in my head, like a light switch flicking on or an e-mail jumping into my computer mailbox. There it was. Pure and simple. I loved Jake Carpenter. All the barriers I tried to erect hadn't stopped the reality, so I supposed nothing would stop the pain if things didn't work out, either. But that didn't seem nearly as important to me now as it had earlier in the day.

I looked up as he squatted down beside me and looked at him. He was carefully dabbing cream onto the cut below my eye, but stopped when I drew back.

"I know it stings, Stel, but it's for your own good." He was smiling, playing with me, even though I hadn't done much to deserve it. Jake had forgiven me and moved on.

"Stel, you all right? You're looking kind of out of it." He held up three fingers. "How many do you see?" he asked.

"Jake, I love you."

His smile grew just a bit wider. "I know," he said, and went right back to dabbing cream on my face.

I pulled his hand away. "Did you hear me? I said I love you!"

He chuckled. "Yeah, I heard you. I know you do. I love you, too."

When he moved to return to his first aid ministrations, I blocked his hand, grabbed his wrist and held on to it.

"Jake, I mean I love you a lot. Like, the whole way, with everything I have. I mean, I want us to be partners. You know, Valocchi and Carpenter Investigations?"

Jake nodded, but I saw a quick flash of something I couldn't read in his eyes. "Partners, huh?"

"Yeah. What you said earlier, about me not trusting you and holding on to the past. You were right. I don't want to be like that anymore. I trust you. I want you to be my partner."

Jake frowned and pretended to examine my face closely. "Sure that fight didn't knock some things loose in there? I mean, what made you change your mind?"

I shrugged. "I suppose I just thought about it. I mean, you were right. We were kids in high school. People grow up. Just because I've had a few bad relationships with jerks doesn't mean you're going to hurt me."

Jake nodded, but he didn't seem to be as excited about what I was telling him as I was. What was wrong? I started to ask but stopped when he began talking.

"I didn't call you last night because I was in Washington with Shelia," he said. "She thought I should talk to a couple of other people and tell them about our quasi-investigation in hopes that it would help with their attempts to figure out who killed Bitsy."

I nodded, careful not to appear skeptical and waited for him to continue.

"She took me to see the agent investigating Bitsy's death, who also was the team leader on Bitsy's last project with the agency."

"So Bitsy was still an operative?"

Jake smiled, leaned back and inspected his first aid work. "Beautiful. Now take these." He opened a small white bottle of over the counter pain reliever, shook out two tiny caplets and handed me a glass of water to swallow them with before answering my question.

"Reading between the lines, I'd say yes. Those guys don't give you anything unless they have to, and then only if it's going to help them out."

I ached all over and felt myself growing impatient. "So, what's the bottom line here, Jake? What the hell is going on?"

"Okay, here's what I was able to piece together with Shelia. David and Bitsy worked under the guise of being a young, diplomatic couple assigned to the embassy in Slovenia. David's real mission was to develop a relationship with a Slovenian biochemist, in hopes of one day paving the way for him to leave Slovenia and come to the U.S. Apparently things went along as planned and the defection was in process when the scientist was killed."

"Killed?"

Jake nodded. "It was a big loss, too. The guy was allegedly in the last stage of developing a biochemical weapon capable of affecting specific DNA targets."

I was straining to make my brain work past the headache my attacker had given me, and the effort must have been clear to Jake because he explained in more detail.

"A weapon that targets a particular genetic code would be capable of hitting highly specified segments of the population, say for example, all people with blond hair or all Asians, or even something far more specific, like…"

"Like freckles?"

Jake nodded. "Yeah."

"But the guy died, so why is Bitsy dead?"

Jake carefully folded the first-aid kit closed and sat down in the chair next to mine at the table.

"That's where reading between the lines is necessary. I think the other agent was leaving out quite a bit. He said Bitsy got hit because the Slovenians were angry and wanted to send the U.S. a message not to interfere."

"So, their guy dies trying to flee his country with our help, it failed and so Bitsy was payback?"

Jake nodded. "Something like that, only I don't buy it. The Mafia might stoop to retaliation, but countries don't do it that way."

"So, what do you think happened? What's the connection with Bitsy?"

Jake shrugged. "I'm not sure. I don't think we have the big picture. It's clear to me Bitsy felt she was in danger."

"Well, Baby's room has been trashed twice. Two men

died in the parking lot of the nursing home, and if my little run-in was any indication, there seems to still be an interest in the place. I'd say they're after Bitsy or something Bitsy had with her. You sure that DNA formula isn't missing?"

Jake stood up and patted my shoulder gently. "Scramble your brains and you still come out thinking," he said. "That's exactly what I'm wondering, only I'm wondering why they were after Bitsy and not her husband."

"Yeah, why aren't they on David?"

"I'm sure they're thinking along the same lines we are, only the agency has more resources at their disposal. It'll shake out sooner or later. I'll let Shelia know there was more activity out at Brookhaven and she'll relay the message." Jake was pulling on his jacket and ski cap as he spoke. When he'd finished, he turned back to me. "Ready?"

I frowned. "For what? Aren't you going to call Shelia?"

"Yeah, later. Right now, it's time to start driving."

"Driving where?"

Jake shook his head softly. "To dinner. Aunt Lucy invited me. I wasn't going to go, but since she said she had an announcement to make, I figured it was a command on her part and not a request." He looked at his watch. "We'd better hustle. She said six."

I rose up slowly and allowed Jake to help me back into my coat.

"I'll drive," he said, wrapping his arms around me from behind, his breath soft on my neck. "We can come back for your car later."

We were halfway to my house before I asked my next question. "Jake, what about Baby? I mean, what are they doing to make sure no one hurts her?"

Jake hesitated. "I'll admit your last tango over there

was strange, but the two men in the parking lot can be explained."

"How?"

We were turning onto my street. In a few moments we'd be inside with the others, eating pasta and trying to make up to Aunt Lucy for spying on her new boyfriend. I had to know Baby was not in danger.

"Stella, sometimes threats have to be neutralized and the results cleaned up later."

"Meaning?" But I had a feeling I knew what he meant.

"Meaning maybe these two guys were responsible for what happened to Bitsy, and someone else handled it."

"Like agency people?"

"Hopefully."

"Okay," I said, taking this into consideration. "Then why didn't they leave after they took Bitsy out? And why was that girl still hanging around?"

Jake considered this. "Maybe they wanted to make sure there were no loose ends. Maybe they wanted to make sure Bitsy hadn't talked to her grandma about anything, or left anything with the old gal. Before they could do that, they were eliminated."

"And the girl? Why was she there today?"

Jake pulled into a parking space in front of my aunt's brick row house and killed the engine.

"Well, I'll admit, she doesn't fit into the picture. Maybe she's totally unrelated to this Bitsy deal. I mean, no one ever saw her *in* Baby's room, did they? Maybe she doesn't speak good English and got spooked when you chased her."

I looked at him and raised a skeptical eyebrow. "She was so scared she snuck back up on me in the woods and clocked me? Come on!"

"Well, maybe not, but I'm not certain that woman has

anything to do with Bitsy's grandmother. Baby Blankenship is fine. No one's attempting to hurt her, not since they tossed her room and didn't find what they wanted." He looked at me and shook his head. "But you're not going to leave it alone until you know for sure, huh?"

I smiled. "What can I say? Maybe I should've been a social worker. But I want to know what your buddies at the agency are going to do to protect her, and if they don't do something, I will. I want to know who those guys were in the car and I want to know more about what Bitsy and David were doing before she suddenly decided to take a 'vacation' to New Jersey."

"Fair enough," Jake answered. "But let's get this over with first." He nodded toward Aunt Lucy's back porch where Nina had come out to stand and beckon us in.

"Guess what?" Nina was hopping up and down on the balls of her feet and appeared ready to spring off the porch in her excitement.

"What?" I answered.

"I can't tell you! Aunt Lucy has to be the one. Come on!"

Did I mention my cousin is a dingbat? I rolled my eyes at Jake and followed Nina into the kitchen. Please, I bargained silently, don't let it be that she's decided to marry that old geezer.

The kitchen had been restored to some semblance of order, and Aunt Lucy was in the process of directing everyone through the last-minute dinner preparations. When Jake and I arrived, Aunt Lucy barely turned long enough to nod and give Jake a quick smile.

"Come everyone! *Mange!* It's time to eat!"

I watched as Spike and Nina carried steaming platters to the table, followed by Arnold, who carried a big jug of Uncle Benny's Chianti. The impulse to rip it from his hands was childish, I knew, but also almost unstoppable.

Aunt Lucy gestured to the table impatiently. "Come on, you two, sit down!"

At least she didn't give Arnold Uncle Benny's place at the head of the table. Thankfully, she still allowed Lloyd to sit there.

"Tell them, Aunt Lucy! Tell Jake and Stella! I can't stand it!" Nina cried.

Aunt Lucy no longer seemed inebriated, but her cheeks were flushed and her eyes were a little glassy.

"The blessing, *cara*! First, the blessing."

Nina sighed. I saw Spike reach under the table to squeeze her hand and wished for a moment that Jake was holding on to me. We bowed our heads and then she did it. Aunt Lucy asked Arnold Koslovski to say the blessing.

I didn't even listen. I was aware of him droning on in his flat, Midwestern-style accent, but I didn't want to hear another man utter the words my uncle was supposed to say. It was a right reserved for the head of the household, not some schmuck interloper trying to get into my aunt's pants.

"Now tell her!" Nina commanded.

Aunt Lucy looked at me and smiled. "I have wonderful news, Stella. We are about to add to the family!"

Don't tell me this, I begged silently. No!

"My *cara mia*, Fang, she is going to have puppies! Soon!"

"What? How did that…happen?"

Everyone at the table watched me as I silently answered my own question. Beside me, Jake choked or else feigned choking to hide how hard he was laughing into his napkin. Lloyd, sitting at his place at the head of the table, barked once. When I looked, he was smiling like a proud father.

Fang was lying on a quilt that Aunt Lucy had prepared

for her and placed beside the pantry door. Fang was most certainly not smiling. In fact, when I looked at her, she snarled.

"What's wrong with her?" I asked.

"Stella!" Aunt Lucy cried. "You don't know what it's like. Your feet swell. Your body is heavy with child. Is not so pleasant to be pregnant!"

"My Ethel," Arnold said, quickly crossing himself. "She nearly died with our last child. It takes a toll," he said. He stared down at the table, as if remembering something that made him quite sad. A moment later he looked up, smiling. "But the babies, they are a joyous occasion, eh?"

He grabbed up his wineglass and raised it, signaling the rest of us to do likewise.

"To new life and the next generations!" he cried. "May they be rich with love and good times!"

I tried to catch Nina's eye, but she was too caught up in the celebratory moment. When we were once again seated, Spike looked around to make sure the others were occupied in conversation before leaning toward me and speaking.

"Listen, I went by the D.A's office today to have lunch with a friend of mine and I picked up on some interesting gossip."

I raised an eyebrow. "Really?"

"Yeah. You know how the feds took over the crime-scene investigation of Bitsy's death?" I nodded. "Well, at the time they said it was a national security matter and because of the terrorist threat, they were exercising their authority to intercede. Nobody was going to fight them on it. I mean, the feds have the ability to do a lot of forensic work we just can't do at the local or even state level. Of course, the police had secured the scene and it was in the preliminary stages of being processed when the big boys arrived and took over."

I nodded, wondering where Spike was heading with all of this.

"Well, anyway, when I arrived to pick up Barry for lunch, the entire floor was buzzing. Seems the feds are telling the locals that foul play is not suspected."

"What?" I put my fork down and stared at her, aware that Jake had been listening just as intently from his place beside me.

Spike nodded. "Exactly. An accident. A defect in the car's ignition system that caused it to explode." She raised an eyebrow and slowly shook her head. "They must think we're yokels up here or something. Barry said he made one phone call down to the lab and they were all over it. They have proof of accelerant use. Furthermore, one of the guys recovered some fibers and human hair samples that he thought might help in tracking the perpetrators." Spike smiled. "They were a little naive in how they handled it, though. They called up the feds and offered their help, thinking maybe the big guys had merely overlooked something. The feds sent someone from the local office to get everything, and I do mean *everything* they had, and then called the county boys back a few hours later to say the evidence still supported their original findings. Now, that's impossible! But of course, how can the county prove it? All their evidence is in federal custody!"

"Damn!" I whispered. The hair on my arms felt as if it were standing at attention. The temperature in the room seemed to have dropped ten degrees, and yet, across the table from where we huddled, the rest of the family laughed and toasted Fang and Lloyd's good news.

"What about the nursing home killings?" Jake asked. "What's happened with those?"

Spike's expression tightened. "Very weird. They were having trouble getting an ID on either vic at first. They ran them on NCIC, AFIS, even Interpol and came back with nothing. Then, two hours later, someone runs the prints again, don't ask me why, and they get two hits, right away, identifying them as Medicaid auditors from Washington. Barry said Chief Weller was starting to get real squirrelly about it all, saying Big Brother was fucking with the little man, now and threatening to call the Department of Homeland Security himself!" Spike shook her head. "You got to admit this is some weird stuff."

Nina horned in on our conversation. "Are you guys talking about Bitsy? Is her grandmother all right? Did you find out who broke into her room?"

Spike, Jake and I must've looked like children caught with our hands in the cookie jar, because we all immediately stopped talking, jumped apart and shoved big forkfuls of pasta into our mouths. Spike at least nodded in Nina's direction, but I could feel Aunt Lucy's suspicious glance sweep over us like the searchlights from a prison guard tower.

Surely Nina didn't think we'd discuss an on-going case with a stranger present? What was wrong with her?

Aunt Lucy turned to Arnold Koslovski and began explaining. "You remember Cynthia Blankenship's sister, Belinda? They called her Baby because she was the youngest. I believe she was a few years behind us in school…"

Then, as I sat flabbergasted, Aunt Lucy began to tell him all the details of Baby's case. I looked over at Nina. She must've caught Aunt Lucy up on the details of the case, and now Aunt Lucy had lost her mind and was blabbing it all to a virtual stranger.

"Actually, Nina," I said, interrupting Aunt Lucy before

"Arnold and I grew up together," Aunt Lucy said. Her eyes were soft as she looked at the little man, obviously enamored by him. "He swore to watch after me, but who knew?" This time when she reached across the table, she did slap him, right upside the head like she always did with us.

Arnold shrugged and turned his attention to me. "What could I do? Love is love. Your aunt chose another, but I forgave her. What is love if it does not forgive?"

"That's why he sent me such unusual flowers," Aunt Lucy gushed. "They were little messages from his heart. They said what he could not say…then."

"Did you know flowers all have symbolic meaning?" Nina said. "Like, code! Is that cool or what?"

"Tell my niece what the violets said," Aunt Lucy urged Arnold.

The little man had the good grace to be blushing as he spoke. "Well, it was only a quote from Mark Twain, really."

"Tell her!" Aunt Lucy urged.

Arnold shrugged again and looked at me apologetically. "It's not that big a deal really. Mark Twain said, 'Forgiveness is the fragrance that the violet sheds on the heel that has crushed it.'"

"I crushed him," Aunt Lucy explained simply and drained her glass. "I didn't marry him and I crushed him."

"But that was so long ago, Lucia," Arnie murmured.

That was enough for me. I raised the glass to my lips and gulped half of it without stopping.

"Arnold brought me fresh lemons. He had them flown in from Sorrento!"

I raised the glass and drank again. It was surprisingly good, but it was not *limoncello*. That would take three months to make. It was a process my uncle supervised she could go any further. "We weren't talking about that at all. I was asking Spike about your house hunting."

Nina and Spike froze, stricken, as my desperate brain caught up with my run-away mouth. Uh-oh. Aunt Lucy obviously hadn't been told that Spike and Nina were thinking about moving out. In trying to keep one secret, I'd given away an even bigger one.

"What is this?" Aunt Lucy said. "House hunting?"

Nina's face was scarlet, and she wouldn't meet our aunt's eye. It was Spike who jumped in to save her by taking the fall.

"No, Aunt Lucy, it was me. I was looking. I…well, you know, you didn't bargain to have me living here when I moved back from California. I just thought maybe I should start looking. You know, I don't want to be any more of an imposition than…"

"Imposition?" Aunt Lucy cried. "What is this? Perhaps you do not feel comfortable here? I have not provided you with—"

"It's not that, Aunt Lucy," Spike remonstrated smoothly. "I have never felt as welcomed or loved as I do in your home. I just thought it was time to establish my own household. I'm going to be staying in Glenn Ford permanently. I'll have to find a place of my own some time."

Arnold was wisely staying out of the dinner table drama, watching it unfold with the air of one who has lived through many such family growing pains and knows they will pass eventually. I was not so certain. After all, Aunt Lucy was in our family, not his.

"I'm sorry," I mouthed silently to Nina, who was looking at me with an expression of complete shock at my betrayal.

"I told you this was a bad idea," Nina said. Her voice

broke as tears welled up in her eyes and she struggled not to lose her composure completely. "Don't worry, Aunt Lucy…"

Aunt Lucy held up her hand. "Stop!" She looked around the table, focusing on Nina, Spike and me. To my surprise she smiled and her eyes were warm with affection.

"It is time we talked. You girls have been very good to me since my Benito died. You watch over me, I know that. Lloyd watches over me."

I realized with a start that my aunt was no longer referring to Lloyd as "Benito" and wondered when she'd stopped, and if this meant she suddenly realized Lloyd was not Uncle Benny reincarnated.

"But life goes on and I must learn to live without my Benny." She smiled at Arnold who smiled back. "You know how it is," she said, and he nodded reassuringly. "I will always have the love of my Benito in my heart and in my memories. No one can take that from us, eh?"

Nina's tears spilled down her cheeks and I felt my own eyes begin to burn and sting. I was thinking not just of Uncle Benny, but of my parents.

"No one lives forever," Aunt Lucy continued. "We do not honor their memory by grieving our lives away. We honor them by continuing on, strengthened by the love they leave in our hearts. Nina," she said focusing on my cousin. "Stop with the tears! What are you crying for?"

"Because it's soooo sad!" she wailed.

Aunt Lucy reached out, smacked the top of her head lightning fast and clucked her disapproval. "It is not sad! It is life! Do you love Spike?"

"What?" Nina frowned, not following Aunt Lucy's train of thought.

"Do you love that woman?"

"Of course!" Nina looked almost indignant.

"Then stop dilly-dallying around. Is time to make a life and a family. What's wrong with you? You think you have all the time in the world? Life moves fast. It could all be over tomorrow! You can't stand around waiting!"

Nina swallowed, hard. "Well, I didn't want to leave you and…"

Aunt Lucy rolled her eyes in a flawless imitation of Nina. "That is so much crap! You will still live in this town. I am right here. I will have—" she paused and winked at Arnold "—a life. You cannot use an old woman for an excuse. Are you worried about your mother? You think she will not like it if you live with a woman?"

Nina shook her head vehemently. "No! She doesn't worry about those sorts of—"

"You are right!" Aunt Lucy interrupted. "She has her own life. She is too busy shopping in Europe to worry about such technicalities! So what is your problem?"

Spike had been watching the interplay between her girlfriend and Aunt Lucy with the same detached air she usually seemed to regard everything and everyone, but now her eyes darkened as she cocked her head and seemed to hold her breath.

Thoughts seemed to be percolating in Nina's blond head because she started to speak several times, stopped, frowned and squirmed in her chair, becoming increasingly uncomfortable. We all waited in silence for her to explode.

"All right! All right! You want to know what it is? Huh? Okay, well, I'll tell you!" She favored us all with a defiant scowl. "I'm scared, all right? You know, like, what if it doesn't work out and like, we have kids or something, or I'm at home with them and she runs off with someone smart or something!"

"Baby!" Spike didn't seem to know whether to laugh or cry at Nina's answer.

I saw Arnold Koslovski nod out of the corner of my eye, as if he'd expected this exact answer.

"Well? How do you know when you've found the right person? How can you be like, totally certain? I mean, I'm only twenty-three!"

"I married Benito when I was nineteen years old," Aunt Lucy said. "And I was terrified. I didn't know. All I knew was I didn't want to be apart from him. He widened my life and my heart until it seemed only natural that we should be together. Still, I was terrified. I married him because I couldn't think of anything else to do *but* marry him."

Arnold had been watching Aunt Lucy talk about the love of her life, the man she chose over him, with a wistful, sad expression on his face.

"And sometimes," he said, in a way that made me uncertain if he were speaking to us or more to himself, "sometimes you marry because you believe a great love is not possible but a good life is. And if you are very lucky, your love grows to fit your life. I have found love is like a garden, carefully tended it flourishes."

Aunt Lucy reached over and took his hand, her eyes shining with unshed tears. For a few long moments there was silence around the dinner table before Aunt Lucy trusted herself to speak again.

"Don't waste your life on guarantees, *cara mia*," said Aunt Lucy. "What is life without surprises? Make something of your love with Spike. Make something of today, don't wait around for imaginary tomorrows. Grow your garden. It will not be easy. Your heart will ache many times over, but it will also learn to sing."

I felt a catch in my throat and didn't dare look in Jake's direction. When the phone rang, demanding attention from its position on the kitchen wall, I almost knocked my chair over in my hurry to answer it.

Chapter 8

Old Mrs. Talluchi didn't want to waste time talking to me. When I answered the phone, she merely sniffed and said, "Put Lucia on the line. We got business. Tell her the fox is in the henhouse."

"Excuse me?"

"*Stracciamanici!* Put your aunt on the phone!"

I held the phone away from my body and summoned Aunt Lucy. As she took the receiver, I cautioned her. "She's in one of her paranoid moods. She says the fox is after the chickens or something and I'm a *stracciamanici*. What is that, anyway?"

Aunt Lucy lifted an eyebrow. "So, she thinks you're a nymphomaniac, eh?" She nodded. "What else was she to think, seeing you and Jake stumble out into the street half-naked in front of my house?"

Nothing good ever came of old Sylvia Talluchi's phone

calls. Now it seemed she didn't even have to speak to Aunt Lucy to turn my day bad.

I returned to my seat at the table, trying to think up a diversion that would keep Aunt Lucy from bringing up my misguided stakeout with Jake when she returned. I didn't have to work on it for long. Mrs. Talluchi seemed to have provided enough of a distraction.

"When was that?" I heard her ask. "How many?" She nodded, listening. "You say you've seen them twice now? Uh-huh." She paused briefly, listening, then drew our collective attention. "What? Now?"

Aunt Lucy leaned into the counter, picked up a remote control and aimed it at a small television screen mounted on top of one of her cabinets. I inhaled sharply and nudged Jake. Apparently Aunt Lucy saw no need to keep her part-time work as a government chemist with a top-secret security clearance a secret from Arnold. Otherwise, she wouldn't have touched the surveillance camera controls. Sophisticated security equipment like that used to secure Aunt Lucy's house and basement is just too difficult to explain as a routine alarm system.

The screen winked on and the street in front of the house took up half the monitor while the alleyway behind the house showed on the other half. I squinted, trying to see whatever Mrs. Talluchi was so excited about. A small white panel van parked two houses down seemed to be the item of interest. Aunt Lucy walked over and stood just beneath the screen, staring hard at the vehicle.

"*Gratzi,*" she said, and hung up.

She looked over at Jake and me, gestured toward the monitor and said, "Who are they?"

We all studied the white van on the screen carefully. Jake shrugged. "Could be anybody. Why's Mrs. Talluchi so worried?"

"Because she said it's been parked there for over an hour and no one ever got out of it. She said it's the second time she's seen it do that today. She said it only shows up when you are here." Aunt Lucy was directing her answers to me with a look that seemed accusatory, like maybe I'd done something and not told her about it.

"When was the first time Sylvia saw the van?" I asked.

Aunt Lucy walked back over to the table and sat back down at her place. "The first time was this morning, after you and Nina came back from the nursing home."

I looked at Jake. "Friends of yours?"

"Not that I know of."

"Good, because I propose rocking their world, and I wouldn't want to do that and have Shelia Martin come tumbling out."

The muscle in Jake's jaw twitched, signaling that I'd hit a nerve. "How do you want to start the van rocking?"

I studied the vehicle's position on the street. It was in front of Mrs. Talluchi's house, two doors down and across the street from Aunt Lucy's, occupying a space right in front of a fire hydrant.

"I have an idea," I said.

Twenty minutes later our plan went into action. Nina, driving Aunt Lucy's aging Buick, slowly crept past the van and came to a stop in the middle of the street blocking the space where the van was parked. This effectively prevented the van from driving away when phase two of the operation began.

Jake and I backed down the street in his red Ford F-450 tow truck, slid into place in front of the van and backed up until we were only a foot or so off the van's bumper. Then Jake, wearing his auto-body shop coveralls, jumped down out of the cab and began the process of hooking the van up to the pickup. He did one thing he usually never did first. He ran a strong Kevlar strap around the outside of the van, cinched it tight and folded the clasp into place.

"No one's leaving that vehicle until I say so," he muttered grimly.

When Jake flipped the switch and the winch slowly began to crank the van's front end up, a startled male face popped up above the dashboard. I didn't have to see an ID badge to recognize a federal agent when I saw one. This guy was the genuine article, unlike the two dead men in Brookhaven Manor's parking lot.

"Hey! Hold up! What're you doing?" The guy's face registered alarm as he looked out the window and saw that his van was headed to the top of the tow truck winch.

Sylvia Talluchi had come up behind us, and when the man in the van began protesting, she shoved me aside to get as close as possible to the vehicle's window.

"So!" she cried. "You think you skulk around my neighborhood, eh? *Stunade!*" Before I could haul her back, she spit on the window, turned around and stalked back up her stoop.

Another bristle-top appeared in the window. This one was older, his hair gray, lines etched deeply around his eyes, an impassive expression on his face. He merely held up a badge and flashed the shiny silver contents in an arc that was apparently supposed to impress us into submission. I guess he didn't realize who he was dealing with. The citizens of Glenn Ford, and in particular the residents of the Italian section of Glenn Ford, have never been overly impressed by dictatorial displays of authority. You have to earn our respect.

Jake, playing the role of tow-truck driver to the hilt, walked up to the window and smiled. "Can I see your badge again?" he asked.

When the gray-haired man produced the badge, Jake

studied it with a serious air and mouthed the words as he read, "U.S. Department of Defense."

He looked over at me and grinned. "Hey, what do you know, these guys are protecting our homeland from terrorists." Turning back to the two men in the van, he grinned. "Ain't that right, fellas? Youse are here looking for terrorists, aren't you?"

He made no move to unhook the van.

"You're interfering with a government investigation," the younger agent said.

"Hmm," Jake said, frowning. "How could that be? We don't have no terrorists on this block. Do you need to tell us something? If there's terrorists here, you should tell us. We take care of our own in this part of town."

You could look at the younger agent's face and practically read everything he was thinking. None of it was flattering to the residents of Glenn Ford.

Jake peered inside the van. "You folks say you're with the Department of Defense, but anyone can have a badge. Can we see some personal ID? You know, technically, you're parked too close to a fire hydrant. That's why I got the call to come out and tow you. See, if there were to be a fire and we couldn't get the trucks in…"

"Jesus!" I heard the older guy swear. He pulled out an identification card, showed it to Jake and said, "There! Will that do?"

"Well, let's see." Jake slowly inspected the laminated card then nodded to the younger man. "Let's see yours."

When the man looked uncertain, the older man sighed. "Just do it and get this over with," he said.

Jake looked at the second card, and I knew he had every detail memorized from both cards.

"Well, it don't much matter anyway," he said. "You still can't park here."

Without another word, Jake turned and climbed up into the cab of the truck with me. As Aunt Lucy's neighbors watched, we slowly pulled away from the curb, the white van in tow.

"Jake, you think they'll shoot us?"

"Nah! How would that look? They won't shoot us, but from the expressions on their faces, I bet they'd sure like to!"

The two of us laughed all the way back to Jake's former auto-body shop. Once we'd backed the van into the bays and lowered its front wheels onto the ground, we got serious.

Jake walked up to the driver's side window again while I slowly undid the Kevlar strap that held the van's doors closed.

"All right," he said cheerfully. "You can come out now."

They came out, weapons drawn and obviously angry. Before either one could speak, I began.

"For some reason, you two seem to have been assigned to watch my house. I can only assume this has something to do with Bitsy Blankenship's death, but I'd like to hear it from you. What were you doing?"

Jake and I weren't surprised when neither man answered us. We hadn't expected them to, nor did we believe their identification was accurate. Our sole purpose in bringing them back to the garage was to put them on notice. We knew about them and they didn't scare us.

"You are interfering with a federal investigation," the younger agent said, clearly angry.

Jake smiled dangerously. "No we're not. We're private citizens concerned about our welfare and the welfare of our neighbors. We thought you were hoods, casing the neighborhood. We merely asked a few questions in an environment that provided all of us with privacy. Run along, if you'd like."

"Of course," I said, "we'd be forced to answer any questions the media wanted to ask us about you. I mean, in a small town visitors are interesting. We love to write up stories in the local paper about their visits. Sometimes it even makes the local T.V. news."

The older agent's jaw muscle twitched just like Jake's did when he got tense. He glared at me. "And if you did that, we might be forced to press charges against the two of you. Kidnapping and impeding a government investigation. You could do time."

I gave it right back to him. "But of course, you wouldn't want to do that. It would only bring more publicity to your presence in town. So why don't you just tell us why you're watching my house, and I'll try and help you out. You know, we could be playing for the same team."

The younger agent looked as if that was not even a remote possibility, but the older guy was listening.

"You know we can't talk about our assignment," he said. "I've got my orders and we have to follow them."

Jake nodded. "Then you'll understand that we'll do what we have to do, too."

It was a standoff. The two agents climbed back into their van and drove out of Jake's garage. They didn't go very far, only across the street where they parked and began watching us again.

I walked to the edge of the garage bay and looked back at Jake who was busy studying his pager.

"All right, let's think this thing through," I said. "This has something to do with Bitsy's death. They're interested in us because why? Our only link is through Baby Blankenship. There's got to be a connection. Either they think we know more than we do, or they think we're going to lead them to something or someone. Do you think they're watching the nursing home? Or her mother's house? Or David Margolies?"

I gestured to the tow truck. "We need to find out, but that thing sticks out like the proverbial sore thumb. Let's go back to the house, get Nina and Spike, lose these boys and go look."

Jake shook his head. "What does it matter if they know what we're doing? Let's ride around, let them follow us and then go back to your place. I'm going to call Shelia and see what she can find out about this, too."

The mere mention of Shelia's name set my nerves on edge, but I didn't let Jake see it. No, I was turning over a new leaf, and jealousy wasn't going to be a part of my relationship.

While I drove, Jake talked to Shelia. The white panel van followed us, maintaining a discreet distance as I cruised along the streets of Glenn Ford. The street leading to the Blankenship family home was lined with cars and the house was lit up as people dropped by to pay their respects to Bitsy's family. There was no white van in evidence, nor was there any car that seemed out of place or government issued.

"It just gets more interesting," Jake said, closing up his cell phone. "Of course the names those two gave us are as fake as their badges. She can't get verification of any agents in this area. In fact, she got the same word Spike's friend got—Bitsy's death was the result of a freak accident. Case closed."

"Well, then," I said, turning onto the access road that ran alongside the nursing home, "someone's lying." I looked in the rearview mirror at the white van behind us. "Who are those guys then?"

Jake shook his head. "If I had to guess, I'd say they're the genuine article, but they're not DOD men. I'd say they're CIA."

I rode slowly up the long driveway to the nursing home, circled through the parking lot and saw nothing that triggered my alarm system. That didn't mean they weren't there, it just meant if they were in the lot, they were good at hiding.

When we returned to Aunt Lucy's the white van ran out of options. Every spot on the street was taken, forcing the van to park illegally in front of the fire hydrant outside of Sylvia Talluchi's row house.

"At least I know they won't be comfortable for long," I said, grinning over at Jake. "How long do you think it'll be before Sylvia comes out to give them another piece of her mind, or calls the cops because the van's parked in front of the fire hydrant?"

Jake chuckled, but neither one of us was too happy. Considering the fact that we had no actual case, we had certainly generated a lot of interest and even more questions. We parked and walked back into Aunt Lucy's house where we found everyone still sitting at the table, everyone that is but Arnold. His place was empty.

"Your friend leave?" Jake asked.

Aunt Lucy nodded. "He is tired. He went home to rest. He says all this excitement is too much for an old man!" She smiled happily. "It was a lovely day, wasn't it?"

While Spike nodded, agreeing with my aunt, Nina wasn't ready to let the subject of Aunt Lucy's boyfriend drop.

"He went home?" she repeated. "Oh, so he's really moved back to Glenn Ford for good, huh?"

I gave Nina a warning look, trying to head her off, but she ignored me and focused on Aunt Lucy.

"Yes," Aunt Lucy answered. "He says there is nothing for him in Michigan. He wanted to be back where he grew up."

"What about his children?" Nina persisted. "Aren't they still out there?"

Aunt Lucy glanced sharply at Nina before she answered. "They live all over the county," she said. "Arnold doesn't worry about them visiting. He sees them when he wishes. They are busy with their own lives." As she said this, she gave Nina a meaningful look, like she should get her own life and quit being so nosy. Of course Nina wasn't good at picking up on even not-so-subtle hints.

"So where does Arnold live?"

"Out in Honeybrook," Aunt Lucy replied slowly.

"In a house or a condo?"

It was obvious now that Nina and Aunt Lucy were engaged in a battle. Nina was like a dog with a bone. She wasn't giving in. For some reason, Aunt Lucy was equally determined to answer her questions, but there was a distinct edge to her voice, a warning tone that spelled trouble.

"How about dessert?" I said, trying to distract them.

"A lovely homelike setting," Aunt Lucy answered slowly, as if she knew Nina already knew exactly where Arnold lived.

"Have you been there to visit?"

"Yes," Aunt Lucy answered. "Whenever Arnold feels like staying in, I go there. Sometimes I go to his home because it is so private. Nobody asks questions they already know the answers to at Arnold's house."

Oh, boy! Here we go, I thought, and settled back in my chair to weather the upcoming storm.

"A friend of mine said Arnold moved into the hospice in Honeybrook," Nina said, a distinct edge of defiance in her voice. "But I told her Arnold couldn't live in the hospice, at least not as a patient. Hospices are for people who are about to die."

Aunt Lucy nodded. "Actually, hospices usually work with people who have six months or less to live. Occasionally people get better and don't need the hospice services, but you're right, you must be diagnosed with a terminal illness to receive their services."

Nina sat back and exhaled in a sigh of relief. "Good. That's like, totally what I thought. You only live in a hospice if you're like terminally ill. So, if Arnold doesn't live in the hospice where does he live?"

Everybody sitting at the table saw it coming except for Nina.

"Nina," Aunt Lucy said gently. "Arnold does live in the hospice. He is dying."

"No!"

Spike leaned over and took Nina's hand. Nina looked at her lover, still not quite able to accept what Aunt Lucy was telling her. "I don't get it. He doesn't even look sick!"

"Well, he is," Aunt Lucy said. She looked suddenly sad. "He has good days and bad. This was a good one. Arnold has an inoperable tumor that is growing around his heart. He found out about it almost a month ago."

My heart ached for my aunt. She had lost the love of her life and now would have to lose Arnold.

"Oh, Aunt Lucy," I said, reaching out to touch her hand. "I am so sorry. It must have been a dreadful shock to find out Arnold was dying."

She shrugged. "He told me as soon as he knew. He even wanted to stop seeing me because of it! I told him, we are not so young, you and me. We will learn to make the most of the time we have together. And so we do. What, I should send him away because soon he will leave me and it will hurt? Bah! Lucia Menetta Valocchi is made of stronger stuff than that!"

"But he doesn't look sick!" Nina protested. "Maybe you should get a second opinion!"

Aunt Lucy shook her head. "Arnold Koslovski could buy the Mayo Clinic if he wanted to. He's seen the best doctors and they all say the same thing. That's why he moved into the hospice instead of buying the farm he wanted. There isn't time for that now. He needs help. He wants to be able to enjoy what time we have left. So, he gave the money he was going to spend on his estate to the hospice and in return, they are putting him in a small suite and taking care of him. Now," she said, rising to her feet and looking down at the rest of us, "I am tired. I have had a long day and I want to go to bed. Arnie and I are going to Longwood Gardens in the morning. He has hired a hot air balloon to take us on a little ride."

"Won't it be too cold?" Spike asked, always practical.

Aunt Lucy giggled like a school girl. "Arnold promises to keep me warm!" She was blushing as she walked out of the room and didn't even turn around as she called back over her shoulder, "Good night!"

"Do you think it just hasn't hit her yet?" Spike asked, concerned. "I mean, clearly she's infatuated with the guy. Don't you think it's going to affect her terribly when he dies?"

Nina sighed. "Maybe she meant what she said about love. You know, that it's like a garden that you have to plant today. Maybe Arnie's her garden or something."

I couldn't listen to any more. My heart was aching and I didn't want to think about it. I didn't want to think about Aunt Lucy's heart breaking or love or Nina and Spike or anything that would make me feel. I had too many questions of my own. I didn't want to think about the scary, unpredictable nature of life and love.

"Okay, listen," I said, turning to Jake. "I don't want to

wait around to see what those guys in the white van do. I think we should be more proactive. I propose we go stakeout the Blankenship house and the nursing home. Maybe David Margolies will do something interesting. Or maybe someone will try to get into Baby's room again. Either way we'll be there, ready and waiting in case anything happens."

Jake gave me a knowing look. "What, all this emotion making you squirrelly?"

I ignored him. "We can slip out through Aunt Lucy's lab in the basement."

"Hey," Nina cried. "Wait! If you guys need to get away, let me and Spike go create a little distraction. I love doing that stuff!"

Spike grinned apologetically. "Be a shame not to let her have a little fun," she said. "You know how Nina likes to amuse the bad guys."

Lloyd barked once, hopped down from his chair and walked over to the back door.

"See!" Nina cried. "Lloyd likes undercover work, too!"

Five minutes later Nina and Spike, wearing push-up bras, low-cut tops and carrying a tray full of hot chocolate and brownies arrived at the van's door and were not content to go away until their banging summoned the two beleaguered agents.

Jake took the nursing home and I got stuck with the Blankenship house. Before we set off in opposite directions he stopped me, grabbing me by the arms and pulling me into him for a long, lingering kiss. When he'd finished, he leaned back and studied my face.

"You know," he said softly, "you're going to have to get used to having me around. Does that scare you?"

I longed to walk into his arms, snuggle deep into the warmth of him and stay there, forgetting about everything else and escaping the reality of our current crisis. But the other half of me cried "Run for your life!" and so I fought off my need for him and coated myself in emotional Teflon.

"I'm not scared of you, Carpenter, and I'll put my money where my mouth is just as soon as we figure out what's going on here."

He didn't buy it. I could tell by the way he smiled. He was letting me off the hook, giving me space to deal with the new terms of our relationship. As I drove across town, I worked to convince myself that I was not running away from Jake. I just couldn't focus on our relationship when I felt personally responsible, maybe, for Bitsy's death and all the trouble that had followed. I knew I didn't have a client per se in Baby Blankenship, but I felt morally responsible for her. I liked her. I didn't want her to get hurt and I just didn't have a good feeling about her safety. On top of that, we seemed to be the object of a government surveillance operation. Who could engross themselves in a relationship with all that going on?

I parked Nina's baby-blue Civic a block away from the Blankenship home and crept across back alleys and lawns until I came up behind the Blankenship garage. Like many of the homes in the older, well-to-do part of town, the Blankenships had a huge stone manor house with a matching detached garage that sat just off the alley. Their yard was surrounded by tall trees planted by the original owners to shield the property from its nearby neighbors. It made a wonderful shelter for me as I snuck slowly around the side of the garage and crouched down at the base of one of the cypress trees.

A few lights were still on inside but it appeared that the crowd of condolence callers had left for the evening. It was freezing. I shoved my hands deep inside my coat and huddled closer to the tree. Now and then I let my hand curl around the butt of my Glock 9 mm, just so I could reassure myself of its presence.

After about twenty minutes I looked over at the garage and began seriously thinking about watching the house from its slightly warmer confines. Just as I stood up and decided to try the door on the near side of the building, the back door to the house suddenly opened and David Margolies stepped outside. While I watched, he lit a cigarette and called someone on his cell phone.

When he sank down onto a wrought iron bench, his back to me, I realized I was too far away to hear what he was saying and decided to move closer. I crouched low and darted from my hiding place beneath the tree, heading for a stone barbecue that stood just off to the side of the built-in pool. When my heart stopped pounding and I realized I hadn't been seen, I decided to risk moving closer. I needed to hear what he was saying.

I scanned the backyard and decided upon a small building to the right of the patio where David Margolies sat talking. I stood up, poised to run, and ducked back down as the back door opened and a short, bleached-blond woman whom I assumed to be Bitsy's mother, Brenda Blankenship, stood framed in the doorway.

"David?" she called, peering out into the darkness. "Are you out there?"

As I watched, David slumped down in his seat and didn't answer her.

"Someone called for you," she said, apparently not satisfied that he wasn't within earshot. "They'll call back in ten minutes."

Brenda walked back inside, closing the door firmly behind her.

The arc of David's cigarette tip glowed as he took one

final drag and flung it out in front of the bench. Immediately, he lit another and resumed his conversation.

I waited until I heard the low rumble of his voice and sprinted across the short distance between the barbecue and the potting shed. I reached the side of the building, breathless, my heart pounding in my throat as I squatted down and positioned myself to listen.

"I'm telling you," David said, "I don't know!"

Behind me, the bushes rustled in the wind and I shivered, suddenly nervous. Even Margolies sounded frightened as he hunched down into his jacket and checked anxiously over his shoulder every few seconds. Instinctively, I pulled out my gun, feeling better with it in my hand instead of in my pocket. I waited for Margolies to make his next statement but never heard it. Something moved just behind me. I started to turn, felt hot, searing pain shoot through the back of my skull and fell forward into the frigid darkness.

I awoke to the sound of sirens. Red and blue lights strobed across the frozen ground where I lay, and I was still holding my gun in my right hand. I struggled to focus, to remember, to wake up, but all I could think about was the shooting pain that seemed to radiate out from the base of my skull. With intense effort I was finally able to stand. The world swirled around me in a sickening cartwheel that made walking impossible.

A moment later the Blankenship backyard was covered with cops, all of them running with their guns drawn. When they saw me, all hell broke loose.

"Freeze! Drop your weapon! Drop your weapon or I'll blow your fucking head off!"

The voice was familiar. I squinted, blinded by the beam of a bright flashlight and dropped my gun.

"Hands up! Up where I can see them!" the irritating female voice insisted.

"Detective, I got a body! One down!"

"Call for an ambulance!" the female directed. *Oh great*. Detective Wheeling, one of Glenn Ford's finest was on the job.

"Wheeling, it's me, Stella Valocchi."

"Keep your hands where I can see them," she answered. "What did ya have to go and shoot him for?"

"What? I didn't shoot anybody. Somebody hit me and knocked me out. What are you talking about?"

"Jeeze Louise! Valocchi, don't pee on my leg and tell me it's raining."

I looked past Wheeling, shielding my eyes so I could take in the body on the ground a few yards away from me. David Margolies lay facedown in front of the bench where he'd been talking. As I studied the scene, the back door flew open. Brenda Blankenship screamed and dissolved into hysterical sobbing.

Wheeling walked over and spoke to the woman. I couldn't hear what she said but I could certainly hear Brenda Blankenship's answer.

"I told you. I saw a woman with a gun in her hand, running. Right after I heard the gunshot. That's when I called 911."

Wheeling motioned toward me and I saw Brenda squint out into the darkness.

"I don't know. She's the same size but it was dark. Maybe it's her."

Wheeling nodded to the cop standing beside me. "Cuff her," she said, unable to keep the satisfied, smirky tone out of her voice.

"What for?" I asked. "It's not like I shot the guy!"

"Take her downtown," Wheeling directed. "Have ballistics check her gun out, ASAP."

"Detective Wheeling, don't be stupid! I'll have my

lawyer slap a police brutality and false arrest suit on you so fast your head'll spin."

Wheeling stepped directly into my line of vision then. She was probably in her late forties, a brassy, bottle blonde who carried an extra thirty pounds on her stocky frame and always looked like she'd just come from a battle with a mountain lion. Her clothes were permanently wrinkled and her stockings always had a run in them. No matter how hard she tried, she always looked frumpy.

But Wheeling's disposition was worse than her choice in clothing. She seemed convinced that the world conspired to rain on her parade. And apparently, she viewed me as the drum major of her misfortunes. She'd tried to pin a murder charge on me once before and been disappointed. If I knew her, she'd do everything in her power to stick one to me again, even if she had to make up the evidence.

"You're blowing smoke up my skirt, Valocchi," she said. "I got a witness and the old smoking gun. We check your hand and find gun powder residue and it's all over but the crying. Go on, you get one phone call. See if Spike Montgomery can get you out of this one!"

Gun powder residue. No problem. I hadn't fired my gun in days. They'd do the test and I'd be home free. Wouldn't I?

Chapter 9

I had a monster headache. I was in an interview room in the Glenn Ford Police Department at 2:00 a.m. sitting across from Detective Wheeling and her partner, Detective Slovenick. We were not happy campers, or rather, Slovenick and I were not happy. Wheeling was ecstatic. She smelled blood. Mine.

Detective Slovenick had some sense about him. He was older, nearing retirement, and years on the force had taught him to trust his instincts. He didn't think I'd killed David Margolies. Why would I?

"She's got gunpowder residue on her hands!" Wheeling crowed. "She did it!"

Slovenick sighed, ran his one hand through his short gray hair and rearranged his large frame in another futile attempt to make himself more comfortable in the hard plastic chair.

"The test results were consistent with her having

handled a recently discharged weapon. If someone knocked her out, took her gun, shot the vic and then placed the weapon in her hand, she'd test out the same way. You gotta ask yourself where she got the bump on the head."

Wheeling scowled. "Maybe she got in a fight. Maybe it's totally unrelated to her hitting Margolies."

"Or maybe I got knocked out and the killer used my gun to kill Margolies so it'd look like I did it." I was looking at Wheeling and envisioning myself kicking her ass and wiping the self-satisfied look right off her face.

A young female cop stuck her head in the door and looked at Detective Slovenick.

"Spike Montgomery's here. She wants—"

The girl didn't get to finish. Spike walked into the interview room, pushing past the irritated officer and plopping her briefcase down in the middle of the tiny table.

"Charge her or release her," Spike said coolly.

"We've got questions…" Wheeling started.

"We aren't giving answers or interviews," Spike answered. "It's two o'clock in the morning. Either you've got enough to charge her or you don't. Now which is it?"

Wheeling stood up. "We're charging her," she said.

"No we're not. She can go, Spike. With the understanding that…"

Spike raised her hand. "I know. She's not leaving town." She put her hand on my shoulder and squeezed reassuringly. "Let's go."

She waited until we were in the car and safely out of the parking lot before she said anything, and then it wasn't at all what I expected.

"Want to hear something interesting?" she asked.

I didn't have the energy to do much more than nod, but it was all Spike needed. She smiled, practically dancing in the driver's seat as she began singing a made-up, off-key song.

"I know you're bumming, 'cause you been slumming, but I got something for you! I saw the D.A. He stopped by today. And guess what he say to me?" She drummed on the steering wheel as she sang, thumping it hard as she came to a halt and looked at me, grinning.

When I didn't answer and instead just stared back at her wide-eyed and slack-jawed, she continued her little song. I was having trouble believing this was the same Spike Montgomery I'd come to know and love, but then I remembered she had left her successful career as a district attorney to move to California and become a performance artist. I reasoned she was probably missing her on-stage days, and this, along with the late hour and lack of sleep, was why she chose to sing a song to me about her D.A. friend.

"The lab took the itsy pieces of Bitsy.... They didn't send to the feds. They used restric-tion frag-ment length poly-mor-phism and they con-cluded it wasn't...Bitsy's itsy pieces that they were stud-y-ing so hard!" She sang, stumbling as she tried to fit the long syllables into her barely recognizable tune.

"What?"

Spike stopped singing, pulled up in front of Aunt Lucy's house and cut the engine. "Thought that might make you feel better," she said. "It just ticked the local guys off when the feds demanded every piece of evidence and basically called them yokels. So even though they'd all be fired, if not jailed, and can't ever admit to anyone they did it, they kept a few minuscule samples. Steve Evans, the lab supervisor, told Barry the results. Is that weird or what?"

I was stunned. "Bitsy wasn't in the blown-up car in the mall? Then who was in her car?"

Spike shrugged. "No idea. They're working on what little they had left to work with, but of course, they can't send any more samples off, not without a good explanation that wouldn't make the feds suspicious. Personally, I'm hoping Jake can use this information as leverage to get his contact to find out more."

My mind was racing with possibilities and questions. Where was Bitsy? Did she blow up her car with someone in it? Did someone take her? Was this staged? Was Bitsy being held somewhere?

"Does Jake know?"

Spike nodded. "I called him earlier, before you got arrested and again after you called me from the PD. He should be waiting on us now."

As if on cue, the front door opened and Nina emerged to stand on the front stoop. She wrapped her arms around her torso and shivered in the frigid early-morning air. She leaned down to peer into Spike's car.

"Are you two like coming inside? It's freezing!" she called. Jake appeared in the doorway behind her, and behind him stood Aunt Lucy.

When we were finally inside, Jake wasted no time in taking me into his arms. He kissed the top of my head, rubbed my arms to warm me and sighed softly when I sagged against his chest.

"You had me worried," he murmured. Then, in a louder voice said, "I know we were going out to try and shake things up, but did you have to shoot the guy?"

Nina whirled around. "You shot him?"

Aunt Lucy shook her head. "*Cara mia*, of course she didn't shoot him. Jake is playing." But she gave me the Italian once-over for confirmation and seemed reassured when I nodded.

What followed was an old-fashioned war council, held

around Aunt Lucy's table over cheese, *suppresatta,* bread and pot after pot of espresso. Everyone had an opinion about what had happened to Bitsy and what should happen next.

Aunt Lucy thought Bitsy had been kidnapped by terrorists or by Slovenian agents sent to make an example of Americans who attempted to help their nation's scientific talent defect to the United States. Jake seemed to think this was a plausible idea and slipped down to Uncle Benny's old workshop in the basement where he stayed for almost half an hour, talking to Shelia Martin.

When he returned and was sitting next to me at the table, I leaned in to him and whispered. "Well, what did she say?" Aunt Lucy and Nina were in a heated debate over Nina's theory that Bitsy had run off with a Slovenian man she'd fallen for and had, herself, defected. No one paid Jake any mind at all, but he was too cautious to answer me.

"I'll tell you later" was all I could get out of him, and in light of the fact that it was almost dawn, I couldn't imagine remaining conscious long enough to hear and make sense of it all.

Spike tried to stay with the conversation, but once she'd revealed all of her news, she'd slowly started drooping. Now she was asleep on the table, her head resting in her cradled arms as she snored softly.

"Well, we can't put any more into this when we're all tired," Jake said, abruptly rising to his feet and pulling me along with him. "I vote we all get some shut-eye and get back to it later, when we're all fresh and rested."

Aunt Lucy nodded wearily and rose to her feet. "You're right, as usual, Jake," she said. She looked down at Lloyd and Fang, both of whom were sleeping at her feet. "Come, children."

The two dogs followed my aunt out of the kitchen as the mass exodus began. Spike and Nina wasted no time carrying dishes to the sink and putting away the food. I looked at Jake and suddenly didn't want to sleep alone.

"Stay here," I murmured. "Stay with me. Please."

I saw his eyebrow shoot up speculatively as a slight grin tugged at the corner of his mouth.

"Why, partner," he whispered. "I didn't know you cared."

"Upstairs, you! Now!" I commanded, gripping his hand tight as I tugged him out of the kitchen.

I started up the stairs thinking about how wonderful it would feel to fall asleep in Jake's warm arms, but somewhere between the second and third floors, my fantasy began to change. Jake stopped me on the landing, pushing me into a tight corner and bent his head to kiss me with a thoroughness that left no doubt about his intentions.

I felt his tongue slip between my lips to meet mine as my hands ripped his shirt free and I slipped my fingers up and across his taut, muscled torso. Below us, Spike and Nina approached the staircase and started up the stairs toward us.

My fingers changed direction, wantonly straying below Jake's waistband, taunting him with the threat of exposure.

"Oh, you are a bad, bad girl," he whispered into my neck and reached, suddenly and with swift proficiency, to swoop me up into his arms. He carried me, effortlessly, up the remaining stairs, down the hallway to my bedroom. He kicked the door open, carried me across the threshold, and dropped me unceremoniously on top of the big iron bed.

I let him think he had the advantage, lay there looking up at him, apparently startled by his take-charge approach as he grinned at me and leaned over to begin undressing me. Then, when I knew he was off balance, I made a counterstrike, pulling him down and rolling as he fell so I emerged on top, seated astride his hips.

"Now," I said, reaching forward to take his shirt in my hands. "It's my turn."

Jake's eyes darkened. His mouth curved into a slow, dangerous grin. "Make your first shot your best, girly," he answered. "'Cause then I'm gonna take you apart, bit by bit, inch by inch. Scared?"

I answered him by ripping his flannel shirt open, spraying buttons everywhere as I bent to answer him with a hot tongue bent on bringing him under my hungry control. He moaned softly and I knew he was mine.

My fingers found a fray in the neckline of his worn T-shirt as I grabbed it and ripped the fabric away from his chest. My tongue, unleashed, covered his nipples as I alternately sucked and nipped, losing myself in his body.

I had him naked before me and was about to enjoy sending him over the edge when he turned the tables.

"Don't think you can have your way with me and escape unscathed," he whispered, pinning me neatly beneath him. "I know who I'm dealing with, and your little playtime is over."

He stretched, reaching for a piece of his torn T-shirt, all the while keeping my wrists firmly gripped in his other hand. With practiced ease he tied my wrists together, secured them to the bars of my headboard, and then leaned back to survey his handiwork, obviously pleased with himself.

"No fair!" I cried softly, but I was thinking exactly the opposite as my body responded to the loss of control with a surge of adrenaline and excitement.

Jake picked up the remaining half of his T-shirt, ripped

it into three pieces and sat back to consider me, slowly running the fabric through his hands as he thought.

"You look like a screamer to me," he said, grinning.

"No," I answered, "don't!"

But it was too late. He tied a strip of fabric across my mouth.

"Now," he said. "If you fight me, I'll use these two pieces to tie your legs down."

With his free hand he slowly trailed his index finger down across my stomach, down lower, between my legs. When it became obvious to both of us that I was enjoying his slow torture, he grinned and lowered his head to take the tip of one breast in his mouth.

He teased my body slowly, working me into a near frenzy of rabid desire as I moaned and longed to be able to tell him to hurry. He worked his way down my torso, pushing my legs apart as his tongue left a trail of fire and longing behind it.

Just before he reached the triangle of dark hair that signaled the point of no possible return for me, he stopped, raised his head and looked deep into my eyes.

"Stel," he said softly. "You know I'll untie you anytime you want, right?"

I nodded, hoping he wouldn't, but welcoming the safety of his words, wanting more than anything now to belong to him, to feel him deep inside me.

"Good," he whispered. "Because, baby, the things I'm going to do to you now will make you beg me to untie you, and I won't do that unless I ask you if you really mean it and you tell me yes, okay?"

I groaned, thinking, Just do me! Jake laughed, reading my body, and as he held my gaze, slipped one finger deep inside me and began slowly teasing me with its agonizingly slow movement. I groaned again, louder, as his movement became more forceful and I arched to meet his hand, my body begging for more.

"Oh," he whispered, still grinning, still looking straight into my soul, "I know what you want. You want me to do you, hard, but I can't. Not yet. Not until you give me what I want."

"What?" I cried, but the word was muffled by the T-shirt gag.

Jake smiled up at me, as his thumb began slowly sliding along in tandem with his index finger, mimicking the soft caress of his tongue.

"She knows what I want," he answered. "Close your eyes and relax. You're going to be here awhile."

I felt him slide lower on my body as his tongue joined his fingers in a symphony of seduction that made me grateful for the muffling effect of his T-shirt. He took his time, edging me closer and closer to the precipice, reveling in his ability to bring me right to the edge and then pull me back, only to start all over again.

I lost track of my surroundings, forgot my earlier fatigue, forgot everything but Jake and the way our bodies joined finally on an ocean of pleasure that crested higher and higher with each succeeding wave of sensation.

I fell asleep finally, my body slick with sweat and spent passion. Jake's arms held me fast as I drifted into a deep and dreamless sleep that held no memory of anything but the uncontrollable emotion I'd felt as he'd brought me to that last, shattering climax and had at last allowed himself to join me. I knew what I was feeling and it was different from anything I had ever felt before, for any lover. It was at once like discovering a new world and returning home after an almost never-ending journey.

I was in love with Jake Carpenter. I was in love for

perhaps the first time in my life. What we had shared in high school couldn't hold a candle to the way I felt now. This was different.

When the cell phone's incessant ringing interrupted my deep slumber, I once again cursed the bright moment when I'd felt compelled to list the number on my business card. I rolled over to the side of the bed, leaned down and fumbled through my clothes to find the offending object.

Jake, lying beside me, rolled over, wrapped his head in the nearest pillow and groaned.

I flipped open the phone, saw who was calling and echoed Jake's moaned sentiment. I was not in the mood for Marygrace Llewellen.

"What?" I snapped.

"I'm at the hospital. You two had better get over here. Now!"

I closed my eyes and visualized Marygrace, surrounded by hordes of clamoring old people, all raising their arms in cries of needy protest, and cringed. What did I look like, the police department? Social Services? Why me?

But then the image of Baby Blankenship's open, trusting face replaced Marygrace and her crowd and I was instantly awake and listening.

"What happened?"

"I don't know if Baby's going to make it," Marygrace answered. "They had to shock her just to keep her around long enough for the ambulance to come and get her. It's been touch-and-go ever since."

"What about Brenda? I thought she was taking Baby home. I thought Brenda didn't want …"

"That was David's doing, apparently. Now she's all

over the idea of Baby needing protection. Furthermore, Baby asked for you."

Jake was awake now, the pillow gone from around his head as he propped himself up on one elbow and listened to my side of the conversation.

"She asked for me? By name?"

Marygrace exhaled an exasperated sigh. "Does it really matter? Don't you think your time might be better spent driving over here? It's a freaking emergency, okay?"

Click. Once again Marygrace Llewellen had hung up on me, and once again I was about to race to the rescue of a little old lady I'd been told had no further need of my *free* services. It defied good business logic, but it didn't defy the hold that woman had on my heartstrings.

I looked over at Jake and felt a similar tug. I was becoming one big sentimental sap.

"Gotta go," I said, throwing back the covers. "Baby's in the hospital and Marygrace says she doesn't know if she'll make it."

To his credit, Jake didn't try and dissuade me. Instead he got out of bed, pulled on his jeans, reached for his shirt and stopped. I looked over, realized what the problem was a second later, and started laughing just as he did.

"I have a couple of your shirts in my closet," I said. "You know, from when you stayed here after Jimmy Spagnozzi shot you?" Like I really needed to remind him of that. The scar was still a livid streak across his left side and the memory of driving him, unconscious, to the emergency room just as indelibly etched in my mind.

He nodded, no longer laughing, and went to the closet while I hastily finished dressing and ran a brush through my hair. I leaned into the mirror, inspecting the damage lack of sleep and hours of lovemaking had done. Jake found me grinning foolishly into the mirror.

"I look like I've been…"

"You certainly do," he agreed, and smacked the seat of my jeans on his way out the door. "I'll go warm up the car."

I glanced at the bedside clock as he left. It was a little after 8:00 a.m. How long had Baby been in the hospital and what had happened to put her there?

Marygrace wasn't much help when we arrived. She greeted us at the entrance to the emergency room and led us back through the rabbit warren of cubicles and curtained-off partitions to the tiny space where Baby lay hooked up to machines and monitors. As we stood, peering in through the glass window at her, Marygrace gave us a sketchy accounting of the circumstances leading up to Baby's hospitalization.

"I guess I got in around six-fifteen this morning. It's the only way I can get my paperwork done. Otherwise, I'm getting pulled in a hundred different directions all day," she explained almost apologetically. "Anyway, the alert went out about five minutes after I got there, and when I heard them call a full code on the north wing, well, I just knew."

Marygrace looked from Jake to me, as if needing validation that instincts were just like that; sometimes one just *knew* things without benefit of factual corroboration. I nodded and she went on.

"By the time I got to her, one of the night nurses had already zapped her with the defibrillator and the ambulance was on its way. There was little else I could do but call Brenda and get my ass over here."

I looked around. "Where is Brenda?"

Marygrace gave me a long-suffering look, like I should know the answer, which of course I didn't. "She got here around seven, stayed long enough to hear the doc say he

thought Baby'd pull through, and then she took off again."
Marygrace shook her head. "In her defense, Brenda's
pretty much out of it. Between Bitsy and then her husband
getting themselves killed, the poor woman's a freaking
basket case. And I mean, who could blame her? Come on,
I mean, she's probably wondering who's next?"

Marygrace seemed to think about this a moment and
then, as if prompted, started up again.

"See, I didn't get to this part yet…I got a call from the
third shift supervisor while Brenda was talking to me.
Anyway, Lisa said she thought I should know they found
Baby's window open when they went in. The nurse closed
it as soon as she found it open, but she doesn't know how
long it was open or if it was what triggered Baby's heart
attack, but she thought she should tell me so I could pass
it along to the attending doctor. So, I did, but Brenda
heard me and that freaked her out even more. She thinks
some maniac wants them all dead! I tried to calm her
down, but she wasn't having it. That's when I said I had
asked you to watch out for Baby but David had pulled you
guys off. I told her you were even doing it as a favor, you
know, in honor of your friend, Bitsy."

Marygrace cocked her head at me. "She asked me if I
thought I could call you guys, and try to persuade you to
come watch Baby again. I said I didn't know, but I really
didn't think you would do it for *free* again. So, guess
what?" Without waiting for us to answer, Marygrace continued, "She said money was no object! Come on, man!
That bitch never gave a shit about her mom until it looked
like maybe the whole family had suddenly become an en-
dangered species. She said tell you she wants you guys to
find out who's doing this and get them locked up."

Marygrace allowed herself a small triumphant smirk.
"See, you put good out into the universe and look how

it comes back to you! Now you'll be working for money, lots of money! And Baby's gonna have somebody looking out for her full-time! Now that's how I like to see a plan come together!"

Baby's eyes were open and she was watching me through the window, frowning and then smiling as she appeared to recognize me. She raised her hand and waved, beckoning me into the small room where she lay.

"Can I go in?" I asked Marygrace.

"Sure, but they won't let you stay long. They're monitoring her. It was a small heart attack but they want to take precautions before they release her. I'm hoping we can take her home this afternoon."

"To Brenda's?" I asked, alarm suddenly overtaking my joy at seeing Baby awake and apparently able to remember me.

"No," Marygrace scoffed. "To Brookhaven Manor."

This option didn't sit any better with me. Baby's room had been invaded at least three times, with each episode worse than the one before. I was beginning to think we needed to come up with a safer location for my friend, Baby. Someplace safe. Someplace where we could have access to good medical care as well as security for Baby.

Jake nudged me and nodded toward Baby. "I don't think she understands why you're not in there," he muttered.

I nodded. When Marygrace's cell phone rang, I used the momentary distraction to clue Jake in privately on my thinking.

"Got any ideas for a location?" he asked.

"Yep. How about calling Aunt Lucy and asking her if she thinks we could use her basement lab for a hospital room. Ask her if she knows any tight-lipped, private duty nurses."

I left him punching in the home number on his cell and went in to see Baby. She looked pitifully small and weak as she lay on the narrow gurney that had become her emergency room bed.

"Hey, friend," she whispered when I took her cold, frail hand in mine.

"Hey, friend," I answered, and bent to kiss her cheek. "Someone told me you weren't feeling too well."

Baby nodded and fingered the crucifix around her neck in the familiar gesture I now knew signaled inner distress.

"I think someone tried to kill me," she said, her voice barely audible over the beeping and ticking of the nearby monitors.

"What do you mean, Baby?"

"My neck hurts. See?" She pulled the necklace aside and gestured to a spot just below the hollow of her throat. An angry red burn in the shape of a cross was clearly visible against Baby's pale pink skin.

"What happened?"

"I just don't know. I was asleep. I was dreaming about Bitsy. She was flying around my room like a little bird and then, all of a sudden, someone opened the window and she flew right out the window! I kept calling and calling for her, but they wouldn't help me! That's when they tried to kill me!"

The monitor started to beep louder and faster. A nurse quickly entered the room, glared at me and said, "Are you family?"

I answered, "No," Baby said, "Yes," and the nurse gave up. "You'll have to leave now. She can't have any more visitors for another half an hour."

I let go of Baby's hand, smiled at her reassuringly and said, "I'll be back, sweetie. Don't worry."

Once I was outside, I went immediately to Marygrace. "What in the hell happened to her neck?"

Marygrace rolled her eyes. "That idiot night nurse forgot to take off her jewelry before she zapped her and Baby got burned. But hey, at least she's alive!"

"But why did she…"

"Oh, come on, Stella!" Marygrace interrupted. "You know how hard it is to get good help in a nursing home on third shift? You think corporate wants to pay what it costs to hire and keep good nurses, when they might make a buck to slide in their slimy pockets? Yeah? Well, no. They ain't paying what it takes to hire someone who'll remember to take off jewelry before they defibrillate somebody. All I can do is be thankful she at least responded to the code."

Damn. I was beginning to really realize how lucky the residents of Brookhaven Manor were to have a bulldog like Marygrace on their side and how scary it was to live in a nursing home run by corporate interests and greed.

Jake had wandered off to stand at the far end of the hallway while he talked on his cell, but now he returned and gave me a quick wink to acknowledge success with Aunt Lucy.

Now we had a new dilemma. If we took Baby and placed her in a secure location, who would we need to tell? I eyed Marygrace. She would need to know that we had Baby, but no more than that. I pictured Slovenian spies torturing Marygrace and felt sorry for the Slovenians, but still, it didn't pay to take a risk like that or to put Marygrace in such a dangerous position. No, she couldn't know where we were taking Baby.

Then I thought about Brenda Blankenship and wondered how we'd get around the issue of family consent.

"Marygrace, how often will we need to check in with

Brenda?" I asked. "For that matter, how often will she come see Baby?"

Marygrace frowned at me, already suspicious. "What are you up to?"

I explained that Jake and I wanted to take Baby to a secure location. I reassured her that well-paid, registered nurses would look after her patient, but that the location would need to remain secret and that we would need her help.

Marygrace didn't hesitate.

"I'll run interference with Brenda," she said. "I'll get her to sign a waver giving you and Jake permission to do whatever is necessary to ensure Baby's safety, and that should clear me and the two of you to do what you need to do. In fact," she said, hitching her purse up onto her shoulder, "I'll go take care of that right now. The doctor told me they're going to set Baby free in another two hours. Will you be ready by then?"

I looked at Jake and when he nodded, gave Marygrace a thumbs-up.

Two hours later a privately contracted ambulance driven by two of our old high school buddies, now EMTs, pulled up to the back bay of the emergency room. Eddie Roman and James Zybelski, "Paint Bucket" and "Weasel," still answering to their junior high school nicknames, asked no questions and could be relied upon to "forget" ever taking delivery of Baby Blankenship. Weasel would forget because he'd spent years and years smoking pot. Forgetfulness was a convenient side effect of chronic marijuana use. Bucket's forgetfulness was more a product of his loyalty to our childhood and the bond we'd all shared as neighborhood kids growing up during tough times.

Of course, as an added precaution, the two men weren't told their patient's name, and they didn't even ask. They were too busy carrying on a debate that had raged between them since I'd returned to town, been knocked out in an explosion and awakened to find them vigorously discussing the possibility that I'd gotten breast implants while living in Florida.

"So, like, Stella, how you been?" Bucket asked, staring directly at my chest.

"Up here, Buck," I said, tilting the short, red-haired man's chin with my index finger. "I haven't trained them to answer yet."

"Told ya!" Weasel cried.

Paint Bucket gave his partner a scornful look. "Real or fake, they aren't trainable, Weasel."

"Boys, let's get on with it, shall we?"

With resigned sighs, the two EMTs took charge of Baby, and while they had been utter idiots with me, they became superheroes with their patient. They moved her gently, effortlessly and with an endearing charm that soon had the little woman beaming. They became her grandsons and they ate it up, all the way across town to Aunt Lucy's house.

Once inside, Paint Bucket and Weasel were grievously offended when they learned their mission was over and their services no longer needed. Aunt Lucy finally took over, stridently ordering them from the house with a crabby Fang nipping at their heels as they fled.

Jake, Spike, Nina and I then took Baby's gurney and transported our fragile patient down the steps, past Uncle Benny's workshop, into the laundry room and through the hidden panel that opened into Aunt Lucy's concealed laboratory.

Baby watched the entire process with undisguised delight, ooh-ing and ahh-ing at each new room, as if we were unwrapping Christmas presents instead of descending into the basement. When we reached Aunt Lucy's gleaming lab with its sparkling stainless steel counters and equipment, Baby stopped smiling and gasped in apparent horror.

"Am I dead?" she asked. "I don't feel dead but this is the morgue, isn't it?"

"Oh, honey, no!" I said, trying to reassure her. "This is where Aunt Lucy makes her—" I stopped, searching for a reassuring image "—soup," I finished lamely. "Her chicken soup."

Aunt Lucy snorted and walked up to stand beside Baby. "Belinda, do you remember me? Lucia Manetta. I married Benito Valocchi. I went to school with your sister, Cynthia."

Baby studied Aunt Lucy for a long moment, her brow crinkling into a frown as she appeared to concentrate.

"Lucy Manetta?"

Aunt Lucy smiled and nodded. "Yes, that's me!"

"Damn!" Baby said, seemingly amazed by this revelation. "You got old!"

Aunt Lucy stiffened. "Well, you're no spring chicken yourself, you know!" she said.

Baby cackled. "What are you talking about, Lucia! You're just jealous because I'm younger and Cynthia's dating your old boyfriend, Arnie!"

There was a moment of silence as Aunt Lucy and the rest of us shifted gears, realizing that Baby thought she was still in high school and decades younger than Aunt Lucy!

Across the laboratory, behind a curtain of starched white bed sheets, I heard a snort of suppressed laughter. Aunt Lucy called out something in Italian to the hidden figure and was answered by a familiar voice. A moment later the sheets were flung back and Baby Blankenship's private duty nurse stood glaring out at us.

"Well," she demanded. "Are you all going to stand there like a gaggle of gossipy girls trying to figure out who's the fairest in the land or are you going to bring my patient over here and let me keep her alive for a few decades longer?"

Sylvia Talluchi was wearing a crisp, white nurse's uniform, complete with cap, which had to have last seen daylight in the 1940s. Her hair, which had been worn in a tight braid and coiled into a bun on top of her head for as long as I could remember, was now down in neatly coifed, shoulder-length, ink-black waves. Her wrinkled skin was rouged and powdered. Her lips were painted bright red and she wore ancient cat's eye glasses to complete the bizarre costume.

"I remember you!" Baby cried. "Mrs. Talluchi, the school nurse!"

Sylvia Talluchi grinned and shook the glass thermometer in her hand with gleeful abandon.

"Bottoms up!" she crowed.

Chapter 10

"Tell me she wasn't the school nurse when you guys were in high school," I demanded, spinning to face Aunt Lucy.

Aunt Lucy shrugged. "It was wartime. She was just out of nursing school. What can I say?"

"That bag of bones couldn't possibly be sane enough to take care of Baby," Jake hissed in my ear.

Aunt Lucy had walked away but stopped midway across the room, spun on her heel and glared at Jake.

"For your information, sir, that 'bag of bones' as you so rudely described my best friend, was not only a decorated war nurse in the Korean controversy, but was also the only surgical nurse Carlos Santoria would allow in the operating room to assist him when he developed the very first procedure for the splicing of pig valves into human aortas! If you can find a more capable nurse, younger or older, I'd like to meet her!"

Jake actually looked ashamed. "I'm sorry, Aunt Lucy," he said.

She was still frowning. "Do you think because we are old we cease to have value? Are you young people so bigoted that you dismiss us because of the color of our hair or the lines and wrinkles on our faces? You act as if we are invisible!" she cried, addressing her remarks to all of us.

I was aware that old Sylvia Talluchi had stopped moving around behind the curtain and was probably listening to Aunt Lucy's every word. The reality of the situation was not so much that we dismissed Sylvia because of her age. No. We were leery of Mrs. Talluchi because in my considered and very much nonprofessional opinion, Sylvia Talluchi was certifiably insane.

The woman was forever calling Aunt Lucy to alert her to some new threat to the neighborhood and half of them were imagined or involved alien invaders. What good would she be with Baby Blankenship? For pity's sake, the woman was wearing a 1940s uniform. What did she know about nursing a cardiac patient in the twenty-first century?

I considered telling Aunt Lucy this, but was too tenderhearted to do so while within earshot of Sylvia Talluchi. Instead, I kept my mouth shut and decided to keep one of us with Baby and Sylvia until a more suitable replacement could be found. Then I remembered Paint Bucket and Weasel. They were potheads, but they were also quite good at their jobs. Perhaps between the three of them, Baby Blankenship could receive reasonably good medical care and the rest of us would be freed up to get to the bottom of the entire Bitsy and Baby Blankenship case.

I caught Jake's eye, noticing as I did the pale color of his face beneath the unshaven stubble of dark hair. He looked every bit as tired as I felt and I longed to take him back upstairs but knew that was not going to happen until Baby was secured and some questions had been answered. With a weary nod, Jake pulled out his cell phone and walked with me out of the lab and upstairs to Aunt Lucy's kitchen.

"I need to call Shelia," he said. "I need to see if she's got a bead on what's really going on with the Bitsy/David investigation."

I nodded and pulled out my own cell phone. "I'm going to call Paint Bucket and offer him a side job for a few days. I'll tell Sylvia they're her assistants because surely she knows one person can't take a twenty-four-hour shift. Maybe that'll fly. I'll give Paint Bucket the real scoop and pray he and Weasel can survive three days with Sylvia Talluchi."

Jake didn't look optimistic, but then, what other option did we have? I made the call, swore the boys to secrecy, and only gave them enough information to allow them to take off from their full-time jobs for three days, pack bags for a short trip and drive to my house. From the expressions on their faces when I opened the door to them a short half hour later, you would've thought I'd granted their fondest wish in the world.

"Stella, I am so totally honored to finally be working with you," Weasel said, before the front door was even closed behind him. He was still addressing his remarks to my chest, but I overlooked it.

"Thanks, Weasel," I said. "Now, I do hope you both know you won't ever be able to reveal the nature of this mission nor the identity of your patient." I looked from one to the other, trying not to laugh as Paint Bucket slowly raised his left hand in what appeared to be the Boy Scout pledge gesture.

"On our honor," he intoned stiffly.

"Lives are at stake," I said.

"Lead us not into any trespassers," Weasel said. "'Cause I will kick their asses!"

"All right, boys. I am about to take you to a secret location and introduce you to your team leader." I looked at the bags they held. "You did bring medical equipment, correct?"

"Yes, ma'am!" they answered in unison.

"Good. Now, this mission is delicate. Your team leader, while a very venerable and esteemed colleague, is prone to certain lapses in…well…judgment. She will require careful handling and a delicacy that might at times be hard to finesse."

Paint Bucket looked at Weasel who in turn furrowed his brow, indicating that neither man understood anything I was trying to say. So I rephrased my remarks.

"Okay. Your team leader is a crazy old bat that you two have to get along with. It's a political thing, but basically, if you don't figure out a way to make her look good, even if she is nuts, I'll lose my ass. Are we clear?"

"Copasetic," Paint Bucket said, grinning.

"Ten-four," Weasel added.

"All right, then there's only one more thing." I whipped two bandannas out from my back jeans pocket and looked at my new employees. "I've gotta blindfold you."

"Whoa! That is so awesome!" Weasel exclaimed. "Aw, man!" he cried, turning to Paint Bucket. "This is the real thing, huh?"

Paint Bucket rolled his eyes at me. "What can I say, Stel? We grew up together."

"I know," I said. "What is friendship without loyalty?"

Paint Bucket shrugged. "I was thinking more along the lines of I could do time if he was ever to turn on me and dime my ass out."

I nodded, looking over at Weasel who was now tying his own blindfold in place and stumbling around Aunt Lucy's kitchen in a happy frenzy of barely contained joy and excitement.

"It's like getting a new puppy every damn day," Paint Bucket said. "You can't housetrain 'em and they're just too damned cute to take to the pound. You just gotta do the best you can with what you got to work with."

I considered Weasel for a moment, wondering what kind of dog he'd be. I finally concluded that Weasel most resembled a whippet crossed with a cocker spaniel. While looking more whippetlike—in a pressed rat sort of way, his personality was pure cocker. He embodied unbridled enthusiasm.

I felt a pang of uneasiness which made me take Paint Bucket aside and point out the potential hazard of his temporary assignment.

"Bucket, I want you to know that people are looking for your patient. I don't know why but they appear to be after her and, well, this could be a risky deal. I'll understand if you and Weasel…"

Paint Bucket stopped me right there. "Stella, we ain't doin' this just for the money. We all grew up together. It's a brotherhood. I'm doin' it for the good of all that's right and decent in Glenn Ford, so don't go talking to me about risk. We're not chickens."

I half expected to see him giving another one of his Boy Scout salutes or offering to exchange a secret handshake, but instead he turned to Weasel.

"Hey, idiot!" he called. "Let's go!"

Weasel, still blindfolded, turned and walked straight into Aunt Lucy's table. Paint Bucket responded with a string of imaginative curses and a yank on Weasel's arm to pull him up beside him.

"Okay, wrap me up and take us off," he said.

I blindfolded Paint Bucket, and was about to lead the two men out to my car when I heard the unmistakable clomping sound of Sylvia Talluchi's sensible shoes coming up the basement steps.

"Oh, hell," I muttered. "This is a big waste of time. They're going to find out about the basement lab, anyway." I put a hand on each man's shoulder, stopping them at the edge of the kitchen and said, "Guys, in a moment I am going to take off your blindfolds and introduce you to your new commander, but before I do, I need your solemn vow that you will never, ever reveal any detail, no matter how small or seemingly insignificant, of what you are about to see or of whom you meet while on this case. Is it a deal?"

Paint Bucket and Weasel both stiffened to attention and simultaneously lifted their left hands high, their fingers folded down identically, and said, "We promise, on our honor, to do our duty to God and our country…" Their voices fell off here as they failed to remember the rest of the oath, and I interrupted.

"Good enough, gentlemen." I pulled off the blindfolds and left them standing in front of Sylvia Talluchi.

Weasel shrieked. "Who are you?" he gasped.

Sylvia, equally appalled, eyed him with a malevolent glare and said nothing.

Paint Bucket hopped right into the fray. He saluted Sylvia and poked Weasel in the ribs until he, too, saluted, then said, "McMasters and Steinbolt, reporting for duty, ma'am!"

This seemed to significantly mollify Mrs. Talluchi, and without further ceremony, I led the little troupe downstairs to Aunt Lucy's secret laboratory. The arrival of the two men absolutely fascinated Baby Blankenship. She took in the knotted bandannas around their necks, clapped her hands and gazed rapturously at them.

"I love Westerns," she said, sighing.

I left, considering my work below ground done for the day. It was time to move on to the next phase of the current operation. It was time to figure out what had happened to Bitsy Blankenship.

Halfway up the basement steps, the emergency red light Aunt Lucy keeps tied to her government-installed security system began to flash. The door opened at the top of the steps and Aunt Lucy stood looking down at me, a worried expression on her face.

"We've got two bogies at high noon," she said cryptically.

"Ringing the doorbell?"

Aunt Lucy nodded. "Suits, crewcuts, badges and bulges."

"Local?"

"I'd say federal."

I reached her side and walked with her to the monitor. Two men I'd never seen before stood on Aunt Lucy's front stoop. They didn't appear to be thinking about leaving, so I supposed they must've had the house under surveillance long enough to know we were inside. The thing that pissed me off was that I hadn't spotted them.

"Where's Jake?" I asked.

"Here."

Jake had entered the room so quietly neither one of us had heard him. He crossed the room, handed me my Glock in its pancake holster and bent to slip a small Walther into the leather holster strapped to his ankle.

"Nervous?" I asked.

"Nah," he muttered. "Just packing an ounce of prevention."

As we walked toward the front door, leaving Aunt Lucy

to monitor things from the security system in the kitchen, I studied the tense set to Jake's shoulders, wondering what he knew that I didn't.

"Shelia tell you anything new?" I whispered.

He shook his head. "She's looking into it."

The way he said *looking into it*, made me nervous. Jake sounded skeptical.

When we reached the door, I took a deep breath and tried to mentally prepare myself.

"I want the tall guy on the left," I said, smiling at Jake. "I think he's my type."

Jake raised an eyebrow. "Getting restless so soon, my pet?"

"See, that's just it. Sleep with a guy a few times and he's looking to buy you a scratching post and a leash. I'm not your pet!"

I swung the door open, still smiling and looked into the cold, deadpan faces of the two men on the front stoop.

"Let's see," I said. "Mormons or Fuller Brush salesmen?"

The tall guy on the left let the bottom of his plastic badge cover fall open. "FBI," he said. "We'd like to talk to you, Ms. Valocchi."

"Oooh, I love it when a guy calls out my name," I said. "You feds are soooo psychic!" Only I didn't believe for a minute that the two men were FBI. They didn't quite have the clean-cut, in-your-face attitude of a true Fibby. No, these two guys were more accustomed to skulking around in the dark, if you asked me.

"Let's see some ID gentlemen," Jake said.

While the two held their badges out for his inspection, I studied them. The tall guy had red hair and a smattering of freckles, a lean, muscular build and large, almost feminine hands. The hands fascinated me, in a macabre way. Slender fingers, nails just a bit too long but manicured. They were the sort of hands you see in horror flicks, wrapping around young girls' necks and squeezing the life from their squirming little bodies. I shook myself and turned my attention to Red's partner.

He was tall, too, but where Red was fair-skinned, this man was dark. An olive complexion darkened by recent exposure to the sun. Small, close-set black eyes. A boxer's nose and knuckles.

The badges identified Red as Samuel Weller and his partner as James Timothy. They might as well have said John Doe and James Smith because I didn't for a moment suppose they were using real names.

"Okay," Jake said, apparently satisfied. "Talk." He made no move to invite them inside.

"May we come in, Mr. Carpenter?" Red asked. "What we have to say is best kept confidential." He looked briefly at the street behind him, as if emphasizing his statement. "It's…"

"A matter of national security," I finished with him. "Yeah, yeah, yeah. Already got that T-shirt, boys. What do you really want?" I wanted to ask, *How do you know Jake's name?* but didn't.

"The FBI has assumed jurisdiction over the investigation into the death of David Margolies. We'd like to interview you about the circumstances surrounding the incident. We can do that here, inside, or at the local branch facility."

In other words, I could either invite them in or take a trip in the back of a sedan with tinted windows. I knew the drill.

"All right, the living room it is," I said, holding the door open.

We filed into Aunt Lucy's small front parlor and sat,

gingerly perched, on the edge of antique chairs and a Victorian love seat while the two men reviewed the events of the night before. Red's partner, the alleged James, asked the questions, and neither man even pretended to take notes. In fact, the entire proceeding had the air of a made-for-T.V. movie. It barely passed muster as an interview, and I had the impression that they were only going through the motions of asking me questions. What in the world was that about? I wondered. And when would they get around to the real reason for their visit?

I didn't have to wait long. After five minutes of phony questioning, they turned the conversation to their main area of interest.

"We understand you and Mr. Carpenter were retained to investigate an alleged break-in and petty theft from Mrs. Margolies's grandmother. Can you tell us what exactly was taken and what you were able to ascertain as a result of your investigation?"

The boys used such long-winded, government-speak! I smiled at them and shook my head. "I'm sorry, gentlemen. That's privileged communication between our firm and our client."

Red bristled. "We are investigating the double homicide of two government employees, ma'am. The laws governing the dispersal of confidential information do not pertain to private investigators."

I raised an eyebrow. "What does my investigation have to do with their murders?"

Red's partner attempted to play good cop to Red's bad. "Well, now, Stella," he said, shooting himself in the foot by talking to me like I was a reluctant three-year-old. "We don't know if your investigation is tied to ours until you tell us about your case. It might have relevance and it might not."

I felt imaginary hackles rise up on the back of my neck. "Well, now, Mr. Rogers," I began. "I don't know how they do things in *your* neighborhood, but around here we just don't go blabbing all of our secrets without little permission slips. You know, maybe you ought to go get a yellow piece of paper that says something like, oh, I don't know, 'subpoena' on it and come back for milk and cookies later."

"All right, I've had enough of this bullshit," Red announced. "Here's how it's going to go down. We're in charge of this investigation and you two are to stay away from anyone having anything to do with it. That includes the family of Bitsy Blankenship, Brookhaven Manor and any and all other relevant parties, including but not limited to, members of the press, both print and other media."

"You can't do that," I said, struggling to keep my voice calm.

"Try us," Red answered.

"See ya," Jake said, standing and gesturing toward the front door.

Red and his partner stood up but Red just had to have the last word before he left. "This is a federal investigation involving the death of two diplomats. I don't think I need to remind you of the penalties for impeding our investigation. Unless you want to do time in a federal facility, you'll follow our instructions and stay away from the Blankenship family."

They left then, filing out the front door and down the steps to their government-issued white sedan. Jake closed the door behind them and stood with his back against the door, studying me.

"Well?" he said.

"Very interesting. Red seemed to think they were investigating a double homicide. Kinda runs counter to what they told the local boys, doesn't it?"

Jake smiled, but the grin didn't reach his eyes. They were a dark, dangerous blue, and his brow furrowed as he seemed to consider the implications.

"Yep, sure does."

"So, what's bothering you?" I asked.

Jake seemed to struggle with what he wanted to say and when he finally came out with it, I could understand his reluctance. "I'm wondering if Shelia's been giving me the straight scoop about what's going on."

I allowed a slight ripple of self-satisfaction to fill me briefly with a smug, "I told you that bitch was no good!" attitude, before I returned my focus to our investigation.

"What do you mean? You think she's lying? Why?"

Jake shrugged. "It's a tight club and I'm a former member. She's probably just doing her job."

And you were dumb enough to think she'd choose you over doing her job? Poor baby!

I nodded. "Okay. Well, then, I guess we take anything she says with a grain of salt and try to verify it before acting."

Jake nodded. I tried to put myself in his place and supposed he was feeling foolish. After all, he and Shelia had worked together for a long time. It's hard to let go of what-was and face what-is-now. I wasn't about to make him stew in it.

"I think we should have Spike talk to the local lab boys. Maybe we can find out more about how Bitsy's car exploded and what made that happen. If we know that, we might get a bead on who was behind it. It might even be that Bitsy blew up her own car."

"That would make a lot of sense. If she felt she was in trouble and needed a distraction, it would be simple enough to do," he agreed.

"So, if that wasn't Bitsy in the car, who was it?"

Aunt Lucy joined us in the kitchen, fresh from a trip down to the basement to visit Sylvia. When she caught sight of the two of us, she immediately launched into one of her lectures.

"I know what you were up to, sending those boys in to assist Sylvia," she began. "Don't think we old ladies can't see your lack of faith." She brushed past the two of us and began pulling out heavy iron pots and pans from the cabinets beside the stove.

"Aunt Lucy, no one can nurse a patient around the clock without help," I protested.

"Be that as it may," Aunt Lucy said, pouring a liberal dose of olive oil into a heavy Dutch oven. "We see through you two." A chunk of butter slid off her knife to sizzle into the pan. Minced garlic followed, then onions and soon the kitchen was filled with the welcoming scents of home. Too bad Aunt Lucy's attitude didn't match the wonderful aroma.

"Well, I'd better get going," Jake said, taking the chicken's way out.

He turned toward the back door but stopped as Aunt Lucy's boyfriend, Arnie, opened it from the outside and stepped into the kitchen.

Aunt Lucy took one quick look and dropped the wooden spoon she had been using to stir the pot.

"Stella, put on a pot of tea, sweetheart." Aunt Lucy was using her crisis-management tone, the overly nice, "everything's just fine" voice that let me know the opposite was in fact true.

I rushed to do as she ordered, watching Arnold Koslovski as I did. He was pale. Little beads of sweat stood out along his upper lip and despite his heavy topcoat, he appeared to be shivering.

The little man took two steps into the kitchen before

his knees seemed to buckle. Jake was there, catching his elbow before he fell and guiding him, along with Aunt Lucy on the other side, to a sturdy wooden chair by the table.

"Whew!" Arnold said, grinning up at us. "I about lost my footing there. Now, Lucia, don't go fussing with me. I'm all right!"

But he wasn't all right. His eyes radiated pain. His face was gaunt and his cheekbones seemed to stick out in sharp contrast to his sunken cheeks. This was not the same man who'd been laughing and drinking with us all just the day before. This man was seriously ill, and I suddenly saw how very sick he was.

"I'm fine," he said again, attempting to wave Aunt Lucy away.

She stuck fast, and after a moment Arnie reached out and gripped her hand in his. She sank down into the chair beside him, watching his face, reading a fresh spasm of pain that had begun and was building to a crescendo. I saw the little man's grip tighten and the knuckles of my aunt's hand turning white with the pressure.

"Stella, could you bring me a cool, wet washcloth, dear?"

I fled down the hallway to the linen closet, panicked by the mute appeal in Arnold's eyes. When I returned, Jake was putting a tea bag into a mug and giving Aunt Lucy and Arnold some privacy.

"Here you go," I said, handing her the cloth.

I was careful to keep my voice pitched to match hers but as I turned away I heard Arnold say, "I'm sorry, Lucia. I shouldn't have come like this. I thought I was feeling better."

Aunt Lucy shushed him. "You think I am your fair-weather friend, eh? You think I only want the strong man? Now I am in charge and you must answer to me!" She turned in her chair to issue another order. "Stella, in my medicine cabinet, there is a bottle labeled nausea. Bring it to me, *cara.*"

Aunt Lucy, famous for her homemade remedies in addition to her government-sponsored chemical formulas, had found something concrete she could do for Arnold.

When I came back into the room, Aunt Lucy was talking to him in a soothing voice.

"This will help you," she said, reaching to take the bottle from me. "You will feel better and then I will put you into a nice bed with feather pillows and a warm down comforter. You are not going back to that place, Arnie. It is time for you to move in."

Behind us a spoon clattered to the floor as Jake, eavesdropping, registered his surprise. Aunt Lucy living with a man? A sick man, at that, a man who was dying? I caught Jake's eye and saw the same worried concern mirrored there. Could my aunt handle this? Even with all of us helping, could she face another loss so soon?

Jake finished making Arnold's tea and carefully carried it across the room to him. Aunt Lucy was talking over Arnold's objections, continuing ahead with her plans despite the man's objections. Finally Arnold could take no more. With a burst of strident energy, he took on Aunt Lucy.

"Woman, listen to me! I'm dying! Dying is ugly and messy and painful. It's not how a man wants a woman to see him. You've been through enough, don't you think I know that? Dying at Honeybrook is the one gift I have left to give you. I don't want you to suffer along with me. I didn't come back here to put you through that. I came back to take care of you, not to have you take care of me! A man needs his pride!"

Aunt Lucy sat staring at him, her eyes brimming with

unshed tears. Arnold pulled his hand from her grasp and repositioned it, so that he was now holding her hand in his.

"I didn't mean to make you cry, Lucia," he whispered. "Don't cry."

Jake and I looked at each other, frozen, wanting to leave but unable to figure out how to do so without distracting the two lovers who seemed to have forgotten us.

Aunt Lucy slowly, visibly, worked to pull herself together. She straightened in her chair, took long, deep breaths and slowly exhaled. After a few moments she nodded and gave Arnold an understanding smile that seemed completely genuine. She stretched out her hand, cupped his face and gently caressed Arnold's pale cheek.

"And so, you think perhaps I have no need to give to you in return? Years ago I didn't wait for you. Now there is a second chance for us. Let me be here, with you, when it is good and when it is dark or lonely. Let me be the one. Now. Today. Don't push me aside because you wish to spare me. Give me the real gift. You."

I had to walk outside then. I slipped out the back door, onto the porch and stood in the frigid winter air, tears running down my cheeks. I heard Jake's quiet footsteps as he joined me, and when he slipped his arms around my waist, I went to him without hesitation, burying my face in his warm chest.

We stayed like that for what seemed a small eternity but was only perhaps a few minutes, then once again the ringing of a cell phone interrupted us.

"Stella, I need you to come over to my house," Marygrace said. "I've kinda got a situation here."

"Marygrace, I've got a lot on my plate right now. Between Baby Blankenship and…"

"Stel, I really need you to come over here. Please?"

Marygrace was talking in a slow, deliberate manner and not at all like her usual rapid-fire self. That was what clued me in.

"Are you in trouble?"

"May...be," she said.

"Okay, honey, I'll be right there."

"Good. Do you know where I live? I'm on Mary Street, you know, across from St. Joseph's? It's number 361."

"Right. Gotcha."

"Thanks, Stel," she said. Marygrace sounded entirely too relieved and very much unlike her normal, brazen self. It sent chills of apprehension through me.

"Oh, and Stel?"

"Yeah?"

There was a brief, perhaps reluctant, pause then "Bring Jake with you, all right?"

"Sure, honey."

I hung up, aware that Jake had been listening intently to my side of the conversation.

"Something's wrong at Marygrace's," I said. "She wants me to get there fast and she specifically asked me to bring you. I think it's a setup. When I asked her if she was in trouble she said 'maybe.'"

We made the trip in less than five minutes and that included taking the precaution of strapping on extra guns, ammunition and assorted other odds and ends that might come in handy should Marygrace's "trouble" include gun-toting bad guys.

Jake stopped the car about a block away from Mary-grace's house. "You want the front or the back?"

"I'll take the back door," I answered. "After all, she specifically asked for you, so you should be the one to ring the doorbell."

Jake put the Viper in gear and began slowly driving

down the alleyway that led to the back of the Mary Street houses. Marygrace lived in a more transitional neighborhood, filled with small bungalows that had once been home to the mill workers who once worked in the abandoned paper factory downtown. The homes, as well as the neighborhood, had gone through several life phases, from well kept to rundown to renovated and made over.

Marygrace's house was somewhere in between the gutted-shell and turn-key finished stage of renovation, but I recognized it instantly without having to count house numbers or study the street long enough to become an obvious newcomer. Marygrace's tiny cottage was painted a pale pink, with teal-blue shutters and a Margaritaville flag flying from her back deck. To further cement the matter, a gaily painted sign hung on the gate leading into what was probably a cottage garden in the summer. Marygrace's Place, it read.

"That, Sherlock," I muttered to myself, "would be a clue."

My cell phone began to vibrate in my coat pocket just as I began edging my way up the neighbor's yard.

"What?" I whispered.

"I can see her moving around inside," Jake said in a low voice. "It doesn't look like there's anyone else in there with her so she's not being held at gunpoint. You got anything back your way?"

"Nope. It's clean and green here." I looked over my shoulder, shivering in the cold.

"Come on around and we'll go in."

I slipped the gun I'd been fingering back into my pocket, closed the phone and slowly made my way up the narrow strip of frozen ground that ran between Marygrace's funky cottage and the one next door. When I reached the sidewalk, Jake practically pounced on me.

"Ready?" he asked. "I'm freezing!"

"All right, let's do it."

Jake and I walked up the steps to Marygrace's front door and didn't even have to ring the doorbell before the little woman appeared.

"Took you long enough," she groused. "I could've been dead and buried."

The slow, elaborately careful tone was gone and while she still wasn't running wide-open as usual, I actually felt relieved to hear the spunk return to her voice. But when she reached out and grabbed my arm to pull us inside, she cut her eyes to the left and wiggled a telling eyebrow. Subtle she was not.

If Jake caught the gesture, he didn't let on. Instead he stepped into Marygrace's small living room, cased the room for the exits and then seemed to relax just a little bit.

"So, what's the big emergency?" I asked.

"Well, I… It's um…" Marygrace stumbled to a halt, this time looking openly at the hallway leading toward what I assumed to be the bedrooms. "How about some herbal tea?" she asked, rather loudly.

"All right," I answered slowly, elbowing Jake as I did so and nodding toward the hall. "That would be fine. Jake, wouldn't you like some tea? Let's all go in the kitchen and have some."

I gave him a tiny shove in Marygrace's direction, nodding toward the kitchen, and pulled my Glock 9 mm out of my pocket.

"Sure," Jake said. "I'd love something hot!" As he said *hot,* he smirked and licked his lips in a mock display of hunger. The man was incorrigible. He was also a phony. I knew he worried whenever I took the front of a search, especially when we both knew there could be trouble at the other end.

"Marygrace, you don't have to send them into the kitchen," a female voice said. "And you don't have to sneak up on me either, Stella. I asked her to call you."

A slim blonde stepped out into the hallway and stood there watching the three of us. Her hair was lighter than I remembered from high school but the brilliant blue eyes and cheerful expression were exactly as I remembered. Bitsy Blankenship wore tight faded jeans, a thick black turtleneck sweater and a jeans jacket. The telltale bulge in her jacket pocket told me she was armed.

"Hi, guys!" she said. "Remember me?"

Chapter 11

"You look good for a dead woman," I said.

"Hey, Bits."

Sometimes being a woman and having that female intuition we're all so proud of comes back to bite you in the ass. Jake said two words to Bitsy Blankenship, but they were all I needed to tell me a wealth of information. For one thing, Jake thought Bitsy looked every bit as good as she had the last time he'd seen her. I had to agree with him there, she looked fabulous. The second thing Jake's greeting told me was that the spark of chemistry or attraction or just plain lust he'd once felt for Bitsy had not diminished over time.

"Hey, yourself, Jake," Bitsy answered. She slipped up beside Marygrace's living room window, turned the blinds closed, then peeked out through a carefully lifted slat to peer out at the street.

While she scanned the street, apparently looking to

see if we'd been followed, I found myself taking a detailed reading of Bitsy's still-hot feelings for my boyfriend. She was more than a little glad to see him. In fact, given time, I was pretty sure old Bitsy would do everything in her power to try and renew their former level of acquaintance.

Marygrace, being the good social worker type she was, jumped right into the fray by closing all the blinds in the small living room before turning to make another offer of herbal tea. The look she got from the three of us must have registered because she quickly revamped the drink menu.

"Well, I do have something stronger if you want it," she said. "I just thought..."

"Tea is fine," I answered. My jaw felt as if someone had wired it shut without my knowledge.

"Okay, then, well, I'll just go boil water!" Marygrace made a quick getaway into the kitchen, leaving the three of us alone. Bitsy was slowly making her way down the hallway, her eyes on Jake.

"How long's it been?" she murmured. "Four years? Five?"

I wanted to puke. If I'd been able to, I would've, and the two of them wouldn't have even noticed, that's how strong the current was. Did Jake have this effect on every woman he'd slept with? Shelia and Bitsy both looked at Jake the same way, like they'd just crawled out of bed after having the best sex of their lives. Come to think of it, I probably looked at him the same way, only I was still sleeping with him, and they allegedly weren't!

"Okay, so several questions are running through our minds here, Bitsy," I said, hoping to pull Jake back down to earth. "One being, if you're not dead, what happened? Another being, if it wasn't you in the car, then who was it? And last, but certainly not least, what in the hell is going on here?"

I felt my voice rising in an attempt to cut through the flying pheromones that threatened to suck the brain functions from both Bitsy and Jake. I finished my questions at a half scream and was surprised when the two of them both looked at me like I was the one losing her mind.

Jake was the first to recover. He looked at me, seemed to note the obvious frustration I was feeling, then glanced back at Bitsy and took action.

"You'll have to admit it's been a confusing few days around here. Why don't we all sit down and hash things out," he said.

Bitsy nodded in the direction of the kitchen. "I think I'd like to keep the circle of insiders as small as possible," she said quietly. "I don't want any more innocent by-standers to get hurt." Her attention shifted to the street outside Marygrace's living room window. "And I also don't want to get myself killed, so we need to leave here after it gets dark. I can't afford to spend too much time in one place. Besides, I'd rather not talk around Marygrace. What she doesn't know won't get tortured out of her if anyone connects her to me."

I looked at my watch. It was almost four-thirty. The northern winter sky would be completely dark in another forty-five minutes making it safe to leave Marygrace's little bungalow, but where could we take Bitsy that wouldn't attract attention? I thought for a moment and finally decided our office would be a suitable, short-term hideout, at least for the amount of time it would take to hear Bitsy's story.

"All right," I said, addressing the two of them. "We'll leave when it gets dark and go to the office to talk. We'll see what needs to happen after that."

Jake looked as if he was thinking of protesting my choice, but he looked at me and appeared to think better of it. Bitsy nodded and seemed relieved to have a temporary plan. As I studied her, I began to realize that Bitsy's past few days had been spent with little sleep and without benefit of soap and water. I wondered where she'd been hiding. She knew Glenn Ford as well as I did. She knew what areas to avoid if she didn't want to be spotted, but it was cold, and that narrowed down her choices. Her eyes were red-rimmed and bloodshot. Her fingernails were dirty and broken. The clothes she wore were dirty and smelled faintly of wood smoke.

I was still puzzling over the possibilities when Marygrace walked back into the living room carrying a large black tray filled with teacups, snacks and various other items. For the next hour we all played generic high school catchup, never mentioning Bitsy's recent past. Instead we focused on old classmates and past misadventures. We never mentioned the brief time Jake spent with Bitsy after our tragic breakup.

Marygrace, playing the role of group facilitator, edged the conversation around dangerous emotional sinkholes and on to happier times. She told us enticing tidbits about former classmates and seemed to recognize that she would not be among the privileged few to know the details of Bitsy's most recent adventure. When darkness finally fell and I signaled Jake that it was time to leave, Marygrace seemed frankly relieved.

"I'll bring the car around," Jake instructed. "Wait until I'm right out front before you leave."

I frowned at his apparent need to appear to be the man in charge of two damsels in distress. Did he really think a former cop, his partner, and a CIA agent would need those kind of precautionary warnings? I bit back a sarcastic retort and said nothing. After all, Jake was now my partner. Hadn't we just been through the big summit on trust and confidence? Bitsy's reappearance was testing the waters of my new commitment to trust Jake implicitly, but I was going to stick to my guns…until, that is, I had proof to the contrary.

Bitsy had played the part of perfect tea party guest for the past hour. She'd laughed and told stories right along with Marygrace, but now as we stood waiting for Jake, she seemed tense and wary. I saw her slip her hand into her jacket pocket and knew she was fingering her gun, the same way I did when I expected trouble and didn't want to be unpleasantly surprised.

Fortunately, neither of us had to pull our weapons. Jake stopped the Viper in front of Marygrace's cottage as planned. Bitsy and I said goodbye to Marygrace, walked unhurriedly down the steps to the car, got in and made an uneventful trip to my office. No one followed us, despite Bitsy's repeated glances out the rear window, and no one was waiting to ambush us when we pulled into the parking lot. It was simple, easy and almost…well, disappointing.

Once inside, I wasted no time getting down to business with Bitsy. The lack of information was making me nervous. I couldn't protect myself, let alone the other people involved, if I didn't know the details.

"What's going on, Bitsy?" I asked.

Bitsy sat on the edge of the chair across the desk from me in my office. Jake had chosen a neutral spot, halfway between the two of us, and was standing, arms crossed as he leaned against the wall. When she looked to him before answering, he gave her an encouraging nod, which only pissed me off further. Jake had a blind spot when it came to women who professed to need him. I'd seen it before and it continued to bother me now.

"Why did you call and want to see me?" I asked, redirecting her back to me.

Bitsy was too smart to play stupid with me. Her attention swiveled back to focus on me and she began talking in a clear, unemotional voice. She could turn the damsel-in-distress act on and off without even trying, it seemed, and I made a note of that as I jotted down the other details of her story.

"To make a long story short," she began, "I was recruited out of college by the CIA. My degree in biochemical engineering is the sort of thing the Company was looking for at the time and, well, I guess the mystique and allure of working for the Agency appealed to me." She gave me a knowing look. "You know, Stel, we grew up in Glenn Ford and both of us left as soon as possible. I heard you became a cop, so I suppose you were looking for excitement just like I was. Anyway, joining the Agency gave me all I could handle."

She slipped Jake a tiny smile, unaware I'm sure, that I knew all about their fling a few years ago.

"Anyway, I wound up in Slovenia, married to a fellow agent and working on an important assignment. David was in the process of helping a brilliant scientist defect to the U.S when all hell broke loose and the scientist we were escorting was killed."

"What went wrong?" Jake asked quietly.

Bitsy looked down at her lap and was quiet for a few long moments, apparently deciding how detailed to be with two outsiders.

"The man we were bringing in was working on the final stages of a biochemical weapon that targeted its victims by their genetic code, their DNA," she explained. "That sort of thing is worth a lot of money if it falls into the wrong hands. There was an attempt to stop us. We managed to escape but lost Gregor in the process."

Bitsy's eyes were bright with unshed tears when she looked up again.

"The Company launched an investigation. They questioned both of us but they zeroed in on David. For a few weeks it seemed as if they suspected David of having something to do with Gregor's death. Then, they suddenly stopped asking questions. I don't know what happened or why. It just seemed as if they'd decided to let the entire thing drop."

Bitsy sighed and picked at an invisible thread on her pants before she continued.

"We were given new assignments. Granted it was busy work, but still it was something. It was a vote of confidence and I couldn't understand why they just seemed to let the entire investigation go away. I had to know what had gone wrong with our mission and why. When I wasn't satisfied with the answers David and my superiors gave, I began to quietly investigate on my own."

Bitsy was looking at Jake, speaking to him as if he would know what she meant when she talked about investigating and left out the details.

"It took a few months, but eventually I realized that I was sitting in the middle of a hornet's nest." Bitsy's face flushed as tears slowly streaked down her cheeks. "Jake, David was a double agent. He was working with people on the inside. Higher ups. He killed Gregor. I know he did and I can prove it!"

"How?" I asked.

Bitsy turned back as if remembering that I was in the room too.

"I found the microchip with Gregor's work on it. I think David killed Gregor, took his work and was planning to sell it."

"How could he get away with that?" I asked. "Wouldn't your bosses know he'd done that? Wouldn't they wonder when the scientist died and the formula was missing?"

Bitsy shook her head. "Not if no one knew the truth. David told me that Slovenian agents ambushed them as he was driving Gregor out of the country. He said he managed to escape but that Gregor was shot and killed. We were left to infer that no one had the formula, that Gregor alone knew it and hadn't written it down."

Bitsy shook her head sadly.

"The news accounts from Slovenia only mentioned that his body had been recovered after a car accident. But I began thinking about all the ways David could have hidden the truth, first from me and later from the agents who investigated the mission."

"But I thought you said your boss was in on…"

Bitsy waved me aside impatiently. "They use independent investigators, like the police have Internal Affairs officers to check out shady cops or suspicious shootings."

My mind was racing, trying to keep up with the pieces of information Bitsy was throwing at us.

"David could only pull off a coverup like that with the corroboration of his immediate supervisor."

"Not you?" Jake asked, surprising me by not blindly believing Bitsy.

"I wasn't in on that phase of the operation. I was running the smoke screen back at our embassy quarters, making it look like David was still home, with me, and not running across Europe."

"What made you decide that David was dirty?" I was still feeling confused, as if a piece of the story was missing.

Bitsy sighed and seemed a little frustrated by my question. "I couldn't think of any other explanation for our plan going wrong," she answered. "I just couldn't believe the Slovenians had any idea that Gregor was thinking of defecting. We played it too well for too long to have it suddenly explode on us."

Bitsy hesitated for a moment, again weighing the necessity of sharing information with us before proceeding.

"I've worked for the Agency too long. I know how to check facts. I know how to glean little bits of information and piece them together into something big and solid. I worked my insiders. I listened to the questions they were asking and finally I found notes David had made, little things that, paired up with phone records and e-mails, led me to the truth."

Jake was frowning thoughtfully and pacing, sure signs that he was having issues with Bitsy's accounting. I watched him stop to look out the front window overlooking the street for what seemed to be an almost imperceptibly short moment before continuing on across the room. When he repeated this walk-and-pause ritual several times in a row, I felt my stomach clutch as a frisson of alarm caught fire deep inside my body. What was happening down on the street?

"Okay, so you figured out what was going on," Jake said abruptly. "How did you prove it?"

Bitsy nodded, as if expecting the question. "I found the formula. David had hidden it in a microchip."

Jake passed the window again.

"How did you find the microchip and how did you know what was on it?"

Bitsy smiled. "Everybody has a weakness," she said softly. "David liked cognac and sex. Lots of cognac. Lots of sex. Over time I came to know him. I knew his habits and I knew his hiding places. It took a while but I found it, and when I did, I replaced it with a blank chip."

"Wasn't it only a matter of time before he found out?" I asked. "Why hadn't he given it to whomever he was working for or with?"

"He wouldn't have any bargaining power then, would

he?" she asked. "I think he was holding on to it. I think he might've been trying to sell it to the highest bidder."

Jake was at the window again. "So, what went wrong? How did you end up running?"

"Once I'd taken the chip I knew I had to get it into the right hands. I have a contact and a safe house to go to but I hadn't arranged the meet when the Slovenians showed up. I don't know how they knew that the government wasn't in possession of the formula, but the afternoon I spotted them shadowing the house, I knew things were about to get nasty. That's when I ran."

It was something in Jake's overall body posture that alerted me, a tiny shift in the muscles of his neck perhaps, an imperceptible tightening of his jawline, something that triggered me into the awareness of imminent danger and the need to move.

"Out the back, up onto the roof or down into the print shop?" I asked quietly. I opened a desk drawer, drew out two extra ammo clips and was sliding them into my jacket pocket before he could answer.

"Print shop," he answered, pulling his Glock.

"All right. I'll tuck her in and follow up from the back. How many?"

"Two crossing the street. I don't know about others. They look like the visitors we entertained this afternoon," he said. "You know, Red and Fred, or whatever they called themselves."

Bitsy was working not to show her alarm but when she pulled her gun I saw it in her eyes. Whatever we were facing, it scared her and she was a seasoned professional.

"Let's get you out of here," I said, rounding the desk and heading toward the trap door hidden in my office supply closet.

"I'll stay," she said. "I can help."

"Do as I say. We're not going to risk losing what you've been trying to safeguard," I said.

"But I don't…"

"Now!"

Bitsy moved quickly to join me and within seconds we were descending the steps that led into the back room of the print shop below us.

"There are two men out front," I said, pitching my voice low. "One has red hair, fair complexion, and he's tall. The other is darker and not quite as tall. They said they were FBI agents but we didn't believe them. Friends of yours?"

"I don't know," Bitsy answered. "I'd have to see them."

We reached the bottom step. I had my gun out and ready as I reached out to slowly open the door. It stuck at first and I had to lean my shoulder into it to loosen the swollen wood from its frame but with a loud squeal it gave, swinging slowly open to empty us into the inky darkness of the print shop workroom.

"All right," I whispered. "Stay here. I'll go check out the rear of the building, then back up Jake."

"Where are we?" Bitsy asked. "I can't see my hand in front of my face."

But there was nothing wrong with our hearing. We both heard the person behind us as he stepped out from his hiding place and cocked his gun.

"There you are!" he said softly. "Drop your guns. Now!"

I sucked in a long, slow breath and tossed my weapon onto the floor. I heard Bitsy's gun drop and knew she realized we were playing with a pro who wouldn't hesitate to shoot us both if we didn't follow his instructions. He had the advantage. He was behind us and his eyes had already adjusted to the darkness.

"We need to talk," the man said.

I knew he wasn't talking to me. Almost simultaneously, I realized that I was only in the way. Unnecessary baggage. How long would it be before he shot me? I closed my eyes, picturing the room before me as it was in the daytime, during business hours. We had stepped through a doorway into the workroom. Shelves lined the room, printing equipment and presses took up the center.

I heard the man move, off to the side and away from the wall. I coughed, using the sound to camouflage my quick, short movement backward, within reaching distance of the shelves behind me. I slid a hand out behind my back to feel the contents of the shelf closest to the spot where I stood and was gratified to feel cool plastic jugs. I was standing in front of the inks and chemicals used to develop the shop's glossy, color prints.

Bitsy coughed, prompting our assailant to say, "Shut up!" There was a brief rustle as he moved then spoke into what I assumed was a walkie-talkie.

"Got the target," he said quietly. "First floor. Come in through the back."

Great. Reinforcements were on the way. I slowly slipped a jug off the shelf, keeping it and my hands behind my back as I worked to quietly remove the cap. I had no idea what was in the bottle. I only hoped it would either wound or at the very least, distract the man with the gun and enable us to escape.

"All right," the man began, stepping closer.

He never got to finish. I whipped the jug around, slinging liquid in a smelly arc that landed dead center on target. He screamed and fired his weapon but the shot went wild as I grabbed Bitsy by the hand and ran forward toward the front of the shop.

His screams followed us as we made our way toward

the store's entrance. Along the way I picked up a paper cutter and carried it with me.

"We'll be trapped," Bitsy cried.

"Maybe not," I said and heaved the paper cutter through the plate glass display window.

The glass dissolved into a thousand tiny beads, triggering the alarm and allowing us to escape out onto the sidewalk.

"Come on!"

Still clutching Bitsy's hand, I led her across the street and into a tiny walkway that ran between a pizzeria and a pharmacy. We were swallowed by the darkened interior of the small, dank tunnel and slowed by the slick, wet surface of the bricks beneath our feet, but we had one advantage: we'd left our pursuers in chaos and triggered an alarm that would bring police reinforcements.

We ran down an alleyway and across backyards, only stopping when I recognized the familiar slumped posture of the abandoned pump house that edged Twin Lake. I could hide Bitsy there and return to help Jake.

"There," I said, pointing to the desolate building. "Wait inside. I have to go back for Jake. I don't want to risk calling him."

We were both out of breath and gasping for air, but Bitsy nodded. Before she started off she turned and squeezed my arm. "Be careful, Stella," she said. "They're very dangerous people."

There wasn't time to ask questions or do anything other than run back toward the office and Jake. Although I heard sirens and knew Glenn Ford's small police force was responding, I was afraid for him. He had no way of knowing where we were or what had happened to us. I didn't want him taking unnecessary risks, thinking he needed to

rescue us when in reality, we'd already escaped. I knew
Jake. I knew he'd stop at nothing to find me.

The problem was I was likely to be more of a liability
than a help. I was unarmed and unless the conflict became
one of hand to hand combat, I was going to need to be very
cautious in the way I approached the situation.

I returned the same way I'd come with Bitsy, aware that
her pursuers were probably searching for us. I stuck to the
shadowy sides of buildings, checking each corner before
rounding it and then darting quickly on toward the office.
When I drew close, I saw blue lights dancing over the
brick front of our building as all of Glenn Ford's tiny
force responded to the print shop's burglar alarm. As I
watched, an ambulance arrived and my guts twisted into
a knot of apprehension.

I scanned the street and saw a white sedan that looked
identical to the one the two agents had driven to visit us
at Aunt Lucy's. It was parked half a block down from our
office, tightly parked between a nondescript passenger van
and an oversize Buick. Was this what Jake had seen that
triggered him to begin watching the street?

I looked back at the print shop interior, now well lit and
crawling with cops. No sign of Jake. Something in my pe-
ripheral vision caught my eye, and I looked back toward
the white car. Had I seen something move? As I watched
the car, I began to move closer to it, trying to stay low and
in the shadows. Someone was inside the vehicle.

I was two car lengths away when the engine suddenly
roared to life. Without thinking I darted toward the sedan,
racing down the sidewalk to come up even with the passenger-side door.

Maybe it was luck or maybe just that it was a cheap,
government-issued car, but whatever the reason, the door
opened when I tried it. Without thinking, I jumped inside,

lunged across the seat, turned the car off and snatched the ignition key from the vehicle. The look Red gave me when our eyes met was unforgettable. It was the clearest telegraphing of intent ever sent my way by another human being. He was going to kill me.

When he moved, it was lightning fast. His left hand dropped from the steering wheel, disappearing momentarily before he raised it again, this time wielding a small handgun.

I don't know what comes over me at times like that. It's not fear. It is most probably a primal survival instinct that bypasses my conscious brain and sends me into action. I don't plan, I just do.

I drove the car keys straight up his nose, following them with the heel of my hand in a Krav Maga move that can only be described as excruciatingly painful and frequently lethal to its recipient. I didn't enjoy it too much either but it was a kill-or-be-killed situation. Red wouldn't have hesitated to take me out, if he'd moved fast enough. I was just lucky.

"Stella!" Jake's voice broke through to me and I realized he was there, opening the car door and pulling the incapacitated Red out of the vehicle. Two uniformed officers followed at a flat-out run, stopping as they took in the unconscious, bloody body of the "FBI" agent.

I looked up at Jake. "He would've killed me."

Jake nodded. "I know, sweetheart." His fingers were pressed hard against the man's carotid artery, feeling for a pulse. "Medic!" he yelled, forgetting and lapsing back into his Special Forces days.

The EMTs who'd arrived with the ambulance joined the cops, pushing past Jake and taking over to begin the work of either reviving Red or declaring him dead. I didn't want to know. I didn't want to believe I could so easily take a life, without even thinking, in order to save my own. It had been too fast, too easy for me to feel that my harsh actions were justified, and yet, I remembered the look on Red's face just before I struck. There hadn't been an option.

I had a new problem now. Regardless of whether I'd killed the man or not, if he was indeed a government agent, I was going to find myself arrested for aggravated assault and possibly murder.

"What happened?" One of the cops asked, bending down to peer into the car's interior at me.

"He's one of the armed men who broke into the print shop," Jake answered. "He was trying to get away when my partner attempted to stop him." Jake's eyes never left my face as he spoke, drawing me into his fictional account of the past thirty minutes.

"He was going to kill me," I said, aware that my voice sounded flat and not at all the way I thought I should sound, given that I'd been threatened with death.

"You chased him?" the cop asked, clearly thinking I was suicidal.

"Not exactly. I just happened to be on the sidewalk when I saw him attempting to get away and as there wasn't an officer close enough to intervene, I took action." I looked at the middle-aged, paunchy man in uniform. "I was a cop. It's not like I didn't know what I was doing."

The officer looked pointedly at the man on the ground. "Obviously," he said.

Jake was through with the uniform. In a brusque tone he said, "I'd appreciate it if you'd put in a page for Joe Slovenick."

The man's eyebrow lifted slightly. "You know Detective Slovenick, do you?"

"You could say that," Jake turned back to me. "Let's go get you a cup of coffee." He reached into the car's interior, took my hand and pulled me out of the sedan. His expression softened into a gentle smile that warmed my heart. "You look like you could use something hot. Let's go down the street to the diner."

The cop saw us begin to walk away and acted as if he might stop us, but I didn't give him the opportunity. "Tell Joe we'll be in the Coffee Cup if he needs to talk to us." Calling the detective by his first name seemed to make the uniform a little insecure about asserting his authority. He turned back to the EMTs without another word and left us alone to walk down the street to the diner. We'd just bought a little time to put together a credible story to tell the detective when he did arrive.

"Oh, shit! Bitsy!" I cried. "I forgot. I told her to wait in the pump house for me."

"The pump house? Down by the skating pond?"

I nodded. "It was close and I figured it was a good place to hide until I knew you were okay."

Jake lifted a skeptical eyebrow and smiled. "You came back to save me? Why, I'm right honored, ma'am!" He tipped an imaginary hat in a mock salute and chuckled. "I'm beginning to like this equal partnership deal."

"What, you think I'm incapable of…"

Jake held up a hand, warding off the inevitable defense from me and intervening. "Now, Stel, you know I'm only kidding." He stopped smiling as quickly as he'd started, apparently remembering Bitsy and the impending arrival of Detective Joe Slovenick. "I'll go get something figured out about Bitsy, at the very least I'll tell her about the holdup and tell her it'll be a bit longer before we get back."

I nodded and stopped in front of the ancient Coffee

Cup Diner. "If Joe shows up, I'll try and hold him off until you get back."

Jake hesitated before he loped off in the direction of the pump house. "I'll call Spike. Get her down here in case we need a bit of legalese thrown around."

I nodded and watched him walk away. When I pulled open the big, green door leading into the diner I was rewarded with a blast of warm, humid air, scented with the smell of freshly brewed coffee and home-cooked food. My throat tightened and for a second I wanted to cry. The diner was a comforting reminder of the reassurance of loved ones and home. It felt safe and far away from the violence down the street.

Delia, one of the night shift's regular waitresses, walked up to the back booth where I sat trying to warm up and stared at me for a long moment.

"Let me guess," she said, cracking her gum in between words. "You and Jake had words and now you're looking to fill the empty place he left in your life with chocolate cream pie." She looked back toward the door leading outside and slowly drew a pencil out of her mop of unruly jet-black curls. "Can't say as I blame you," she continued. "But it'll take more than a slice of pie to forget that man. You need coffee and probably a fifth of Jack Daniels."

Delia didn't even wait for me to correct her. "I can get you two out of three. That'll be a start, but the liquor store closed two hours ago."

She walked off, never having taken my order, and returned a few moments later with a thick white mug of coffee. She placed it on the table, then slid into the bench seat across from me.

"Men," she said. "Can't live with 'em, can't rip their heads off!"

"Delia, Jake and I aren't fighting," I said.

Delia reached across the table and patted my arm sympathetically. She wore heavy gold rings on each finger, and her acrylic nails were airbrushed red with tiny white coffee mugs detailed into the center of each one.

"Sure, hon," she said, affecting a soothing, motherly tone. "You just keep on believing that, but I've just been expecting him to show his true colors and run off with some trashy bimbo. Skunks can't change their stripes any more than they can stop stinking!"

Frank, the night cook, peered out at the two of us from his kitchen pass-through window.

"Hey, Delia!" he shouted. "If you can tear yourself away from giving advice to the lovelorn, your order's up and the gent's burger is getting cold."

The waitress scooted out of the booth and over to the window, giving Frank hell for disturbing her and loudly reassuring her customer at the counter that his food was indeed hot and fresh.

I watched her, thinking surely my life would be easier if I had her job. I tried to think of a place where I could move and start over on a diner waitress's salary. It would have to be somewhere small, without a newspaper that could run my picture along with the headline, Wanted for the Cold-Blooded Killing of an Undercover CIA Agent. I was just sure tomorrow's newspapers would all have that exact headline.

I was still plotting my "virtual" escape into anonymity when Spike arrived with a very tense-looking Jake right behind her. They slid into the seat across from me as Delia caught my eye and mouthed the words, "I told you so!"

I rolled my eyes at her and almost missed Spike's report.

"You didn't kill the guy," she was saying. "But you

came damned close. He's in surgery now. I called Joe on my way over and he's already heard. I'm afraid it's going to get messy. The sedan's got government plates and given the Bitsy and David Margolies angle, Joe felt he had to go ahead and contact the local FBI office."

I groaned and buried my head in my hands. What else was going to go wrong?

I raised my head slowly and looked at Jake, remembering the grim expression on his face as he'd entered the diner.

"There's more, isn't there?" I said.

"Yeah. It's Bitsy," he answered. "She's gone."

Chapter 12

"Gone? What do you mean, gone?" I demanded, more in disbelief than for information. How had they found her? Or had they found her? And who were "they" anyway? The CIA? Slovenian agents sent to recover the stolen formula? Wasn't that a little like closing the barn door after the horse has escaped? I could feel myself beginning to panic as I realized that we'd stumbled into something that was way beyond our abilities.

"I checked the pump house," Jake continued. "It was empty and as far as I could tell, Bitsy never made it inside. I don't think she would've left on her own. She needs our help too badly to risk going solo again."

I pictured the ancient wooden structure sitting at the edge of the local skating lake, a shell of the building it had once been. The door was missing, so the place afforded no security if Bitsy had been attacked.

"No sign of a struggle?" I asked.

Jake shook his head. "It snowed last week. The area around the place is shaded by the roof overhang. I looked at the ground. Aside from worn tracks, there's nothing. No sign to indicate Bitsy ran into any trouble."

Spike was frowning. "Stella, you saw her making a beeline for the pump house and that was right before you ran approximately two blocks back to the office?" I nodded. "Could someone have gotten past you and found her? Could you have been followed?"

I hated to admit it. "Yeah, either one of those things could've happened. I didn't see anyone, but hell, we were running. It was dark."

Spike's cell phone rang, playing an Indigo Girls song that signaled a call from Nina.

"Hey, sweetie," Spike murmured. As she listened, the lines of her forehead creased into a concerned frown. "What? Okay. Okay, stay calm, honey. I'm on my way." Spike listened a few more moments before responding. "No, they're kind of tied up. They'll come when they can."

Delia approached the table carrying a small tray loaded down with my coffee, three glasses of ice water and a huge slab of chocolate cream pie. When she reached the booth, she carefully set the pie and coffee down in front of me, followed by a glass of water.

"There you go, hon," she murmured.

"Hey, Delia, how you doin'?" Jake said.

My misguided, avenging angel wouldn't even look at him. She set the remaining two glasses of water down with loud, sloshing bangs, turned to walk away and appeared to accidentally hit Jake in the side of the head with her tray.

"Ouch!" he yelped, surprised.

Delia smiled, satisfied she'd made her point and stalked off without another word.

Jake, still rubbing his head, looked at me, baffled. "What's up with her?"

"For some reason known only to her, Delia's decided that I'm upset because I've discovered you're having an affair with Spike."

"What?" Jake stared after the retreating Delia, and Spike, pausing in her conversation with Nina, lifted a puzzled eyebrow.

"Did I miss something?" she asked. "Did you say Jake and I are sleeping together?" Spike quickly spoke back into the phone. "No, honey! Of course not!" She listened a second, then added, "Yeah, like *that's* gonna happen! Let me call you back, okay? Yes, baby, I'm coming!"

Spike closed the phone, slid it into her jacket pocket, and shook her head slowly. "Just what we need, a little more chaos! Nina said Arnie's having a pretty bad spell of it and she's worried about Aunt Lucy. I told her I'd be back as soon as we got things cleared up with the police."

She nudged Jake to let her out of the booth, stood up and slowly buttoned her heavy coat in preparation to return to the cold night air.

"Rather than wait for them to finish up at the scene and come on down here, I think I'll just slip around the corner and see if I can't speed things along. All right?"

She didn't wait for us to answer her. She turned to walk out, took a few steps, turned back around and gave Jake a sly, seductive grin. Delia, watching from her post beside the cash register, gasped audibly, and I realized Spike was creating "performance art" for the sole benefit of the suspicious waitress.

"Oh, and Jake, sweetie?" she called in a husky, come-hither voice.

"Yeah?"

Jake was practically salivating at the teasing, sexy,

come-on Spike was affecting and seemed completely unaware that she was performing for an audience.

"In your dreams, baby!" Spike called and walked right out the diner door.

This pleased Delia no end and would have completely distracted me had the door not opened again and ushered in an icy blast of air and a new problem. I groaned under my breath, making Jake look over his shoulder just as Shelia Martin spotted her quarry and zeroed in on us.

"It just keeps getting better and better," I muttered.

Shelia Martin walked like a jaguar, lean and muscular, tall with a waterfall of sleek black hair that slowly caressed her back and shoulders as she moved. But if Shelia's body seemed like an invitation to sensual pleasure, her cold, ice-blue eyes would freeze the desire in any man stupid enough to approach her. Of course, the hands-off attitude evaporated with Jake. They had an obvious history and from the look on her face, even a few hours away from him would've been too long.

No, now stop that! I cautioned myself. He said that's all in the past, and if you love him, you'll trust him. Out of the corner of my eye, I saw Delia take off her apron and disappear into the kitchen. So much for allies and support, I thought glumly.

"Hello, Shelia," I said, when she was finally standing beside our table. "I'd ask you to join us, but I know you're busy."

She ignored me and focused her attention on Jake. "I thought our agreement was you two were going to stay out of this until I had a chance to find out what was going on?" she said.

Jake appeared to be thinking it over, his brow furrowed into deep lines. "You know, that's not how I remember it," he said finally but he was smiling, trying to charm her.

"Jake, don't play me," she said, sliding into the booth beside him and turning to face him. "You've really stepped in it now."

My self-appointed bodyguard was watching the tableau at my booth and seemed to have decided it was time for intervention. She swooped up a coffeepot and began bearing down on us, unseen by Jake and Shelia. For a second I was tempted to let Delia loose, but my conscience took over and visions of Delia, every bone in her ample body broken, lying on the floor beside the table took over and brought me to my senses.

"Delia!" I cried. "Look who's here! Jake's cousin, Larry."

That stopped the erstwhile waitress in her tracks. "Larry?" she said, wrinkling her nose.

I nodded. "Well," I said, smiling at Shelia, "I suppose it's no longer Larry, is it, dear?"

Delia put the coffeepot down on the table, leaned in and inspected Shelia closely. "It's a freaking miracle what they're doing with medical science these days," she said, shaking her head. "A freaking miracle! You want some coffee?"

Shelia could only nod.

When Delia walked off to get a mug, I explained. "For some unknown reason, Delia thinks Jake's unfaithful to me. Can you believe it?" I said, smiling and reaching over to take Jake's hand in mine. "So, sometimes she spills ice water or hot coffee on potential troublemakers. I was just trying to spare you."

Shelia gave me an appraising once-over that let me know she didn't believe a word of what I was saying before turning her attention back to Jake.

"The guy she attacked is a federal agent, all right, but no one seems to know what he was doing here. Are the cops right? Was the shop below your office being broken into when the alarm went off, or was there something more going on? Have you two found out any more about Bitsy Blankenship's disappearance?"

I waited for Jake to launch into the full explanation but to my surprise, he didn't.

"That's right," he said. "Stella and I were working on some paperwork when the alarm went off. I went out the back door. She took the inside stairs to the print shop. When she saw someone running away out on the street, she noticed the broken window and followed. As she was returning, she noticed a white sedan leaving and attempted to stop the man who then drew his gun. Stella's actions were purely in self-defense."

I tried not to let my facial expression give away what I was thinking. Jake's account sounded like a police officer's written report and he delivered it in the same matter-of-fact, impartial tone. He was lying to Shelia Martin! What in the hell did this mean?

Shelia's expression never changed and if she suspected him of lying, she didn't say. Instead she just sat there in silence, studying him. Jake, too wise to give her enough information to hang him, stayed equally quiet.

Delia's return was almost a welcome relief.

"Here you go, hon," she said, placing a mug of coffee in front of Shelia. "You want some pie, too, or are you watching that girlish figure of yours?"

"No, thanks," Shelia murmured.

"I'd like some, Delia," Jake said, but the waitress ignored him with a pointed little sniff and flounced back to her post by the kitchen window.

"She doesn't really think that…" he began.

I rolled my eyes at him. "There's just no accounting for the way some women think," I said. I slid out of my bench seat, pulled my down jacket closed and smiled at the two "cousins."

"If anyone wants me, I'll be at home," I announced. "It's been a long day and suddenly I need a nice, hot shower, you know? I just feel like I've been rolling around in something nasty." I smiled at Shelia. "Nice to see you again, Larry. Let's do lunch sometime soon!"

I left them there and walked out into the winter evening, intending to return to the office. Instead, I found myself retracing my steps in the opposite direction, back to the half-frozen skating pond and the pump house. I circled the lonely wooden building and saw nothing more than Jake had reported. Bitsy was just gone.

I kept on walking, finishing my circuit around the pond and heading in the general direction of home while I mulled over the strange possibilities of Bitsy Blankenship's predicament in an endless loop of questions that had no answers. An hour later I walked into Aunt Lucy's house and found myself almost grateful for the familiar chaos of my Italian family.

Weasel, looking even thinner and more rodentlike in one of Aunt Lucy's white aprons, stood at the stove stirring something in a pot while Spike, Nina and Jake sat at the kitchen table watching him and apparently critiquing his culinary skills.

"Did she tell you to add garlic salt?" Nina was asking. "All I heard her tell you was stand there and stir the pot. She didn't say you should tamper with her recipe."

Weasel, a wooden spoon in one hand and a spice jar in the other, had turned and was about to offer his rebuttal when I stepped in through the back door and provided the distraction he needed.

"Where have you been?" Jake said. The muscle in his jaw twitched, a sure indicator of his displeasure.

"Walking home."

Nina exhaled loudly. "There, you see? I told you she was all right, Jake!" She turned back to me. "He thought foreign agents had snatched you up like they snatched Bitsy. I told him you were way smarter than some girl who can't even go shopping at the mall without blowing her damned car up!"

Aunt Lucy appeared in the doorway looking very tired but still as peppery as always. She sniffed the air and frowned as she slowly walked across the room toward the stove. Weasel, seeing her, dropped his right hand behind his back and smiled nervously as she approached.

"Hi, um, ma'am," he stammered.

"Where is the garlic?" she asked quietly. "I smell garlic."

Weasel's eyes grew wide. "Garlic?"

Aunt Lucy reached out, snatched his arm and with a quick tug pulled the offending bottle from his hand.

"You stir, you don't tamper!" she said.

"Well, I just thought…" Weasel began.

Aunt Lucy stiffened. "That is exactly the problem," she said. "You didn't think and I don't expect you to, because I am the cook and you are not!"

Mrs. Talluchi appeared at the top of the kitchen steps, a gnome in a vintage World War II nurse's outfit.

"Ah!" she cried. "So you can't do anything with him, either! I want to shoot him!"

Weasel, panicked, looked to the rest of us in a mute appeal for salvation.

"How about you take me downstairs to see our patient?" I said, pulling him away from the stove. "Nina can take over. I haven't seen Baby all day. How is she?"

Weasel, happy to be anywhere but in between the two old ladies, instantly transformed himself back into an

EMT. "BP's slightly elevated but we're watching it," he said, cautiously cutting a wide path around Mrs. Talluchi as we started down into the basement. "She seems fairly alert and somewhat oriented to person but not place or time."

I nodded, half paying attention to what he was saying and half listening out for the sound of Mrs. Talluchi's footsteps following us. I wanted to see Baby by myself, without interference.

"Paint Bucket's with her," Weasel added. "She likes him. She thinks he's her son. I wish she thought I was her son. Maybe then they wouldn't keep sticking me with KP duty. I'm a trained medical technician," he said, clearly irritated at not having his value appreciated. "I can't be stuck stirring a pot of chicken soup!"

"I'm sure this has been difficult for you," I murmured, attempting to soothe his wounded ego. "I don't know how you manage people so well. I think it's a gift."

Weasel's scowl softened. "Aw, it isn't that awful hard. I just wish they'd smoke a joint or something and loosen up! I'd be all twisted, too, if I didn't smoke a doobie…"

"Weasel!" Paint Bucket emerged from behind the curtains of Baby's makeshift hospital room and frowned, his finger held up to his lips in an exaggerated shushing gesture.

I waited until Paint Bucket reached us before speaking. "Is she sleeping?" I asked. "I was hoping I'd get to talk to her."

How Baby mistook Paint Bucket for one of her offspring was beyond me. He looked like a biker, with his long, red hair caught back in a ponytail and his Fu-Man-chu mustache and goatee. If I hadn't grown up with him and known him to be harmless, I would've crossed the street to avoid encountering him. The fact that Baby saw through the outward appearance and found the essential goodness that was Paint Bucket amazed me.

Bucket smiled. "You can go sit beside her for a while, if you want to. Me and Weasel could use a smoke break."

"You won't go too far off, will you? I mean, in case I need you."

Paint Bucket nodded. "But listen, even if you couldn't find us, Sylvia's a right good nurse. I believe she can handle just about anything...unless she's pissed off about something else. That's when you see most of her delusions taking over. She's batshit when she's mad, I'll tell you that right now!"

Weasel shuddered. "I'll say!" He looked over his shoulder nervously. "Come on, Bucket, let's get out of here before she catches us and makes us do something goofy again."

I didn't wait to hear what Sylvia Talluchi had done to Weasel that could possibly fall under *his* category of "goofy" behavior. I was too anxious to see Baby and know that she was all right. I couldn't put my finger on exactly why I felt she needed my protection but I wasn't about to ignore the instinct driving me. It had been right too many times before.

I slipped behind the curtain and sat down in the chair next to Baby's hospital bed. Her eyes were closed and she snored softly as she slept. I watched her carefully, noting the faint traces of pink in her cheeks, a distinct improvement from the pale pallor she'd had when she'd arrived at Aunt Lucy's.

I glanced around the small cubicle, noting the meticulous handwriting on lined paper clipped to an old-fashioned clipboard that had to belong to Sylvia Talluchi. I picked up the makeshift chart and read the careful notations of blood pressure, temperature and pulse rates.

"Is he gone?" Baby's whisper startled me.

I looked back at the woman lying against the crisp white sheets and thought for a moment I'd imagined the sound. Baby's eyes remained closed and her breathing even, including the soft snoring sound I'd heard only moments before.

Then Baby's nose twitched and a slight smile played over the corners of her mouth.

"He thinks he's my son," she whispered, popping one eye open to watch me. "Can you believe it?"

I stepped to the bedside and took Baby's soft, bony hand in mine. Her skin was tissue-paper thin, and dull purple bruises colored her hands and arms, the result of blood thinners and too many hands hurriedly rushing to turn and move her when she'd been taken to the emergency room. At least, that's what I hoped, knowing full well that demented elderly patients were prime targets for abuse and that in Baby's case, there was the added threat of outsiders searching her room.

"I call him Paint Bucket," I said, giggling. "When he was little, his dad was a painter and Bucket wanted to be just like him."

Baby's eyebrows shot up and she opened both eyes. "Oh, dear! I don't remember that at all! I did marry him, didn't I?"

"Who?"

"The painter," Baby said. "It would've been the right thing to do!"

I was trying to follow along but Baby was losing patience and it seemed better to switch to a new topic, something hopefully familiar, and something that might just help me figure out what was going on with Bitsy.

"Guess what? I saw your granddaughter, Bitsy, today." I stopped, waiting for the words to sink in and become attached to meaning.

"Bitsy?" Baby was frowning.

"You were worried about her, remember? She came to see you and she gave you something."

Baby nodded slowly. "Yes, I was very worried."

"Well, she was fine when I saw her, but then I lost her."

Baby smiled. "She used to love hide and seek as a little girl. Was she playing with you?"

Who knew the answer to that one? I nodded. "I think she was," I answered. "I wonder where she could've gone this time."

Baby slowly shook her head. "She's a wily one, that girl is. One time she ran all the way to the old library. They didn't find her because she knew about the secret room. The library was a stop on the Underground Railroad during the Civil War, you know. Of course, they tore it all down. Now it's a bank."

Baby lay back against her pillow and seemed to be worrying about something. She frowned, shook her head slowly and sighed.

"What's the matter, Baby?"

"I just can't understand something about Bitsy," she said slowly. "How could a girl that pretty have someone like that man for a father?"

"That man?" I echoed.

Baby raised her head and glared at me. "Honestly, honey, sometimes you can be so short-minded! That son of mine! The one with the beard! They just don't look a thing alike!"

When I left she was sleeping. Paint Bucket was sitting beside her, reading a book on advanced cardio-pulmonary diagnostic procedures. Weasel was once again relegated to the kitchen, and Sylvia Talluchi was in my uncle Benny's former basement workshop, napping on his worn-out sofa.

I tiptoed past her, up the stairs and back into the kitchen where Jake sat watching Aunt Lucy ladle bowls of savory chicken soup into ancient crockery bowls. Lloyd the Dog sat at her feet, torn between his desire for a handout and his devotion to his new love, Fang. The wolf-dog lay on the pallet Aunt Lucy had made for her beside the warm stove, snarling softly whenever Lloyd appeared to edge closer to her resting place.

"It's what they do," Aunt Lucy was explaining to Jake. "They nest right before it is time to give birth. Until then, she is resting. Imagine how crabby you'd be with a belly full of puppies!"

Jake looked at me and grinned. "I can't even imagine," he said, but it seemed to me he was imagining plenty and none of it had to do with puppies.

Before the conversation could continue any further, his cell phone sounded. He answered, listened a few moments, stood and walked out of the room, away from the two of us. Aunt Lucy gave me a questioning look and I shrugged.

"How's Arnold?" I asked.

She turned back to the stove before she answered. "He is comfortable. They have medicine for him when the pain gets too bad. Now I will feed him soup and he will feel much better."

I watched my aunt prepare a tray and carefully place a bowl of soup on it. I hoped she didn't think Arnold's cancer could be cured with something as simple as a bowl of chicken soup. I doubted she thought this, but Aunt Lucy had fallen into such deep denial of my uncle's death. It worried me to see her facing another loss so soon.

Jake came back into the kitchen, pulled his jacket off the back of the chair across from me and gave me an apologetic look.

"I've got to go take care of something," he said, glancing at Aunt Lucy's back and shaking his head quickly. "I shouldn't be long. Will you still be up if I stop back by?"

Right. Like I could sleep not knowing where he was or what was going on.

"Want me to come with you?"

Jake shook his head again. "No, I'd better do this by myself. I'll be back."

I sighed. "Okey-doke, then," I said. "I guess I'll see you when I see you."

I got up and left the kitchen before he could walk out the back door. At least I could be the first one to leave, I thought, and knew I was being childish. How come "we" had trust issues but I was the only one who had to ante up by trusting? Why didn't I ever do anything that pushed his trust envelope?

I trudged slowly up to my room, feeling my body grow heavier with each step. The sound of female voices arguing stopped me. Spike and Nina, the couple voted most likely to resemble lovebirds, were fighting.

"Guess I'm not the only one feeling the stress," I muttered to myself.

"I know we'll have to paint it, but it's wood. I hate brick!" Nina was saying.

"It'll be too expensive and who's going to keep up with all the maintenance? You don't know anything about renovating houses," Spike countered.

"I can learn," Nina said. "I want to be original. You're selling out."

"Selling out?" Spike sounded wounded.

I tried to slip past their room without listening but it was impossible.

"Who's thinking of taking a job in the D.A.'s office again?" Nina said.

I stopped. Was Spike thinking of going back to the D.A.? Didn't she have any faith in Valocchi and Carpenter Investigations? What about her private practice? She certainly couldn't work for us or have a private practice if she returned to the D.A.'s office.

"Nina," Spike argued, "we need a steady, reliable income. We need health care and security, especially if we're thinking about starting a family."

I froze, blatantly eavesdropping. Spike and Nina with children? Why hadn't they said something?

"Why can't you just go with your gut," Nina cried. "Why can't you have faith that things will work out for the best?"

"Because I'm just not like that," Spike answered. "I need to have a plan. I need to be logical and sensible. I can't live with my head in the clouds."

"Oh, so now I'm not sensible? You think I'm an airhead!" Nina's voice cracked as she began to cry.

I dashed down the hallway past their room, knowing the argument was rapidly moving from bad to worse and not wanting to hear the hurtful things that would probably follow. I slipped into my room, closed the door and sank down onto my bed. So, just because the two members of a couple were female, it didn't mean they were any better at resolving their issues than Jake and I seemed to be. Damn. I'd just assumed heterosexual couples argued because men were unreasonable. Oh, well, another theory shot to hell!

I lay back on the bed and closed my eyes, intending to rest for only a few minutes. Instead I fell into a deep sleep, awakening only when Jake arrived. I felt his hand on my shoulder, heard him softly calling my name and opened my eyes reluctantly.

"What are you doing back? I thought you said it might

be an hour or two?" I asked, feeling groggy and somewhat cranky. All I wanted was a nap.

Jake smiled. "Stel, it's almost midnight. I've been gone a little over two hours."

I sat up and peered at my bedside clock—11:48 p.m. How had that happened?

"Okay, so where were you and what's going on?"

Jake chuckled. He was wearing his bomber jacket, and when I touched it, the leather was still cold from the outside.

"Marygrace was the one who called earlier, wanting me to meet her out by McConnell's farm, only she wouldn't say that. All she'd say was she wanted to see me where we had our keg parties. Almost everything she said was in this convoluted code of clues made up from things we'd done in high school." He grinned. "She thinks she's the next superspy or something."

"Well, hell, Jake! Why didn't you just tell me she was the one who called?"

He shook his head. "She made me swear I wouldn't tell you, and she wouldn't even let me call her by her name over the phone! She thinks my phone and the house are bugged."

I shrugged. It could well be true, I reasoned. "So why are you talking to me now, then?"

Jake raised an eyebrow. "What, you think Marygrace is right? You think your bedroom's bugged?" Before I could answer, he pulled a small device from his pocket and fiddled with it. A second later the box began to hum. "Audio jammer," he explained. "Blocks any outgoing audio signals."

"Okay, so what did Marygrace want?" I asked, returning to the matter at hand.

Jake took off his jacket, tossed it on the chintz-covered

slipper chair in the corner and stood up. "Bitsy called her," he said, and began unbuttoning his shirt. "She wanted Marygrace to get a message to me."

"What are you doing?"

Jake had removed his flannel shirt and was now sitting on the bed again, pulling off his lizard-skin boots.

"Well, I'm just realizing how security conscious you are," he said, grinning. "And I know you'd want me to take every possible precaution against high-tech surveillance techniques compromising our transfer of sensitive material, so I'm being careful. It would be too risky to simply sit beside you and tell you about my conversation with Marygrace, even with the audio debugging device. So I propose to narrow the space between us by slipping under the covers and whispering in your ear."

I raised an eyebrow. "And the reason you're taking off your clothes to do this is?"

"Well, Stel, bugs come in all shapes and sizes. What if someone slipped a tiny device into one of my pockets? Worse, what if an even smaller bug, say shaped like a seed or a briar, was clinging to my shirt or my pants? What if it fell off between your sheets? Why, then every sound you made in this bed would be monitored."

Jake turned to me and slowly ran one finger along my chin, tracing the line of my jaw and sending a shiver of anticipation through my body. "We wouldn't want that, now, would we?" he whispered.

"No," I murmured, and reached past him to unbutton his jeans. "We certainly can't have that!"

Less than a minute later we were naked and under my warm blankets. Jake pulled me to him, spooning me into his body and nuzzling my neck with the scratchy, late-day stubble that covered the lower half of his face. His hands began to move, exploring every curve and plane of my skin, teasing and arousing me with well-proven moves.

Jake was avoiding something. I realized with a start that Jake had no intention of continuing the report of his conversation with Marygrace and had hoped to distract me by making love to me! Damn, that man!

I pushed away from him, turning as I did to face him. "Talk, Jake," I demanded.

"Bitsy's fine. She got nervous and pulled a rabbit, that's all," he said. "Now come back here."

I stiff-armed him. "Details, Jake."

He sighed, apparently resigned. "All right. I went to the field by McConnell's farm and met Marygrace. She said Bitsy wanted me to know she was all right and that she'd call again tomorrow to arrange a meet."

What wasn't he telling me? I knew there was something, felt it and trusted my instincts. When Jake reached for me again, I looked at him and frowned.

"What else?"

"What do you mean what else?" he asked, looking puzzled.

"Come on, Jake. You were gone two hours. What aren't you telling me?"

Jake seemed irritated. "I told you, it's not important, certainly nothing I couldn't have told you in the morning. Bitsy's just paranoid, that's all. She left the pump house because she felt it wasn't secure and she wouldn't tell Marygrace where she was. She said she'd call the pay phone outside Reeder's Newsstand tomorrow morning at 7:30. Then she'll arrange a meet."

"And?" I said, as he showed signs of clamming up.

"She doesn't trust anyone in the Agency now. She doesn't want us talking to any of them."

"In other words, she doesn't want *you* talking to anyone. I don't have CIA connections."

"Right."

"Does Bitsy know you talk to Shelia Martin?" I asked.

Jake seemed uncertain. "She seems to know I talk to someone."

I propped myself up on an elbow, feeling even more uncertain about Bitsy and her predicament. "Do you think Bitsy's holding something back or do you think she might be right in not trusting Shelia? Are you having doubts about her? Is that why you lied to her earlier?"

The lines on Jake's forehead deepened. "I don't understand why she's here if she's not involved in this. Shelia says she's not, but why else would she keep popping up whenever something happens that involves Bitsy or her grandmother?"

"Good question. What do you want to do?"

"I think I'll wait and hear what Bitsy has to say tomorrow," he said. "Then we can take it from there." Jake hesitated for a moment then added, "I think I'll back off Shelia for a while, too—you know, not necessarily report everything I hear of or know about Bitsy."

This was a huge step for Jake to take, I realized. He had to have significant doubts about Shelia to take that sort of action. Jake started to reach for me again but I still had questions.

"Why did Bitsy ask for you and not me?"

Jake shrugged. "I don't think it was anything personal," he answered. "Marygrace said she seemed very paranoid and suspicious about everything. She's scared and fighting for her life," he said. "That tends to make you hypersensitive. Besides, Bitsy and I do have a deeper connection than she has with you."

You certainly didn't need to remind me of that, I

thought. I looked hard at Jake, watching his every reaction as I followed up with another question.

"So, you're telling me Bitsy didn't say anything to Marygrace about not wanting me there tonight or tomorrow?"

Jake broke eye contact with me for the briefest possible second. It was all I needed to know what he'd been avoiding.

"What did she say?"

Jake sighed. "Baby, you know you can't take…"

"What did she say, Jake?"

"All right. Marygrace asked Bitsy if she wanted her to call you if she couldn't reach me, and Bitsy said no. According to Marygrace, Bitsy just feels safer because she knows I've had agency training."

"And?" I prodded.

Jake looked uncomfortable. "Marygrace said Bitsy thinks you might have some old resentments about her that would keep you from being as effective at safeguarding her."

"Bullshit! I do my job and I don't let my personal feelings ever get in the way!"

Jake reached out and grabbed my arm in a firm grip. "Stel, I know that. Even Bitsy probably knows that when she's thinking straight, but like I said, she's freaked out right now. Don't take it personally. I'll handle it with her when I see her."

I was steaming. I'd risked my life to protect her and done a damned fine job of it, too. How dare she question my abilities?

"Come here," Jake coaxed, this time pulling me up on top of him. "Come on. Let it go, Stel. She doesn't know you like I do and she's scared to death. Let it go."

If he said, "Trust me," I was going to have to kill him.

But he didn't. Instead he began talking with his hands. He rolled me across his body, back onto the bed and onto my stomach.

"You've had a long day," he whispered, slowly kneading my shoulders with magical fingers. "Just relax."

I felt my body respond, against my will, to his skillful touch. I felt the tension slowly leaving the tight muscles, felt my body melting into the mattress as Jake rubbed and stroked my back. I heard him reach for something on my bedside table and moments later heard him unscrewing the lid to my jar of body cream. I closed my eyes and sighed as Jake began his massage in earnest.

"Tell me where it hurts," he asked, leaning close. His breath tickled my ear and I giggled softly.

"It hurts all over," I answered.

"Mmmm…" he sighed. "Poor baby, I'll take care of it if it takes all night."

I smiled into the soft cotton sheets. It was going to be a very long night indeed!

Chapter 13

I woke up in an empty bed. My last conscious memory was of relaxing into the comfortable mattress as Jake slowly massaged me into a stupor. That was it. No passionate night of lovemaking, just a Jake-induced coma that kept me unconscious and unaware all through the night and into the morning.

I sat up, remembering Bitsy, and grabbed the clock off the bedside table. Jake was scheduled to hear from Bitsy at seven. It was after eight now. Where was he? Why hadn't he gotten me up?

By the time I made it downstairs to the kitchen for coffee, my mind was racing. I wasn't only worrying about Jake; I was making mental lists of everything I needed to do. I needed to know more about Bitsy. I needed to check on Baby. I needed to check in with Detective Slovenick. I felt as if the day had started without me and I was already too late to catch up to it.

Nina was ahead of me, already sitting at the kitchen table and drinking her coffee. I poured a cup, crossed the room to join her and quickly realized someone was having a worse morning than me. Nina's eyes were puffy and swollen; her nose was red and chapped and it seemed she barely had the strength to lift her head in answer to my greeting.

"Rough night?" I ventured.

Nina's eyes filled with tears as she nodded.

"Want to talk about it?"

A tiny sob escaped her throat as Nina struggled to speak. "It's hopeless!" she wailed finally.

I took a big sip of coffee and tried to wake up enough to help my cousin. "What's hopeless, honey?"

Nina reached into her bathrobe pocket and brought out a thick wad of tissue. "My life," she said. "It's me. I'm not like other people, and I used to think that was a good thing but now…now…" Nina broke off, unable to finish.

"Nina," I said, reaching over to pat her arm. "Does this have anything to do with you and Spike buying a house? Because if it does, you know, it's normal for couples to find that a little stressful. I mean, sometimes you have different tastes and…"

"They do?" Nina interrupted. "It is, normal I mean?"

"Sure," I said, hoping I sounded reassuring. "Happens all the time. You two will work things out." I felt like I should break into "The Sun'll Come Out Tomorrow," and tap dance my way across the kitchen. That's how hard I was trying to make Nina believe me, when in reality I had no idea if couples worked these sorts of things out all the time or not. I mean, my track record didn't indicate many happy endings, but maybe I was just the victim of circumstance.

"I hope so," Nina said, brightening a bit.

"You can count on it. Like I said before, just try not to take everything too personally. Maybe Spike's just feeling a little scared."

Nina frowned. "Not Spike. She knows what she wants and she goes after it."

I nodded, feeling Nina's insecurity begin to rise again. "It's one thing to know what you want but it's another to know what you feel. That's why Spike loves you. You make her feel."

I looked at the clock and couldn't help feeling worried about Jake. Why hadn't he called in yet?

"What's wrong?" Nina asked.

I shook my head. "Jake's supposed to meet Bitsy this morning but I don't know where and I haven't heard from him."

Nina frowned and pulled her fuzzy, tie-dyed bathrobe tighter around her small frame. "That's not like Jake, is it?" she asked.

"Nope. I'm beginning to wonder about Bitsy, too," I admitted. "I don't know if she's told us the full story yet."

"What full story?" Spike wandered into the kitchen looking every bit as tired and unhappy as Nina had been. She poured herself a cup of coffee and took her place at the table next to Nina. She looked distinctly uncomfortable and I could tell she was avoiding looking at my cousin.

Nina reached over and placed her hand on Spike's leg, whispered something in her ear and I saw Spike's shoulders relax.

"Really?" Spike asked softly.

Nina smiled. "Normal," Nina said. "I don't care, brick, wood or adobe, as long as I'm with you, who cares?"

I busied myself at the coffeepot, giving the reconciling lovebirds a few moments. I turned back around as

Aunt Lucy and Arnold made their appearance. Arnold was wearing one of Uncle Benny's bathrobes.

"Good morning," I said stiffly.

Aunt Lucy frowned, saw me looking at Arnold and ignored me. Arnold, on the other hand, didn't miss a trick. He looked down at the paisley flannel robe then over to me.

"I'm sorry," he said. "I shouldn't have…"

"Nonsense!" Aunt Lucy interrupted. "Benito would have given you the robe to wear himself. He is not here. It hangs in the closet, waiting, and for what? My Benny is never coming back to me. He loved me and I loved him something awful! His bathrobe didn't love anybody. Why not wear it? It doesn't make you into Benny. It makes you my Arnie wearing my dear Benito's robe. What is wrong with that, eh?"

Aunt Lucy looked around the room at each of us, daring us to say something to contradict her.

"I'm sorry, Arnold," I said and I really was sorry. "I saw Uncle Benny's robe and…"

"And you missed him," Arnold finished. "Of course you did." He started back toward the door. "I'll just go get dressed. That's what I meant to do anyway."

"No, wait!"

Arnold stood quietly in the middle of the kitchen, looking smaller than ever and very frail. I felt like a total heel.

"Aunt Lucy is right," I said. "Uncle Benny would've been the first one to put that robe on you, and I dishonor his memory by acting like a baby. Sometimes I forget that my uncle is gone and all I have left are the things he taught me. Please don't get me in more trouble with him," I said, smiling. "He'll haunt me if you go change!"

Lloyd, standing by Aunt Lucy's side, barked suddenly.

"See!" Aunt Lucy cried. "My Benito is agreeing with her!" She looked at Arnie and gestured to my traitorous canine. "Benny speaks through him, you know."

In the face of that revelation, the entire bathrobe issue seemed a bit small, I'm sure. Arnold looked at Lloyd questioningly and Lloyd, on cue, trotted over to lick his hand.

"Well, if you insist," Arnold said, patting his head. "Thank you."

My entire family was nuts, and now everyone they brought along into the inner circle seemed to join in to the insanity.

Soon the kitchen was filled with people and the smells of breakfast cooking. Arnold insisted on making the pancakes, over my aunt's objections, and the two worked side by side filling orders and happily bickering about their different culinary habits and techniques.

Poor Weasel wandered up and into the kitchen just in time to be put to work cleaning the pots and pans.

"You know," I heard him mutter, "I have lots of other skills. I can save lives, you know. I can make a computer do things you never dreamed were possible. I know the Latin name of every herb in your garden but what do you want me to do? The dishes, that's what!"

He stood at the sink, mumbling to himself while Sylvia Talluchi sat at the kitchen table watching him with a malevolent eye.

I signaled Nina and the two of us quietly slipped out of the kitchen and back upstairs.

"We need to learn more about Bitsy," I told her when we reached the third floor. "Can you get online and see what you can find out?"

Nina nodded. "Anything in particular you want to know?"

I thought for a moment before nodding. "Yeah, I want to know more about that scientist that died while they were trying to get him out of the country," I said. "His name was Gregor something and he was a biochemist working with DNA-related weapons."

Nina grinned, back to her old self again. "Okay, boss. I'm on it!"

I left her, returning to my room to get dressed for the day. I pulled my cell phone out of my bathrobe pocket, flipped the lid open and stared at the blank display. No messages. I carried it into the bathroom with me while I showered. No messages. Dressed and dried my hair without it ringing. Finally, right before I decided to go looking for Jake on my own, it rang. When the Caller ID said "Restricted," I answered.

"Where are you?" I demanded.

Detective Joe Slovenick sounded disconcerted. "In my office," he said. "Where are you?"

"Oh," I said, recognizing his voice. "It's you."

"Sorry to disappoint you but yeah, it's me. I need to talk to you about last night. How soon can you get down here?"

I felt my pulse kick up a few notches. I didn't need this now. I needed to find Jake.

"How about this afternoon?" I said.

"How about in twenty minutes?" he countered. He sounded like the offer was nonnegotiable.

"Twenty minutes it is," I said and severed the connection.

Nina met me in the hallway, carrying her laptop. When she saw me she frowned and held the tiny computer out for my inspection.

"You pay good money for these damned things and

what happens?" she said, clearly not happy. "I'll tell you what happens, they overheat. Now, in addition to that, something's interfering with my cable reception and I can't get online. I'm going to try downstairs, but if that doesn't work, I guess I'll have to go into the office."

"Okay," I said cautiously, wondering what was wrong with the office.

"You don't want me to use the office computer for this, do you?" Nina's eyebrows raised an extra half inch as she placed one hand on her hip and waited for me to catch on.

"No, of course not," I answered.

Nina sighed. "Good! For a minute there I thought you were losing it! I mean, you totally don't want your computer vulnerable to the feds. They could seize it, you know, and like, find out what you're thinking. I thought you were trying to keep this confidential, but I just wanted to be sure."

"Absolutely," I murmured. "We can't risk a security breach." But I was wondering why she thought her computer was so impenetrable, or indeed immune to government seizure should they decide to investigate Valocchi Investigations.

Nina tapped the laptop and smiled knowingly. "Weasel showed me a couple of tricks yesterday. By the time I'm through, you couldn't find a fragment of text if you tried." Nina bit her lower lip and frowned again. "Hey, you don't think that's why I can't get online, do you? I mean, if he's screwed up my computer... Hell, it's not even really my computer. This is the one Spike uses for..."

Abruptly Nina left, running down the steps and calling Weasel's name in a panicked tone. Nina was going to be a force to reckon with if he'd ruined her girlfriend's laptop.

I continued on down the stairs after her, checking my

essentials as I went. Gun, cell phone, money, car keys...
They were all where they were supposed to be. The only
thing missing was Jake, still.

I used the ride to the police station to clear my head
and get focused. I could use my time with Detective Slovenick to try and find out what he knew about the man I'd
stopped as well as anything else that might lead me to
Bitsy or the people looking for her.

I was prepared for Glenn Ford's finest. What I was not
prepared for, however, were the two people sitting next to
Detective Slovenick in the cramped interview room.
Shelia Martin, dressed in a tailored black pantsuit, her
shiny black hair pulled back in a stiff ponytail, nodded
coolly when I walked into the tiny office. A dark-haired
man, who could've been in his forties or fifties, sat next
to her. He was wearing a charcoal-gray suit and had the
shut-down, emotionless demeanor of a federal-level cop.
The telltale bulge under his armpit only served to confirm
my suspicion. My morning was about to go from dreadful
to godawful.

I looked around the room and forced a smile. "How de-
lightful," I said. "A breakfast club meeting?"

Slovenick, who hadn't seemed any happier than I had
been to see the two agents, bit down on the left side of his
lower lip and suppressed a small smile.

"Thanks for coming, Ms. Valocchi. We'd like to talk
to you about the events of last evening."

I took the seat he indicated, still smiling and sighed.
"You know," I said, "I would like nothing better than to
chat with you folks but I'm feeling significantly under-
represented here. I mean, it's looking like three to one, and
my team thought we were playing singles. How's about
we call my lawyer. She loves to play by the rules and she's
good at it, too."

Shelia tried to smile, but it came off more like a grimace. "Stella, we'd really like to keep this on more of an informal level. We're not looking to charge you with anything."

I held up my hand. "Ahh-ahh! No! Don't do it! Either I call my attorney or I'm leaving."

The man in the charcoal suit had apparently had enough. Without appearing to move any facial muscles other than his lips, he spoke. "Ms. Valocchi, under Section 218 of the federal Patriot Act, you can be detained and interrogated without benefit of an attorney should we feel your information constitutes a significant purpose of one of our ongoing investigations. As a member of an agency sworn to defend this country against internal and external terrorist threats, I can assure you that it is in your best interest to cooperate with our investigation."

I raised an eyebrow and looked right into the man's face. "All that and he smells good, too. They sure shine 'em up good before they turn 'em loose on us ordinary citizens, huh?"

Shelia Martin stirred slightly and focused her attention on me. "Stella, this is Randall Megan. He's with the Department of Homeland Security and I am attached to him for the duration of this current investigation. It really would help if you could tell us where Jake Carpenter is and what involvement the two of you have had with Bitsy Blankenship."

It was as close to begging as Shelia was likely to get and it also told me several things. They knew we knew Bitsy was alive. They couldn't find Jake, either, and lastly, it seemed to confirm that at least part of what Bitsy had told us was true. Maybe she did have a formula for a biological weapon and if so, she probably was in danger. Of course, I still didn't know whether Shelia and her fellow agent, Randall Megan were trustworthy or bad guys.

"Okay," I said. "We'll forgo the attorney for a few minutes. Now, what is it you want to know?"

Randall Megan began by asking me to review the events surrounding and including the break-in to the print shop. He listened as I detailed the fabricated story Jake and I had used on Shelia without saying a word. When I'd finished, Shelia asked, "Where is Jake now?"

I shrugged. "I have no idea. I suppose he's at his apartment."

Shelia gave me an "Oh, come on!" look. "You didn't call him this morning?"

I didn't hesitate. "Of course I did, but he didn't answer. Maybe he was in the shower or out running."

This didn't seem to satisfy her but Randall Megan didn't give her a chance to follow up.

"Where's Bitsy Blankenship?" he asked.

"Dead," I answered.

"When's the last time you saw her?" It continued to amaze me that the man could fire off question after question without changing his facial expression or moving.

"Let's see, I believe it was the keg party right after our high school graduation," I said.

"Try again," he said. "Start with last night in the print shop."

"Bitsy had a sex change operation?"

That got Megan moving. He jumped forward, slamming his hand, palm down onto the surface of the metal interview table between us and startling everyone in the room with the sudden sound. "This is bullshit!" he roared.

I looked up at the tinted glass mirror separating us

from the room beyond and wondered who else was watching this interrogation. I waited for my heart to stop racing and decided to give Megan as little information as possible.

"She appeared in our office yesterday, without an appointment. Before she could explain what was going on, Jake spotted a white sedan with three men inside. They started toward the building before Bitsy could tell us anything other than someone had tried to kill her and she wanted our protection. That's when Jake and I decided to hide her downstairs, only there was a guy already down there waiting for us when we got to the bottom of the steps. That's all I know. Honest."

I tried to look scared, which wasn't a big stretch given Randall Megan's sudden explosion. I needed the two of them to believe me, at least until I could figure out who was working for the home team and who wasn't.

We went back and forth for another twenty minutes with the two agents trying to trip me up and me trying to avoid stepping in deeper shit. I tried to sandwich in a few questions of my own in an attempt to assess whether they were worried about Bitsy or interested more in catching her.

"Do you think Bitsy had anything to do with her husband's death?" I asked at one point.

Shelia gave me a sharp glance and snapped back. "Why, do *you* think she does?"

It was a frustrating Mexican standoff that only ended when Spike somehow managed to figure out where I was and decided to put in an appearance. She threw around enough phrases like "show cause hearing" and "habeas corpus" to finally wear Shelia Martin and her cohort into allowing us to leave. This was accompanied by the usual warnings, instructions and miscellaneous crap that always surrounded investigations that weren't about to involve me as a real suspect but instead were designed to intimidate me into thinking I was in trouble.

Spike seemed to be enjoying herself, which also troubled me when I recalled overhearing Nina accusing Spike of returning to her old job with the district attorney's office. What would I do if Spike switched sides?

Neither of us said a word as we left the police department, reserving our conversation for the warmth and security of Spike's Landrover.

"Did Jake send you?" I asked.

Spike shook her head. She was wearing a cream-colored turtleneck sweater and black wool dress pants. Tiny gold hoop earrings and a light coating of lip gloss were her only accessories. She looked absolutely beautiful and nothing at all like the wild performance artist Nina had bragged about in the early days of their relationship. Of course, there was little chance of Spike reviving her performance art career in tiny Glenn Ford, but she had seemed happy with her decision to return to law in her old hometown. Was this another performance by Spike?

"Actually, no one sent me, Stella," she answered. "Nina told me where you'd gone and I got worried."

"Well, I'm glad," I said. "I was feeling a bit worried myself. What's going to happen if they find out I wasn't telling the entire truth?"

Spike sucked in a long, slow breath before answering. "Stel, they're going to find out. Those guys are good and let's face it, when it comes to going up against the CIA or the FBI, we're rank amateurs. All you can do now is damage control. First, get to Jake and make sure his story dovetails with yours."

I glanced at the clock on her dashboard and felt pinpricks of anxiety ripple across my skin. It was almost eleven. I pulled out my cell phone, opened it and then noticed for the first time that it wasn't my phone. Somehow, I'd picked up Jake's phone and he probably had mine. At least, I hoped so. I hit one on the speed dial and waited. It went straight into my voice mail. The phone was either turned off or dead.

"Great!" I muttered.

"What's wrong?" Spike asked.

"I have Jake's phone and I think he has mine. I can't reach him and I don't know where he is. He was supposed to call Bitsy from a pay phone and then meet her. That was almost four hours ago and I haven't heard a word from him."

Spike's expression reflected the worry I was feeling. The people looking for Bitsy were dangerous professionals. If something had gone wrong, it had gone very wrong.

"I'm going to pay a visit to Marygrace Llewellen," I said. "If you talk to Nina, tell her to call Jake's cell if she has anything to report, okay?"

Spike nodded and laid a reassuring hand on my arm. "Try not to think the worst," she said. "You know how Jake is. He's as independent and impulsive as you are. Sometimes he just doesn't think to report in."

It was true. Jake and I were alike in that respect, but it was little comfort to me now. I was beginning to realize what it felt like to be on the receiving end of my independent streak.

I left Spike, climbed into my car and drove to Brookhaven Manor. If I couldn't find Jake, I'd have to work on finding Bitsy. How hard could it be to find one person in a town the size of Glenn Ford? Okay, damned hard, but it was my only option.

I found Marygrace in her office, staring blankly at a stack of paperwork that sat on the desk in front of her. Her normally perky appearance was markedly diminished today. Her hair hung limp on her shoulders, she slumped over her work and instead of wearing her characteristic bright colors, and she was dressed all in shades of beige.

"Maybe it would help to talk about it," I said softly. "Even social workers need to talk to somebody."

Marygrace jumped like I'd shot her. "Aw, man!" she cried weakly. "You scared the crap out of me! What are you doing here?"

"I came to check on you," I said, stepping into the office and closing the door behind me.

Marygrace looked uneasy. She kept looking to the door behind me, as if hoping someone would open it. She pointed to the chair next to her desk, indicating that I should sit down.

"Baby's all right, isn't she?" Marygrace licked her lips, which I took to be another sign that my visit was making her uncomfortable.

"Baby's fine," I assured her. "It's Bitsy I want to talk about. Where is she?"

Marygrace closed her eyes and took a deep breath. When she opened them she said, "I can't tell you. I promised."

I nodded. "I figured you'd say that," I said. I leaned in close to the frightened woman, looked back over my shoulder, as if I were about to tell her a secret and didn't want to be overheard and proceeded. "Marygrace, I think Bitsy and Jake are in trouble. I think it may even be life threatening."

Marygrace jerked away from me. "Bitsy said people would say that and I shouldn't—"

I snatched the front of her oatmeal-colored, woven top and pulled her in so close to me I could count the freckles on the bridge of her nose.

"Listen, I don't have time to play around with you, Marygrace. If you don't tell me where Bitsy is, I'm going to beat the skin right off your body! I can kill you twelve different ways, Marygrace, and every single one of them will cause you pain like you've never felt before in your life. So before you decide to play all noble and holy with me, think about what it feels like to hurt so bad you soil yourself, and then decide if you can withstand hour after hour of that kind of agony. Okay?"

For good measure, I slid my hand down her arm and let my thumb slide over the pressure point at the edge of her wrist. As I squeezed, Marygrace's eyes widened and tears sprang to her eyes.

"Okay! I'll tell you!" she gasped.

I eased up but didn't release Marygrace's hand. She was just the type to suddenly scream out and I wasn't about to let that happen.

"Bitsy came back to my house last night. I didn't know she was coming. She was just suddenly there, in my bedroom. I don't know how she did it! One minute I was watching a *Law and Order* rerun and the next, there she was!"

"Go on," I coaxed.

"She said something went wrong at your office and people were after her. She wanted to see her grandmother."

"What?"

Marygrace attempted to jerk her hand away and I let it go as a sign of good faith. While she rubbed her wrist, she talked in a rapid, almost unintelligible, stream of words.

"Yeah, she said she had to get out of town, but she couldn't go without seeing Baby. She said it was all her fault that Baby was having such a hard time. Bitsy said she just needed to see Baby for a few minutes. Bitsy wanted to be sure her grandmother was all right. I know, it's crazy and that's what I told her, but she insisted. Finally I had to tell her that Baby was really safe and that you had taken Baby someplace where no one would hurt her. Well, as soon as I told her that, Bitsy just went off!"

Marygrace paused for breath and I broke in. "You mean she was upset that I had Baby hidden away?"

Marygrace nodded; her eyes wide. "Oh, hell yes! She wanted to know why and who'd approved it and then she wanted me to send an ambulance to bring Baby back over here. Well, I told her we just didn't do stuff like that and besides, I didn't know where you'd taken her. I told her it was for Baby's protection."

Marygrace shuddered. "Bitsy got so mad I was almost afraid she'd have a heart attack or something! But really, even if I'd known where Baby was I couldn't have sent for her. We don't do that sort of thing. For one thing, we don't have the staff. Even if we did, we don't have a fleet of ambulances standing by. Come on, man, we're a nursing home not a private foundation! Finally, I told her she should call you and arrange to go see Baby. I said I was sure it was fine but Bitsy said she couldn't take a risk like that on account of how the people looking for her were probably watching your house 24/7."

I remembered the white panel van old Mrs. Talluchi had discovered parked in front of her house and realized Bitsy was probably right about that. Then I wondered why Bitsy thought visiting Baby in the nursing home would be any safer.

"So then what happened?" I asked.

Marygrace shook her head. "That's when she had me call Jake."

All throughout our talk Marygrace's phone had been ringing. When she didn't answer it the people trying to reach her must've decided to come looking for her. They knocked on her office door repeatedly. They called her name. Some even opened the door and peeked inside the room, but all of them left when they saw Marygrace talking to me.

Marygrace, having decided that I wasn't dangerous, waved them all off like errant children. "It's like they can't read the Do Not Disturb sign on the door or something!" she said. "Now, where were we? Oh, yeah, I called Jake but he didn't answer. Then Bitsy left. She said it wasn't safe to stay with me. She said she had a good place to hide and she was going there."

"Do you have any idea where that might be?" I asked.

Marygrace shook her head. "Who knows? I mean, she hasn't lived around here in years and the place has changed a lot. I mean, most of the places we used to hang out are gone now, or they've been turned into subdivisions. She could be anywhere!"

She was right again. The Glenn Ford we'd known as kids was slowly succumbing to urban sprawl. Our farms and pastureland were now filled with fancy brick houses and swim-tennis communities. Bitsy must've found herself a new hiding place.

Marygrace leaned forward, studying my face anxiously. "Okay, I've gotta ask you this—are people really after her or is she nuts? I mean, we grew up in Glenn Ford, for God's sake! Superspies and government agents just don't come around here that often. What's going on with her? Is Bitsy a spy?"

It was time to leave. Marygrace had told me everything she knew and I couldn't tell her anything.

"You know how it is," I said, "I'm bound by the same confidentiality rules you are. I can't say a word about Bitsy, wish I could," I said, backing out of the office. When my cell phone rang, I snatched it off my waistband and tried to look apologetic. "See," I said. "Our lives are just so alike! It's probably another client in crisis." I held the phone up to my ear and adopted an exasperated expression. "Hello?"

Nina's voice was shrill with worry. "Stella, I think you'd better come home," she said. "Bitsy Blankenship just called on the house phone. She said you have ten minutes to come home and be here waiting by the phone. She said you can't call the police or talk to anyone, just come home."

A thousand needles pricked the surface of my skin. My heart raced and Nina's voice seemed to echo as if coming through a tunnel.

"Because why?" I asked softly, already knowing the answer in my heart.

"She says if you don't she'll kill Jake."

Chapter 14

I made the trip across town to Aunt Lucy's house in just under four minutes, courtesy of my '98 Camaro Z28, adrenaline and a blinding desire to get to Jake. Bitsy Blankenship has crossed the line with me. Whatever she needed, whatever trouble she was in, it didn't justify threatening me with Jake's wellbeing. And I fully intended to tell her this, right after I kicked her scrawny little behind from here to Texas.

I was inside Aunt Lucy's house sitting by the phone with three minutes to spare. While we waited, Nina filled me in with every detail of her brief conversation with Bitsy.

"I didn't hear any background noise," she said. "The Caller ID said the call came in from a pay phone. She didn't sound mad or anything, either. She said she needed to leave a message for you and I said 'okay,' and then she told me just what I told you and hung up."

"Nina, did she ask for me first or just want to leave the message?"

Nina hesitated for a moment, thinking. "No, she just said she wanted to leave a message for you."

So she'd known I wasn't home. How? Had she followed me? Had she driven by the police station and seen my car? Had she driven by the house and noticed it wasn't in the driveway? My mind raced, trying to figure it all out and be one jump ahead of Bitsy before she called but that was impossible.

When the phone rang I snatched it off the hook before the first ring ended.

"Where is he?" I demanded.

Bitsy's voice, cool and detached, floated through the line to me. "There's no reason for anyone to get hurt, not as long as you do exactly what I say. Do you understand?"

"Let me talk to Jake," I said.

"Later."

"Bitsy, why are you doing this? Jake and I were trying to help you."

Bitsy's answering laugh was cold and angry. "Some help you two are!" she said. "I'm beginning to wonder why I ever called you. I try to come see you before things get crazy and you can't fit me in to your busy schedule, even though I told you it was an emergency. I finally come to talk to you and the feds show up. I go to see my grandmother and you've taken her out of the nursing home. You just happen to be on the scene when David gets killed, too. Well, I'm not taking any more chances. I don't trust you two and I'm not going to trust you. All you have to do is follow my instructions."

Bitsy had to have cracked under the strain. She was delusional if she thought we were out to do her harm.

"Bitsy, we—"

"Shut up!" Bitsy yelled. "Now listen to me. You have something I need and I have something you want. Tonight at 3:00 a.m., I want you to take the necklace my grand-mother is wearing and go to the pay phone next to Sheel-er's garage. If you call the police, Jake's dead. If you don't show, Jake's dead. In short, if you don't do what I say exactly, I'll kill your boyfriend bit by bit and mail you the pieces. You only have one chance to get this right, Stella. Don't fuck it up."

Click. Bitsy was gone.

I hung up the phone and turned to Nina who'd been lis-tening on the cordless extension.

"So Bitsy did leave something behind in Baby's room," I said, trying to keep my voice level and calm.

Nina nodded. "What are we going to do?" she whis-pered.

I took a deep breath. "Well, the first thing we do is call Aunt Lucy and Spike. Then we sit down here at the kitchen table and come up with some ideas. After that, we work our plan."

I made it sound simple, but neither of us believed that. To avoid using a phone that could possibility be tapped, Nina sent a text page to Spike telling her she was needed at home on a 911. I sought out Aunt Lucy and finally found her in Uncle Benny's study, doing the newspaper crossword with Arnold.

"Um, Aunt Lucy, could I speak to you in private for a moment?"

This clearly irritated Aunt Lucy. I could tell she thought I was being rude to Arnold.

"You can say what you need to say here," she said.

"Well," I said, giving Arnold an apologetic smile. "It's kind of a personal issue, you know a female problem."

Aunt Lucy just stared at me, like I couldn't possibly

be trying a ruse that thin, but Arnold seemed to fall right for it.

"Sure, honey," he said. "You two go on. I'll just work on this puzzle a while longer."

When I got her out in the hall, I quickly filled her in. Her expression grew more worried as I told her about Bitsy's threats and demands.

"What do you need me to do?" she asked quietly.

"We've got to all sit down and figure out what our options are."

She nodded, turning back toward the office.

"Where are you going?" I asked.

"To get Arnie, of course."

I reached out to grab her arm. "No, Aunt Lucy, we can't. Arnold's a nice guy, don't get me wrong, but this is too dangerous, too risky for—"

"Stella," she interrupted. "Arnold is going to be with us until he dies. I trust him and I want him in on this. He's smart and he has resources. Let him help us."

I started to argue with her, but stopped when she touched my shoulder and looked into my eyes. "Please," she said.

I gave in. After all, Aunt Lucy was a smart woman and she loved Jake. If she trusted Arnold Koslovski, I had to trust her judgment.

However, a short while later, when she showed up with Arnold and Sylvia Talluchi, I had to question her choice in confidants. I raised a questioning eyebrow behind Sylvia's back and Aunt Lucy immediately defended her.

"I asked Sylvia to come because of her expertise in espionage. You remember, Sylvia was in the O.S.S. during World War II," she said. "And she's kept up with things."

I could only imagine what "things" Sylvia Talluchi kept up with, but I let it ride. It was too late now. Aunt Lucy had already told her about Jake.

Spike was the last one to arrive. Nina, waiting for her in the driveway, hurried to the passenger side of Spike's Landrover and hopped inside the vehicle. As I watched from the window over the kitchen sink, Nina began talking earnestly to her girlfriend. When they finally got out of the car and came inside, Spike came immediately to me and wrapped me in a warm embrace.

"We'll find him," she whispered. "Don't worry."

Less than thirty minutes after Bitsy's call, we were all sitting down around Aunt Lucy's kitchen table to formulate a plan of action.

I started by giving them all a thorough overview of the situation, starting with my initial call from Bitsy and culminating with her phone call. The kitchen was pin-drop quiet when I finished as each of us thought about the seriousness of Jake's predicament.

Spike, a thoughtful expression on her face, spoke up first. "So if I'm hearing you correctly," she said, "Bitsy found out her husband was a double agent. He killed a Slovenian scientist then took his plans for a biochemical weapon that targets specific populations according to their DNA and was returning to this country where he and the other agents helping him planned to sell the weapon. Bitsy found out about all of this, took the formula herself and now she is allegedly being pursued by corrupt CIA agents as well as maybe noncorrupt CIA agents and agents from Slovenia who want to recover their scientist's work?"

I nodded. "She told us that David might have been trying to start a bidding war, but in doing so, it sounds like he brought all kinds of hell down on himself. And then Bitsy got tagged 'It' when she took the microchip with the formula on it."

"And that's what my patient has around her neck?" Sylvia said, her voice suddenly an octave higher than usual. "She's wearing a formula for a weapon that could destroy entire segments of the world population?"

"Yes. But it's not like the necklace itself is dangerous," I said. "She's just got a chip somewhere in that piece of jewelry."

Nina, who had been listening to Spike's rehash of the details, frowned and got up from the table and crossed the room to grab a sheaf of papers from the counter.

"Wait a minute," she said, the worried look on her face deepening. "Something doesn't seem right about this." She riffled through the pages in front of her, discarding some and pulling others. "Yeah, this is like, totally weird, okay?"

I waited, knowing Nina would reveal all in her own space and time.

"Okay, so like, you asked me to get online and see what else I could find out about David and Bitsy in Slovenia, right?" she said, looking to me for confirmation.

When I nodded, she continued. "Okay, so look at this. Here's an article about a scientist named Gregor Ryzhov who died in an automobile accident about three months ago in Slovenia. The article says Dr. Ryzhov is from the Ukraine, not Slovenia, and it also said he was big into something called nonlinear dynamics and Chaos Theory. It doesn't say a thing about him being a chemist."

Nina passed the copy of the article across the table to me and returned to her stack of information.

"Here's a picture of David and Bitsy at the opening reception for the conference on Nonlinear Dynamics that Dr. Ryzhov was attending at the University of Maribor. Okay, so like this isn't the world's greatest picture, but that dude standing next to that older dude in front is Gregor Ryzhov. That's what the caption says."

I took the grainy copy she handed me and stared hard at the tall man in the photograph. He was young and had a friendly smile on his face. Bitsy was smiling up at him, but he was staring out at the camera and apparently didn't see her.

Aunt Lucy had the first article and was shaking her head as she read. "I can't see why a biochemist developing such sophisticated weaponry would attend a nonlinear dynamics conference," she muttered. "It's such an esoteric area and not really practical for what he was working on."

I put down the photograph. "All right, I give! What is nonlinear dynamics?"

Nina fielded the question instead of Aunt Lucy. "I wanted to know the same thing. Apparently it's a way of studying systems. Chaos Theory is the biggest part of it. Basically, it starts with the Butterfly Theory and shoots off from there. The thinking is that sometimes little random events can cause other, seemingly nonrelated, larger events to occur. So, like, if a butterfly flaps its wings in China, this might eventually cause little fluctuations that lead to shifts and changes in the atmosphere and bam! On the other side of the world, there's a hurricane!"

I was lost. "Honey," I said. "What in the hell does that have to do with Bitsy and Jake?"

Nina nodded, pulling yet another sheaf of papers out of her stack. "I don't know, but I did find this out. Slovenian scientists don't need to run away from their country. Slovenia is friendly to other democratic countries including the United States, but the Ukraine and

Belarus are still longing for the old days of communism and authoritarian leadership."

She shoved more papers across the table in my direction.

"The United States doesn't like the leadership in those countries and a couple of months ago there was a big stink in the U.N. Belarus and the Ukraine accused the United States of spying on them and financing plots to overthrow the government. If that Gregor dude had developed a bio-chemical weapon for those people, they'd be really pissed if he tried to leave or if his formula disappeared."

I nodded, beginning to understand what Nina was trying to tell us. Bitsy and David both had lied to us. They'd left out some information that shifted Bitsy's dilemma into a whole new level of danger. Now I understood why she was in such danger. If Ukrainian agents were chasing her, she was in deep shit. They played hardball, whereas little Slovenia wasn't even in their league. No wonder the CIA was looking for Bitsy.

Arnold was sitting next to Aunt Lucy, writing notes on a legal pad and listening to everything that was being said. I had the feeling he was quietly formulating his own opinions and would in time voice them, but not before he felt confident he had something to offer.

"All right," I said. "We have a job to do. This is a small town. Bitsy shouldn't be that hard to find, but she's also a professional and apparently damned good at her job. If we could find her then I feel certain we'd find Jake, too. I don't think she'll kill him until she absolutely has to." I looked around the table at my friends and family. "But don't get me wrong," I said. "When he becomes a liability, Bitsy will kill Jake. He's a risk she can't afford to take. He knows too much and he's good. I don't know how she managed to overpower him, but I can assure you, if Jake gets free he won't give her a second chance. That's why she'll kill him…before, during or after the exchange."

Arnold broke the tip of his pencil on the crisp white paper in front of him. Suddenly I remembered the Internet article we'd found when we were investigating him. His only daughter had died as a result of a kidnapping.

"I have experience with kidnappers," Arnold said softly. "You are right, she will kill him. If you need cash or surveillance equipment or manpower, I can get it for you, quickly and discreetly, remember I own an electronics kingdom. I've got the inventory of over sixty Computer Digitech stores at my disposal. You just say the word, Stella."

Aunt Lucy reached over, laid her hand on top of his arm and squeezed gently, silently reassuring him.

"What do you need us to do?" she asked me.

I pushed back the tears that threatened to make speaking impossible and met Arnold's earnest gaze.

"Thank you for your kindness, Arnie," I said. "I don't deserve it after the way I've treated you."

Arnold chuckled. "Don't be ridiculous! You did what any good niece would do, you investigated me. You were making sure your aunt was safe. And then you gave in to your feelings. You loved your uncle and I was stepping into his territory. Who could blame you for thinking it is too soon for your aunt to love someone new? Who could fault your loyalty, eh?"

Arnold's smile became rueful and his eyes looked sad.

"If my circumstances were different, I would have waited, moved more slowly. But as you all know, time is not on my side. I only have right now, today, to make up for years without my Lucia." He shrugged, picking up my aunt's Italian mannerism without seeming to be aware of it. "But, I have no regrets. We have had wonderful lives without each other and now we have the gift of this brief time together."

He paused to smile at my aunt before continuing. "So," he said, placing his hands, palms down on the table and slowly extending his arms toward us. "I do not want to replace your uncle. I just want to be here…for Lucia and for all of you, for as long as we have together."

Nina burst into tears and buried her face in Spike's shoulder. I inhaled deeply and struggled to keep myself together. Between the stress of losing Jake, and Arnold's sweet openness, I was coming damned close to losing it.

"Thank you, Arnold. Maybe if we could develop a list of possible places where Bitsy could be hiding we could fan out and drive past those locations," I said. "Then we might have an idea of what kind of resources we'll need."

It wasn't much of an idea, but the others threw themselves into the task. Spike played secretary and the rest of us tried to list places in and around Glenn Ford where Bitsy might be hiding. We'd been at it for five minutes when Sylvia Talluchi cried, "Bogies at high noon!"

All of us, with the exception of Arnold, scrambled like the on-deck crew of an aircraft carrier. Aunt Lucy grabbed the remote for the front surveillance monitor. Nina scampered down the steps to the basement to make sure the door into Aunt Lucy's underground laboratory was closed and secured. Spike quietly folded her notepad over and put it in a drawer.

"How did you know someone was at the front door?" I asked Sylvia, wondering what high-tech intruder-alert mechanism she and my aunt had come up with now.

She rolled her eyes. "The front door bell is broken," she rasped. "Instead of ringing it makes a click, click, click sound. You were all talking. I was listening."

Duh. It's always the simple explanations.

The monitor flashed on, the picture came into clear view and there she stood, Shelia Martin, without her sidekick. As we watched, she took a slight step back, looked up at the spot above the door where the tiny surveillance camera was hidden, and stood staring up at it as if she were watching us watch her.

"Damn!" I swore under my breath. "Now what?"

I walked slowly through the house to the front door, mentally preparing myself to do battle. When I opened the door, Shelia didn't mince words.

"We need to talk," she said, sweeping past me into the hallway.

I closed the door behind her, praying Bitsy didn't somehow have the row house under surveillance, and stood with my arms folded tight across my chest.

"Shelia, didn't we cover everything back at the PD?" I asked.

She looked at me with frosty blue-eyed intensity and sighed. Her shoulders slumped just a little bit as she shook her head in frustration.

"Stella, could we just sit down and talk for a minute? Why do you have to treat me like I'm the enemy? You know Jake and I are close. I'm not here to do anything other than help."

I cocked an eyebrow at this statement, but brushed past her to lead the way into Aunt Lucy's front parlor. I gestured to the sofa, took the wingback chair across from her and decided to go on the offensive.

"So, you want to help," I said softly. "Why should you think I need help? And what sort of help are you thinking I need?"

Shelia smoothed an invisible wrinkle in her immaculate black wool slacks before answering me.

"Jake came to me asking questions about Bitsy Blankenship's death. I did some poking around and found out that she and her husband could've been in possession of a formula for a biochemical weapon. At first we thought Bitsy had been killed in retaliation for the loss of the scientist who was developing the formula."

Shelia looked directly into my eyes. "That was before we found out she wasn't dead and before we learned that she visited her grandmother shortly before her disappearance. It was also before two men purporting to work for the CIA were killed in the nursing home parking lot and Bitsy's grandmother's room was ransacked not once, but three times by apparently different individuals."

Throughout Shelia's monologue, I made sure I kept my expression flat and didn't give her any nonverbal cues.

"Then, last night, there's a disturbance at your office. Armed men break in. You and Bitsy break out. The police arrive and find one man almost blinded by chemicals and a weird tale of a break-in to the print shop. Then you return and attempt to single-handedly take down one of the suspects as he's driving away. He pulls a gun and you almost kill him."

I nodded when she paused, but when I didn't say anything, she continued.

"We find Bitsy's fingerprint at the scene and all you have to offer is some piecemeal story of Bitsy coming to you for help and intruders interrupting you before you can find out what's going on."

Shelia turned her hands over on her lap, palms up and shook her head. "Now Jake, who's usually glued to your side, seems to have vanished. Where is he, Stella, and why aren't you worried?"

I smiled, but I was far from enjoying our little cat-and-mouse game. "Jake's a big boy," I answered. "Why should I be worried about him?"

Shelia's frost-blue eyes darkened into a brilliant aquamarine as the intensity of her emotions began to show. Telltale pink spots blossomed on her cheeks, letting me know she was working to contain her irritation with me.

"Why should you worry?" Shelia asked. "Because you're a smart woman and you've managed to ferret out Jake's past relationship with Bitsy. And you know how Jake is when he thinks one of his women, past or present, is in danger." Shelia leaned toward me. "He's a knight in shining armor, and right now he's with Bitsy Blankenship, a damsel in very big distress."

Shelia waited for her words to sink in and have an effect while I sat across from her, trying as hard as I could to outplay her by staying cool. All I really wanted to do was jump the short distance between us and kick her ass. Of course, that would be all the evidence she needed.

I was thinking hard and fast, wishing I could tap into her expertise while knowing I couldn't confide in her. Jake had doubts about Shelia. He questioned why she was suddenly so available and willing to help him find out about Bitsy. For the first time since I'd known him, Jake was unsure about Shelia and I had to honor that. "Don't trust, don't talk, don't feel," became my silent mantra.

Shelia was watching me like a cat watches a field mouse, waiting for me to move so she could pounce.

"Jake doesn't know what he's up against," Shelia said softly. "He doesn't know what kind of danger Bitsy's in, not really. Jake thinks he's invincible, but Stella, he hasn't come up against people like the ones chasing Bitsy. They'll stop at nothing to get what they want. Jake won't be any match for them. It's one man against an army."

She shook her head slowly. "I know you think I still have feelings for Jake. I know you don't trust me, but

Stella, I'm begging you, if you know anything about their whereabouts, tell me. Let me help them get to safety!"

She was damned believable and I wanted to let down my guard, but I just couldn't. Not yet.

I sighed. "Shelia, I know you mean well, but Jake's fine. Tell you what, when I hear from Jake, I'll tell him to call you."

Shelia's face hardened into a look of stony displeasure. She was pissed.

"Both of you are making a very big mistake," she said. "I don't understand why you won't let me help."

I shrugged. "Shelia, let's lay it all out here, all right? You didn't come to see me out of some sudden sense of sisterhood. You came because all of your usual advanced technological methods for locating people aren't working. You only want to find Jake because you suspect he's with the person you really want to talk to, Bitsy."

When she started to protest, I held up my hand and stopped her. "I'm sure you care about Jake, but bottom line…you're a cold-hearted bitch on a mission, and that comes first with you. If you could help me by finding Jake, you would have done it by now. You're just fishing to see if you've left any stones unturned and, honey, believe me, you haven't."

I stood up and looked down on her. "I think you'd better leave now."

Without waiting for her to say anything further, I started out of the room toward the front door. She followed me but stopped in the doorway, unable to leave without one final parting shot.

"You're too smart to be so foolish, Stella. Yeah, I'll take Jake away from you if I get the chance. But now isn't the time to be worrying about that. We have to think about what is best for Jake. If you really loved him, you'd be doing that and not playing games with me."

I stonewalled her, held the door open and waited for her to walk through it and out onto the stoop before I slammed it shut behind her. When I walked back into the kitchen, they were all waiting for me.

"Are you sure she can't help us?" Nina asked.

"Yes."

Nina frowned. "I thought the CIA could find anybody," she muttered.

Aunt Lucy shook her head. "Only in the movies."

I looked up at the clock on the wall above Aunt Lucy's sink and felt my stomach lurch. It was almost three. We only had twelve hours to find Jake, if that.

Arnold and Sylvia were huddled together at the far end of the table, holding a whispered conference that ended with Arnold nodding and squeezing her arm before looking up at the rest of us.

"We've been talking," he said. "Does Jake's cell phone have a global positioning system installed in it?"

The first flicker of hope ignited and was quickly extinguished as I remembered. "We just upgraded our phones, but the GPS only works if you dial 911 and only the emergency operator gets that readout. I asked about that because I was thinking it might come in handy for us." I saw Sylvia, and Arnold's faces brighten and quickly added, "We can't call the police or EMS. If Bitsy's monitoring their scanners or Jake's phone—my phone—rings, he's dead."

There was a moment of absolute silence and then Nina sat up in her seat, practically tingling with excitement.

"Okay, okay, so like, we just hack into the phone and get the GPS coordinates!"

I couldn't help rolling my eyes. "Nina, none of us know how to do that!"

The smile never left her face. "I know we don't! But I know someone who does and he's right in this house!"

I frowned. "Paint Bucket?"

Nina shook her head. "No, Weasel. Remember I was all pissed off at him 'cause I thought he ruined my computer, but instead, he made it do things I didn't even know it could do. He, like, knows where there's this Web site that has tutorials on how you can hack into all kinds of things, like video game consoles and computers. I'm pretty sure he could find a way for us to hack into your cell phone and get the GPS readout ourselves!"

She hopped up out of her seat and ran to the basement steps, heading down toward Aunt Lucy's lab. I started to stop her, but didn't when I realized Weasel might hold the only key to finding Jake. When it came right down to it, I trusted Weasel more than I trusted Shelia Martin.

A few moments later she returned with a leery Weasel. He followed her to the kitchen table, sat in the chair she pulled out for him and stared around at the rest of us with a mistrusting gaze.

"This is about the dishes, isn't it?" he said.

Nina pushed the laptop over to him and laughed. "No, silly! I told you. We want you to do something for us, you know, like what you showed me yesterday on that site. I want you to hack into Stella's cell phone so it can tell us where it is!"

Weasel's eyes widened. He looked to me for verification and when I nodded that this was indeed true, he raised an eyebrow and nodded his head slightly in Mrs. Talluchi's direction. "Is it all right with her?" he asked.

"*Stunade!*" old Mrs. Talluchi cried. "*Stupido!* Just do as she says, boy!"

Weasel looked at the elderly woman and shook his head slowly. "Dude," he said. "This is some sensitive work here. I can't work with negative vibes draining my energy levels, you know? Maybe if we could like fire up a joint together or something sometime, you could find something to like about me."

Old Mrs. Talluchi glared at Weasel.

"Weasel, just do it please! Time is of the essence here!"

"All right, all right!" he said, turning his attention to the computer. "This thing connected?" he asked, then apparently answering the question for himself, looked over at me again. "Okay, so like Jake has your phone and you have his?" he asked.

I nodded.

"Let me see it," he said.

Arnold had left his chair and was now standing behind Weasel, looking over his shoulder. As Weasel inspected Jake's phone, Arnold was watching. When Weasel turned back to the computer and typed something in, Arnold leaned even closer.

"Can you circumvent the A5 algorithm?" he asked.

Weasel grinned up at him. "My brother!" he cried. "Pull up a chair and let us get to work!"

Apparently Arnold had said the password into Weasel's good-natured karmic neighborhood.

"I don't know shit about hacking into cell phones," Weasel confided. "Do you?"

Arnold nodded shyly. "Well, not personally, but I spent a little time at the Technion Institute in Haifa a few years back. They were working on tightening the encryption then. I don't suppose much of that is relevant now, but have you tried this site?" Arnold reached across to type something into the computer.

"Damn, Sam!" Weasel cried. "Would you look at that!"

He studied the screen a few moments, then looked up and grinned. "We'll have this puppy up and running in no time!"

"Weasel, what are you doing?" I asked.

"Dude, this is going to be so totally awesome! We're going to change the settings on your phone, then switch phones with Jake's by changing the numbers. His features will be automatically updated through Big Bro, the global positioning option will be activated whether the phone's turned on or not, and we'll be set."

"Big Bro?"

Weasel rolled his eyes and grinned at Arnold. "Big Brother, you know, dude, 1984, George Orwell. The cell company's satellite!"

"Oh," I said, nodding like I got it.

"Then we hack the phone, read the GPS coordinates and go pick up the boy!"

I looked over at Arnold, who nodded like he'd understood every word of Weasel's explanation. "How long will this take?"

Weasel, back at the keyboard and typing away, cackled. "Arnie showed me a shortcut. It shouldn't take us more than twenty minutes."

I looked up at the clock again—3:16 p.m. What if she'd taken his phone? What if it was lying in a field somewhere, miles away from their location? Was Jake still alive? If he was, how long would Bitsy let him live before she killed him?

Chapter 15

"Well, I'll be damned," I said, looking up from the map. "He's out off Harmon Road. Isn't that where the…"

"Proctor place is," Nina finished. "Jake's somewhere on the Proctor estate!"

"Maybe," I said. "At least that's where the phone is. If we're lucky, Jake's there too."

I tried to remember what I knew of the huge estate. Set on fifty-three acres, the original home had been built over a hundred years ago and used as a summer house for the wealthy Proctor family. Over the years several additional homes had been added to the site to house additional extended family. Outbuildings and barns peppered the land, built to support the more recent and failed attempt to start a winery. It was a logistical nightmare for someone planning a rescue mission, but it was the perfect location for someone who wanted to stay hidden.

I looked back down at the map and sighed. Nina had to be right. There were no other properties with homes along that road. It was a perfect hiding place—remote, secluded and full of alternatives. Damn!

"You know," Arnold said, "I almost bought that place a month ago. I have the plat map of the property, a real estate booklet showing the buildings and their floor plans and some pictures. Do you think those would help? They're sitting on the desk in my room at the hospice."

Spike stood up and grabbed her keys from the hook by the back door. "I'll go get them," she said. "Arnie, call and tell them I'm coming, okay?"

The little man nodded. He looked pale suddenly and worn-out. Aunt Lucy seemed to notice this, too, because she put a protective hand on his shoulder.

"You can call from the bedroom," she said firmly. "But then you must have some soup and a nap."

Arnold might have thought about protesting, but Aunt Lucy circumvented this by issuing a string of commands to Nina and Weasel while leading her patient gently but firmly from the room.

With a worried look on her face Sylvia Talluchi watched the elderly couple leave. "We must watch him," she murmured to me quietly. "His spirit is light. I don't think he has much longer."

Lloyd whined and barked once, a shrill yip quite unlike his usual bark. He was watching the doorway leading from the kitchen to Aunt Lucy's bedroom and standing beside the pallet where Fang lay, clearly torn between the two loves of his life.

"They'll be fine, Lloyd," I said, walking over to pet his head and scratch behind his ears. "She'll be back in a few minutes. You stay with Fang."

Fang raised her head and growled softly, probably wishing the overly anxious father-to-be would indeed follow his adopted mistress. Fang didn't seem like the type of woman who took kindly to smothering attention.

I found myself pacing around the kitchen, out onto the back porch and back inside again. I needed a plan for finding and rescuing Jake. I walked through the house, circling each room, and finally wound up following the basement steps down to Uncle Benny's old workshop.

I surveyed the room, running my fingers over Uncle Benny's workbench, feeling the metal and wood surfaces and missing the man who had become a second father to me. I crossed the room, sat briefly on the worn sofa that was his home base during baseball and football season. I closed my eyes and tried to think. I was one woman trying to save one man from a dangerous mixture of professional killers.

I closed my eyes and had a sudden memory of fishing with Uncle Benny. It was the summer after my parents had been killed in an airplane crash and I was a grief-stricken teenager. I blamed myself for my parents' deaths, thinking that somehow my anger at them for leaving me and my burgeoning attempts at autonomy had somehow caused their airplane to fall from the sky. I was miserable and Uncle Benny knew it.

He never forced his wisdom upon me, never tried to hurry my grieving or argue me into moving on with my life. Uncle Benny just sat quietly by my side and waited throughout the long months of my recovery.

On this one day in particular, we were in his skiff, floating quietly in the middle of Kerr Park Lake. Our rods trailed in the lazy wake of the drifting boat. Cicadas sang songs of midsummer heat, and the occasional fly buzzed our ears.

Mango, my ten-year-old mutt, lay in the bottom of the boat, snuggled up as close to me as possible. Her head rested on my foot and even when I moved it, she followed, plopping her heat back on top of my toes as soon as I resettled.

"Why does she keep doing that?" I asked. "She won't leave me alone. It's a zillion degrees out here and Mango has to keep her head right on top of my foot. I'm hot!"

Uncle Benny looked at the elderly cocker spaniel and smiled gently. "Why, Stella, she's only doing what she has to do."

I hadn't expected an answer. I looked over at my uncle, waiting to hear what would follow.

"Dogs are like people. They only do what they feel they must do in order to survive."

When Uncle Benny didn't elaborate, I couldn't help asking, "Mango won't survive if her head isn't on my foot? Why?"

Uncle Benny chuckled. "No, *cara*, it's not that Mango won't survive. She will. She'd be fine, in fact. She just doesn't believe it, that's all. You see, if you want her to change, you must first understand why she feels she must keep her head on your foot or die."

I remember thinking my uncle was nuts.

"Look at things from Mango's point of view," Uncle Benny added. "She is a happy dog in a happy family. Everybody loves her. Then one day, two of the three people in her life disappear and never come back."

Uncle Benny stopped for a long moment, watching as I reached out to stroke Mango's hot black fur. Mango, sensing something in my touch, sat up and began licking the salty tears from my cheek.

"Mango can't understand our words," Uncle Benny

said softly. "She doesn't know what happened or why. All she knows is that she doesn't want to lose you. That's why she has to keep her head on your foot."

Years later, when I became a cop, I used Uncle Benny's philosophy on a daily basis. Once I understood Why, I could understand Who or How. It wasn't going to be any different with Bitsy. Why was Bitsy so certain Jake and I were against her? Why did she think she needed to hold him hostage in order to get me to bring her the microchip?

I got up and walked through the laundry room entrance into Aunt Lucy's laboratory. Baby Blankenship was awake and lying up in her hospital bed talking to Sylvia Talluchi.

"Do you know I worked as a car hop down at Miller's Drive-In?" she was saying.

"All through high school, up until I met Milton," she added.

"My father," Sylvia said. "He wouldn't let us outta his sight. I had to sneak just to see the movie down at the Saturday matinee!"

"You were such a pretty girl," Baby said. "Your father was smart!"

When they saw me standing at the edge of the curtained doorway, Baby's smile grew even wider. "There's my girl, now," she said. "Brenda, come in here!" She turned to Sylvia Talluchi. "She's so bashful these days. I tell her, who cares if you're rich or you're poor. Money isn't everything!"

I frowned. Why would Brenda Blankenship worry about money? The Blankenships lived in one of the nicest homes in town. Bitsy had never lacked for a thing while we were in school. She was always dressed in the latest hot outfit. She'd even driven a candy-apple-red mustang, given to her on her sixteenth birthday.

I hesitated. "Money's not everything?" I echoed.

Baby looked to Sylvia again. "I tell her everyone will understand, but she just doesn't listen. I gave her everything I had. What else could a mother do? At least he didn't go to prison."

I approached the bed. "Who, Baby? Who didn't go to prison?"

Baby frowned, held her finger to her lips and shushed me. "Benton," she whispered.

"Benton?" I repeated.

Baby frowned up at me. "Hey," she said. "You aren't who you are!" She studied me harder, squinting as she tried to place me in her memory. "Who are you? Where is my girl?" Baby's voice rose as she became more anxious.

Paint Bucket appeared in the doorway, a glass of water in one hand and a small paper pill cup in the other.

"Hey, sweetheart," he said, smiling at Baby. "How's my favorite girl?"

Sylvia Talluchi seized my hand with her talonlike fingers and yanked me out of the makeshift bedroom.

"You upset my patient!" she cried in a hoarse whisper. "What's the matter with you, eh?"

"I'm sorry," I said. "I was just trying to— Who's Benton?"

Sylvia scowled. "Her son, Benton. Bitsy's father."

"Bitsy's father?" I tried to remember Bitsy's father and couldn't come up with a face. "I thought Bitsy's father died when she was little? Wait a minute. I thought Brenda was Baby's daughter. You mean she's her daughter-in-law?"

Sylvia cast a worried look back toward the curtained-off area and shook her head. "Benton was Baby's son, but no one talks about him anymore. It was such a shame. Such a waste."

"What happened?" I could feel myself getting increasingly anxious as the knot of details surrounding Bitsy and her family grew more complex. This was taking up valuable time, time I didn't have.

"Benton had a gambling problem. By the time Brenda found out about it, he was in trouble with the loan sharks and was on the verge of losing everything he owned. He was *stunnade!*"

Sylvia made a gesture that left no doubt as to her opinion of Benton Blankenship.

"He ran like a yellow dog! He left his wife and small baby with nothing but the clothes on their backs! It was a disgrace!"

I stared at Sylvia, not believing what I was hearing. "But they lived with Baby. Brenda is still in the house. I don't understand."

Sylvia shrugged. "What is to understand? Baby took them in. What else could she do? Brenda worked in the bank and they tried to pay off the debt."

"But we all thought Bitsy was rich. She had the clothes and the car. How…?" I stopped, realizing how hard Baby and Brenda had to work to make Bitsy's life look easy and privileged.

"Did Bitsy know?" I asked.

Sylvia Talluchi shrugged. "Who knows?"

If she had known, I thought, she never let on. None of us ever saw Bitsy as anything but carefree and air-headed. Only years later did I learn she was brilliant and playing at being stupid so she'd fit in with the popular kids. If she'd been that concerned about her image, imagine how she'd feel if people learned about her father.

"Listen," I said, "I need Baby's necklace. I figured if I exchanged the one I'm wearing for the one Bitsy gave her, she wouldn't get upset. But I didn't expect her to think I was Brenda. I need to go back in there. Will you help me?"

Sylvia Talluchi eyed me warily. "I do not think you should go back in there at all," she said. "Give me the necklace. I'll take care of it."

When I hesitated, Mrs. Talluchi reached up, grabbed a lock of my hair and yanked my head down hard until we were face-to-face at her eye level.

"Look, kid, I know you think I'm a crazy old woman, but I'm all you got at the moment. Now give me the necklace!"

Three minutes later I was walking up the stairs to Aunt Lucy's kitchen, Baby Blankenship's necklace in my hand. I was examining it, looking for anything that could resemble what I supposed was a microchip, when Aunt Lucy found me.

"Arnold wants to see you," she said.

I looked up and was shocked to see how tired and worried she looked.

"Is he worse?" I asked.

Aunt Lucy seemed puzzled for a moment. "Worse?" she repeated. "No, Stella. Arnold isn't worse. He is just very, very tired. It is hard sometimes to die."

She turned and began walking back down the hallway with me close behind her. When we reached her bedroom, she stopped outside the door and cautioned me. "Don't stay too long. He wants to help but…" Her voice trailed off as she slowly opened the door to reveal a small form lying in the middle of her bed. Fang lay at his feet, guarding her new friend.

"Stella," Arnold called. His voice was barely above a whisper. "A friend of mine is going to bring you some tools that might help tonight. Do you need manpower?"

I shook my head. "No, Arnie. If Bitsy found out it would be disastrous. I need to go in alone. It will be easier to slip in that way."

Arnold's bright-blue eyes were dull with pain and the medication used to fight it. He nodded as his eyes slowly closed, and he seemed to be sleeping.

"Thank you, Arnie," I whispered.

"It's...nothing," he answered.

Aunt Lucy was sitting on the bed beside him when I left the room. She was holding Arnie's hand and crooning a tune that sounded vaguely familiar. It wasn't until I had almost reached the kitchen that I recognized it. "Keep on the Sunny Side."

Spike arrived a few minutes later carrying a portfolio stuffed with brochures and information about the Proctor estate.

"Stel," she said. "I've got something else for you. While I was picking up Arnold's portfolio, one of Arnold's employees arrived. He said to tell you to look in Aunt Lucy's back alley trash can right after as it gets dark." She looked outside at the overcast sky and turned back to me. "That shouldn't be too much longer, huh?"

A frisson of adrenaline lifted the hairs on the back of my neck. Darkness wouldn't come soon enough.

I spent the next two hours poring over maps and floor plans before deciding on my course of action. Nina and Spike would have to come along, as getaway drivers and lookouts if nothing else. There was just no way I could search the entire Proctor estate, find Jake and escape without help.

As soon as it was dark enough, Spike and Nina retrieved the heavy box from Aunt Lucy's back-alley trash can. Arnold Koslovski had played high-tech Santa Claus.

"Would you look at that!" Spike cried, holding up a set of night-vision goggles.

"I claim this thing!" Nina called. "It's like, totally too cool! What is it?"

I took the small, gray device she held in her hands and inspected it.

"See all those cute little twinkle lights?" Nina added. "I bet they do something way interesting."

"Nina," I said. "This is too cool! Do you know what it is? This is a universal RF transmitter locator and minibug detector. If Bitsy uses her cell phone or any communication device, this thing will not only pinpoint her location, it'll listen in! It'll detect any surveillance devices, too. Oh, this is great!"

Nina turned to Spike, her face glowing with excitement. "Honey, wouldn't this be cool in our new house? We could like, always know who's knocking at the front door. We'd never be interrupted when we're…well, you know! We could just turn this on and listen to what they're saying. That way we'd know if it was the Jehovah's Witnesses or one of your cop friends coming to visit!"

Spike actually blushed. "Whatever you want, baby," she murmured.

Nina started to giggle, clapped a hand over her mouth and looked dismayed. "Oh, man, I'm sorry, Stella. For a second I guess I forgot about how serious— I mean, before Jake got— Well, I think Spike and I found a house. Next door to Mrs. Talluchi… It's perfect and it's not far away, either."

I reached out to pat her arm. "That's great, sweetie. Of course I understand."

Spike shook her head. "Let's get back to this. We can talk about the house later, okay?" She smiled softly at Nina. "We've got to get Jake back home so we can really celebrate."

We returned to our work, searching through the box and uncovering electronic treasure after treasure. Tiny two-way encrypted radio transmitters, cell-phone jammers, a silent drill, video transmitters. It was amazing. We left for the Proctor estate an hour later, dressed in black fatigues with black greasepaint covering our faces. We wore state-of-the-art bulletproof vests and carried an arsenal of weapons that included Arnold Koslovski's magical box of equipment.

I rebriefed Nina and Spike on the drive out into the county, mainly because I was so pumped up with nervous energy I had to talk in order to keep myself calm and focused.

"All right," I said. "You two will drop me at the north-west quadrant of the estate and proceed to the southern vector. As soon as you're parked, send the signal and we'll make sure you're reading my transmission."

Nina wrinkled up her nose and looked over the front seat at me. "Stella, like, could you just say that in English please? I mean, the northwest quadrant, where is that?"

I sighed silently. "Drop me at the corner of Connell Road and Freeman Mill."

Nina smiled. "See? That wasn't so bad, was it?"

I was actually relieved to get out of the car. They dropped me at the far corner of the estate, amidst a stand of scrawny pine trees and overgrown, ice-glazed brush, and drove on, headlights off, to find a secure place to wait for my hopeful return.

I pulled out the night-vision goggles, slipped them on and began to slowly survey my surroundings. According to the map and plans, the main house stood close to the middle of the property and the other three homes were at the end of long drives that fanned out from the main house in wheel spokes of gravel. No one had lived on the property in over two years, but a caretaker's cottage sat out by the main road and the gates to the estate were padlocked.

Arnold assured us that when he toured the property the electricity was working, as well as the heat and plumbing.

"It was shabby and needed a lot of work as I recall," he'd said. "But it wasn't abandoned."

I set off, walking quickly across the frozen ground, trying to avoid the main drive and stick close to the covering shelter of the surrounding woods. Within moments the massive main house came into view and I pulled the tiny remote listening device from my jacket pocket, hoping to hear something that indicated people were inside the darkened house.

But there was no response on the digital display. I studied the house, not seeing anything but darkness in front of me and was about to move on to search the smaller surrounding houses when I saw the tiniest flicker of light from a second-floor window. Someone was inside.

I crept closer and closer to the mansion, careful to look around for signs that others had found Bitsy's hiding place, but the woods were pin-drop silent. When I was within a hundred yards of the house, I saw the faint flicker of light again. I moved closer still and began to plan my entry.

I closed my eyes, visualizing the layout of the house. The second floor housed eight bedrooms and baths, a small kitchen, two lounges and two staircases, front and back.

I looked up at the second floor again and noticed this time the thick curtains covering the windows. Blackout curtains? The light flashing from the second-floor window seemed to come in little jerks and twitches. As if someone were rhythmically signaling perhaps?

I stared up at the window. Indeed the short flashes of light were coming in a pattern of threes. I grinned. Damn that Jake, always thinking! Was he flashing SOS in Morse code? He knew I'd come for him. He was trying to let me know his location. I started toward the house with a surge of determined confidence. I had a plan and it was time to work it.

I slipped around the side of the house, counted the tiny windows that lined the basement and stopped at the third one. The electrical panel box was located inside this room. I knelt down, quietly taped and broke the glass panes, removed the broken glass and slid through the frame to drop down into the room below.

"Panel box and main cutoff are to my left," I whispered softly. Even with the night-vision goggles, it was difficult to make out much in the darkened basement. I edged forward slowly, saw the gray box a few feet away and walked toward it.

"Lights out, everybody," I whispered as I opened the box and reached for the main circuit breaker.

I pulled the switch down, struggling a little as the ancient handle resisted my attempts, but ultimately succeeding. There was a rewarding hush as the furnace hissed to a halt. I listened but still heard nothing to indicate anyone but me was in the old house.

"Here I come," I whispered. "Ready or not!"

I put my hand in my jacket pocket, pulled out my Glock and froze.

Bitsy Blankenship's voice whispered in my ear. "Having fun, Stella?" The cold metal ring of her gun barrel bit into the base of my skull. "I'm wired, so if you try anything, Jake dies before I hit the ground. Now drop your gun, nice and easy."

So Bitsy wasn't working alone. Great. I remembered the blonde from the nursing home, Aida, and wondered if she were Bitsy's partner in crime.

"Let's go upstairs, shall we?" she said, nudging me forward.

Bitsy reached past me to the panel box, pushed the circuit breaker back up and slammed the metal box door shut.

"We've been waiting for you," she said. "I even let Jake watch you on the monitor while I signaled you. I thought the SOS was a nice touch, didn't you?"

I didn't answer her, I couldn't. I was too busy thinking about how we were going to overpower her and escape to come up with a snappy comeback.

Bitsy pulled the night-vision goggles off my head and tossed them onto the floor as we walked. "You won't need those where you're going."

She pushed me ahead of her, leading me up the sweeping staircase and down a wide hallway, stopping finally outside a bedroom door.

"Go ahead, open the door," she said. "Let's get this party started."

I took a deep breath, reached out and pushed the door open. We entered what once must have been a lavish suite but now was just a shabby and quite dirty space filled with broken furniture and shredded wallpaper. Jake sat alone, in a small, antique chair in the middle of the room, eyes closed. His face was streaked with dirt and sweat and he was pale. Was he unconscious? Why hadn't he moved when he'd had the chance? Where were the others Bitsy said were watching him?

"Where's your buddy, Aida?" I asked, hoping I'd guessed correctly, hoping Bitsy wasn't hiding an entourage of battle-hardened commandos to aid in her escape.

"Aida?" Bitsy echoed.

Great. No Aida. So who was working with Bitsy?

"Who's with you?" I demanded.

"Smoke and mirrors," Jake mumbled.

Jake sat with one leg straight out in front of him, and when I looked closer I saw dried blood crusted around a small tear in his pants leg. His eyes flickered open. He looked at me, attempted to sit up, but slumped back against the chair's uncomfortable back with a soft moan.

"Jake, you're hurt!" I darted to his side, not caring if Bitsy shot me for moving.

Jake struggled to open his eyes and reached out to touch me lightly with one light tap of his forefinger.

"S'nothin' to it," he mumbled. "Just a little flesh wound."

I whirled around, glaring at Bitsy. "Why? All he did was try to help you. Why did you shoot him?"

Bitsy rolled her eyes. "Please, spare me the frantic-girl-friend routine, all right? Give me the necklace."

I stuck my hand deep inside my jacket pocket and felt the miniature radio transmitter. I pushed the talk button down and held it open while I stuck my free hand in the other jacket pocket and pretended to search for the missing jewelry. I was hoping the microphone in the walkie was sensitive enough to transmit at least some of what I was saying to Spike and Nina.

"Why do you want the necklace, Bitsy?" I asked, stalling. "What's on the microchip?"

Bitsy smiled. "Wouldn't you like to know?" she answered.

"David wasn't a double agent," I said. "You were the one, weren't you? You stole the formula and now you and your partners are going to sell it to the highest bidder, aren't you?"

Bitsy frowned. "Oooh, that's scary sounding, isn't it?" Bitsy shook her head. "You people watch too much T.V. That formula's just the beginning. I hold all the cards now!"

"What do you mean, you hold all the cards?"

Bitsy smiled coyly. "Thought old Bitsy was just a little dumb blond cheerleader, huh? Guess y'never know, huh? Well, it's too late now. Just toss me the necklace. I've got a bird to catch."

In the distance I could hear the faint whir of a helicopter. Bitsy was going to take whatever she had hidden inside Baby's necklace, kill us and disappear if I didn't stop her.

I pulled out Baby's necklace and dangled it from my left hand. Bitsy was so proud of herself, so pleased to have pulled the wool over our eyes.

"This can't be too important," I said, giving the piece a very skeptical appraisal. "I bet you stole some designer's fall fashion line. I mean, what could little, blond you possibly stumble on that would be that valuable? And why leave it with an old lady for safekeeping?"

"You stupid bitch!" Bitsy snapped. "I left it with her because no one would look twice at her. Besides, what choice did I have? They were on my ass—I couldn't risk them finding me and taking it. I wouldn't have any bargaining chips—no pun intended. Besides, you and Jake put me off for hours or I would've left it with Jake."

The sting of guilt bit into my gut. Because of my foolish insecurities, Baby had become an innocent victim. I swallowed hard, pushing the bitter emotion down to be dealt with later, after Jake and I were safe.

"So who was after you, Bits, a couple of puny agents from a tiny third world country? You couldn't handle them?"

Bitsy's face reddened but she didn't take the bait. "Toss the necklace over here or I'll shoot his other leg," she snapped.

"Oh, let's not play make-believe, Bits. You're going to do a lot more than shoot Jake in the leg. You're going to kill us both and then you're going to fly away. Then what're you gonna do, Bitsy, follow in your old man's footsteps? Fade away into the sunset and leave your mom and grandmother to face everybody when they learn you're a thief and a traitor?"

I swung the necklace back and forth, like I was considering whether or not to toss it. I looked back up at her, saw the barely contained rage ready to spill over and pushed the last button harder.

"Way to go, Bitsy! The apple doesn't fall far from the tree, does it? Tell me something, Bits. Did you kill David and the two Ukrainian agents who followed you to the nursing home so people would know you were a bigger criminal than your old man? Or were their deaths just more of the stupid mistakes made by Bitsy, the wannabe super-agent?"

"Don't be ridiculous," Bitsy spat. "David was a liability. And the others?" Bitsy shrugged. "Insects. Flies in the ointment. I couldn't risk letting them lead the others to my hiding place."

"So you killed them. Tell me, Bits, are you even human?"

She lunged for me then, crossing the space between us with lightning-fast precision, the gun held level with my face as her finger slowly squeezed the trigger. She wanted to be right up close when she blew my head off, and that's what I'd been counting on her to do.

I tossed the necklace, ducked down and came up under and inside her two-handed gun stance, butting her hard in the solar plexus with my head. Bitsy grunted as the air rushed out of her lungs and she staggered backward. The gun fired, the bullet going wild and shattering the window behind us.

Bitsy had lost her mind. She was fighting as hard as she could, working to bring the gun back close enough to connect with my body, and she fought with a Herculean intensity. I hit her wrist, numbing the radial nerve with the flat side of my hand and loosening her grip on the weapon. The gun skittered across the floor, stopping almost at Jake's feet, but Bitsy didn't seem to notice. She was more intent on killing me with her bare hands.

She flipped me, tossing me onto my back and straddling me. She wrapped her hands around my throat and squeezed. "You stupid bitch!" she cried. "I'm going to have more money than God tomorrow and you'll be dead!"

The room spun as Bitsy's hands squeezed tighter but I brought my arms up, snaking between hers to catch her under her chin and knock her off me. Somewhere above us the helicopter hovered, probably waiting for an all-clear signal.

Bitsy rolled and came at me again, knocking the side of my head with the heel of her hand and momentarily stunning me. I heard the crackle of a radio but I was having trouble getting my body to respond to the signals my brain was sending. Bitsy took advantage of my sluggish responses to jump up onto her feet and kick me hard in the side.

I gasped, retching reflexively as my body coiled into a defense posture. Bitsy pulled a hand-held radio from her pocket, keyed it and spoke. "I'm clear. Set down on the lawn behind the house."

She turned, bending to pick up Baby's necklace and searching for her gun. I marshaled what little strength I had left, pushed up onto my feet and launched myself at her. She went down, hard, with me riding her back. When she hit the floor, I grabbed a fistful of her hair, pulled her head back up and slammed her again, face-first into the floor. Bitsy's body went limp beneath me. Finally.

I got off her and reached down to pry the necklace out of her hand, then looked for the gun.

"Got it," Jake gasped. "It's under my chair."

I turned and looked. Jake had managed to snag the gun with his foot and push it back out of sight behind his injured leg. The fact that he hadn't been able to bend down and pick it up told me volumes about his condition. He was badly hurt.

"Nice work," I said, stooping to retrieve the semiautomatic. "I'm going to make sure she's not going anywhere, and then we can blow this pop stand."

Jake grunted. When I looked up at him, his eyes were closed and he appeared to be unconscious.

I bent down over Bitsy, pulled her arms back behind

her back and grabbed a filthy curtain cord to tie her hands together. Outside, the chopper had landed on the back lawn. I hit the light switch by the door, plunging us into darkness and crossed the room to look out at the yard below.

An ugly black helicopter sat on the ground, its rotors spinning. Great. Now who was in that and how was I supposed to get Jake out of the house without the copter's occupants stopping us? Were they Ukrainians, Bitsy's coconspirators at the CIA or higher bidders from yet another country looking to buy what Bitsy was selling?

I pulled my radio out of my pocket and depressed the talk button. "Nina, can you hear me?"

The radio crackled. The sound of the helicopter's engine seemed magnified in the cavernous room, and Spike's voice answered me.

"We're in the woods just outside the house. We've sent for help but I don't know how long it'll take to get here."

I looked back at Bitsy lying on the ground and an idea came to me. I ran over to her, felt through her pockets and withdrew her walkie.

"Spike," I said, keying my own radio. "Here's what I want you to do. When I give you guys the signal, shoot the ground around the helicopter."

"What?"

"Just trust me!"

I picked up Bitsy's radio and spoke into it. "They've got us surrounded," I said, trying to sound as much like Bitsy as possible. "They want you to turn off the engine and stay where you are," I said.

I waited a moment and then picked up my radio. "Shoot now!" I said. "If anyone attempts to leave the copter, kill them."

A second later a small barrage of bullets ate the ground in front of the helicopter. A few moments later the rotors and engine went quiet.

"Good, okay, that's a start," I whispered. "Now what?"

I looked over at Jake. Could I carry him out alone?

"Stella?" Nina's voice called softly. "Spike's got 'em covered from the front. Do you need help?"

Five minutes later Nina and I had Jake and were almost out the door when a sea of black-garbed commandos suddenly materialized outside. My walkie went off, and Spike's voice reassured us.

"Those are our people coming out of the woods," she said. "Stay inside."

As Nina and I watched, the helicopter was surrounded. Black vehicles, Jeeps and Hummers rocketed through the estate entrance and flooded the lawn around the Proctor mansion.

"Damn!" Nina breathed. "Look at that!"

"Nina, who did you guys call?" I asked.

She shrugged. "Aunt Lucy."

"Stella?" A familiar figure in black strode across the lawn and up the steps. Shelia Martin stepped out of the darkness, carrying an assault rifle. "Where's Bitsy?"

"Upstairs, all wrapped up and topped with a bow," I answered.

"Good work," she said. And then she saw Jake. "Medic!" she shouted.

She looked at me and in that one exchanged glance we reached an understanding. I was the one who'd brought Jake out alive, not her. I was the one on top and she would have to defer to me…for now at least.

"How badly hurt is he?" she asked.

"He'll be all right."

"Good." She smiled and I realized she was issuing a

challenge. She was attempting to put me on notice. *Let Jake heal and then we'll see who comes out on top. You won this round, but I'll be back to try again.*

I nodded and managed a tight smile. *Bring it on, bitch. I'll be waiting.*

Chapter 16

Arnold Koslovski died two days after I brought Jake home from the hospital. He slipped away in the early-morning hours, holding Aunt Lucy's hand and listening to her whispered reassurances that he should "Go on now, honey. Let go and rest."

In the few days after Arnold's death, we all watched Aunt Lucy very closely, waiting to see if the loss of yet another love sent her once again over the edge, but she surprised us. It was as if this expected passing, done right, set her free from the doubt and agony that surrounded my uncle's death. And besides, Aunt Lucy had another patient to tend to.

We returned from burying Arnie and found Lloyd in a near panic. As soon as she came through the door, Lloyd grabbed the hem of Aunt Lucy's black silk dress and tugged urgently.

"What is it, Benito?" she murmured, following the dog as he tugged her toward the basement. "Is it time?"

Nina, Spike and I followed the pair down into the basement where we discovered Fang, nestled on Uncle Benny's ancient sofa, giving birth to her second of five pups.

"Oh, puppies!" Nina cried. "Look!"

Lloyd, reassured now that Aunt Lucy was on the scene and in charge, relaxed into proud-papa mode and seemed to puff his chest out with canine pride in his accomplishment.

Later, when I sat beside Jake on the downstairs guest room bed, telling him about it all, he laughed. "Poor guy, he has no idea what he's in for!"

"What do you mean by that? All Lloyd has to do is run around preening," I said. "It's poor Fang who'll be doing all the work!"

Jake, realizing too late that he'd stumbled into dangerous territory, backed up. "Well, I didn't mean…I mean, his life is going to change, that's all!"

"And that would be a bad thing?" I asked.

Jake shook his head. "Poor baby," he said, pulling me down next to him. "Always on the defensive! Of course it's not a bad thing. Children are wonderful but they are also exhausting and they change your life forever…wonderfully, but forever."

I was going to argue with him, but Shelia Martin's appearance in the doorway, accompanied by Spike, put a halt to our discussion.

"So, you're better," she said softly. She was carrying a basket filled with movies, sports magazines and junk food snacks. Just the sorts of manly items Jake loved, damn her!

"Yeah, I'm almost ready to get back to work," he said.

Shelia nodded. "I figured you two might like a progress report," she said, acknowledging my presence for the first time since her arrival. "We recovered the microchip from the necklace, but for some reason it was corrupted."

"Corrupted?" I echoed. "You mean there wasn't anything on it?"

Shelia smiled. "Oh there was plenty on it, but it was in bits and pieces of jumbled data. When Mrs. Blankenship was in cardiac arrest and shocked with the defibrillator, we think the chip was compromised. However, we were able to recover enough to realize what Bitsy had stolen from David that was worth so much to the Ukrainians though."

Shelia's smile vanished as her expression grew grim.

"Bitsy had stolen a list of every CIA operative in both the Ukraine and Belarus. If that had fallen into their hands, there's no telling how many lives would've been lost or what it would've done to our country's relationships with the eastern European countries who stood by us when we denied actively planning a regime change."

"There was no formula for a biochemical weapon?" I asked.

Shelia shrugged. "We're not sure. The bits of text we've recovered indicate that it is work involving cold fusion and Chaos Theory as it applies to the development of nuclear technology. If Professor Ryzhov had developed this into something quantifiable, it would've been invaluable to the U.S. and deadly in the wrong hands. That's what your friend, Bitsy, was banking on."

Jake shook his head. "I can't believe she thought she could elude the Ukrainians and the CIA long enough to engage them in a bidding war. What was she thinking?"

I listened to the two of them and I tried to imagine myself in Bitsy's place. Her father had disgraced the family, leaving Bitsy to grow up surrounded by shame and secrecy. Her mother made sure Bitsy had the trappings necessary to perpetuate the illusion, but when your life is a sham, how secure can you really feel?

"Bitsy wasn't always like she is now," I said. "Jake, didn't you tell me you worked with her once and that she was a good agent?"

Jake nodded, frowning. "I wonder what happened?"

"Maybe Bitsy got disillusioned," I said. "Maybe she found out her country didn't always play by the rules, so why should she?"

Shelia had grown very quiet, listening as we tried to sort out Bitsy's tangled thought process.

"Well," she said finally. "I think there might be one more factor at play here."

Jake smiled up at her. "What's that?"

"Bitsy had a miscarriage shortly after she and David returned from Slovenia."

I frowned. "I thought she and David were a couple in name only?" As quickly as I said this, my memory brought up the photographs of Bitsy and Gregor that Nina had found. I remembered the way she'd smiled up at him and how her eyes had filled with tears when she told us he'd been killed trying to leave the country.

"Oh, damn! That's why she did it. She blamed David and the agency for failing to get Gregor out of the country."

Shelia shrugged again. "I'm not sure. She hasn't told us everything, but I'm guessing that's one of the reasons she shot David, in addition to not wanting him to find her. Anyway, I've got to go. One of our people caught up with a young, female Ukrainian agent and I need to interview her. She was posing as an aide at the nursing home."

Aida, I thought, but didn't have time to ask.

Shelia stood up from the wing chair where she'd been sitting and put the basket she carried down on the seat behind her.

"I just wanted to make sure you were on the mend and give you what little bit of information I had. Maybe we'll do lunch when I'm in Philadelphia next month."

Shelia was only looking at Jake as she spoke, and the clueless goon seemed oblivious to the intent behind Shelia's casual offer.

"Sure, that'll be good," he said. He smiled at her, and she licked her lips like a hungry alley cat.

"Bye, now," she said. "You take care!"

I watched her go, waited until I heard the front door close behind her and then whirled around to find Jake silently laughing at me.

"You are so clueless!" I cried. "You don't even see what she's doing, do you?"

Jake's eyebrows lifted into two amused question marks. "Don't I?"

"Jake, she's playing you! If she were a caveman, she'd clobber you over the head and drag you off to her cave! She wants you!"

Jake nodded, still grinning. "Yeah, I know." He grabbed me, pulled me back down beside him and rolled over on his side to face me. "The question is," he said, bending his head to kiss me. "What do you want?"

"What do I want?"

Jake feigned frustration as he lifted his head to look around the small bedroom. "Is there an echo in here, Stel? All I hear when I ask a question is you repeating it back to me. Yes, Stella, I asked you what you want. What do you want from me? Do you want to keep on doing the dance or do you want to settle down and get serious about us? Do you want what I have to offer or should I keep on looking?"

The room was suddenly still. My heart was pounding so hard in my chest I was certain he could hear it, but if he did, he was doing a good job of ignoring it. I had the urge to say, "Did you just ask me if I wanted to settle down?" but knew I couldn't. Jake was ready for answers, not more questions.

I felt light-headed and realized I'd forgotten to breathe. I gasped, drew in a deep breath of cool air and looked up at him.

"I love you, Jake Carpenter, with all my heart," I said.

Jake's expression didn't change. "That's not enough, Stella. I'm asking you if you're ready to make a commitment to me and I don't mean a business partnership, either. I want it all. I want you day in and day out, in the morning, all through the night, when it's good and when it's awful. I want you in my bed, in my arms and in my life, Stella. I want babies and meat loaf and dirty dishes in the sink. I want you on family vacations and when the kids are carsick. I want you watching my back and I want you needy and vulnerable. Do you understand what I'm saying here, Stel? I want a life with you."

At some point I felt the tears begin and knew they were streaming down my face even as I was laughing and crying, "Yes, Jake, yes! I want you! I want my life with you!"

"I want you when you're stupid," I said, "and I want you when you're stronger than me. I want you today, now, yes, Jake, yes, I want you!"

"You're sure, then?" he said, pulling me close and kissing me softly.

"Oh, yes, Jake," I said, feeling it bubble up from the very depths of my soul. "I want you!"

"Good," he said, running his thumb along the line of my jaw. "Then get up and close the door. I don't know about you, but I'm not getting any younger."

When I'd not only closed the door but locked it as well, I turned around and walked back over to his bedside, careful to stay just out of his reach. Slowly, ever so slowly, I started taking off my clothes, one piece at a time, teasing him with a provocative smile that let him know just what he was in for when the last item fell to join the others on the floor.

* * * * *

BRINGS YOU THE LATEST IN

Vicki Hinze's

WAR GAMES

MINISERIES

Double Dare

December 2005

A plot to release the deadly DR-27
supervirus at a crowded mall? Not U.S.
Air Force captain Maggie Holt's idea of
Christmas cheer. Forget the mistletoe—
Maggie, with the help of scientist
Justin Crowe, has to stop a psycho
terrorist before she can even think of
enjoying Christmas kisses.

Available at your favorite retail outlet.

Stability is highly overrated....

Dana Logan's world had always revolved around her children. Now they're all grown up and don't seem to need anything she's able to give them. Struggling to find her new identity, Dana realizes that it's about time for her to get "off her rocker" and begin a new life!

Off Her Rocker

by Jennifer Archer

Join Sheri WhiteFeather in The Trueno Brides!

Don't miss the first book in the trilogy:

EXPECTING THUNDER'S BABY

Sheri WhiteFeather

(SD #1742)

Carrie Lipton had given Thunder Trueno her heart. But their marriage fell apart. Years later Thunder was back. A reckless night of passion gave them a second chance for a family, but would their past stand in the way of their future?

On sale August 2006 from Silhouette Desire!

Make sure to read the next installments in this captivating trilogy by Sheri WhiteFeather:

MARRIAGE OF REVENGE,
on sale September 2006

THE MORNING-AFTER PROPOSAL,
on sale October 2006!

*Available wherever books are sold,
including most bookstores, supermarkets,
discount stores and drugstores.*

Page-turning drama…

Exotic, glamorous locations…

Intense emotion and passionate seduction…

Sheikhs, princes and billionaire tycoons…

This summer, may we suggest:

THE SHEIKH'S DISOBEDIENT BRIDE
by Jane Porter
On sale June.

AT THE GREEK TYCOON'S BIDDING
by Cathy Williams
On sale July.

THE ITALIAN MILLIONAIRE'S VIRGIN WIFE
On sale August.

With new titles to choose from every month, discover a world of romance in our books written by internationally bestselling authors.

HARLEQUIN *Presents*

It's the ultimate in quality romance!

Available wherever Harlequin books are sold.

www.eHarlequin.com

HPGEN06

HARLEQUIN® *Romance*

A family saga begins to unravel
when the doors to the Bella Lucia
Restaurant Empire are opened...

The Brides of Bella Lucia

**A family torn apart by secrets,
reunited by marriage**

AUGUST 2006

Meet Rachel Valentine, in
HAVING THE FRENCHMAN'S BABY
by Rebecca Winters

Find out what happens when a night of passion is followed
by a shocking revelation and an unexpected pregnancy!

SEPTEMBER 2006

The Valentine family saga continues with
THE REBEL PRINCE by Raye Morgan

**Hidden in the secrets of antiquity,
lies the unimagined truth...**

Introducing

a brand-new line filled with mystery
and suspense, action and adventure,
and a fascinating look into history.

And it all begins with DESTINY.

In a sealed crypt in
France, where the
terrifying legend of
the beast of Gevaudan
begins to unravel,
Annja Creed discovers
a stunning artifact
that will seal her destiny.

*Available every other
month starting
July 2006, wherever
you buy books.*

GRA1

COMING NEXT MONTH

#101 HAUNTED ECHOES by Cindy Dees
The Madonna Key

Assigned to recover a stolen Madonna statue with mysterious powers of life and death, Interpol art expert Ana Reisner and her sexy art-thief-turned-professor partner fell prey to strange visions, ghostly visitations and even a bogus murder rap. Soon time was running out, as the thieves' misuse of the relic threatened to bring a nation to its knees....

#102 COMEBACK by Doranna Durgin
Athena Force

Less than a year after defusing a hostage crisis, Selena Shaw Jones was back in the Middle East to find a missing ex-terrorist and his case officer—her own husband, Cole Jones. Could Selena overcome traumatic memories of her last mission and the mistakes of her current partner to recoup the men...and avert a major strike against America?

#103 TRACE OF DOUBT by Erica Orloff
A Billie Quinn Case

Forensic pathologist Billie Quinn's TV appearance in a rape case drew unwanted attention from an unexpected quarter— the serial killer who'd murdered her mother all those years ago. Now Billie turned to the DNA to catch a cold-case killer—but would revisiting the doubts of her past save her in the here and now?

#104 DETOUR by Sylvie Kurtz

Hard-driving private investigator Sierra Martindale was at the top of her game—until she needed a heart transplant. But this second lease on life came with an unwanted side effect—being haunted by nightmares about being murdered! Soon recovery took a back seat, as Sierra took a detour to Texas...to hunt down her heart donor's killer.

SBCNM0706